STOLEN HEARTS

"Do you think we can start over and do it right this time?"

Andre heard the resigned tone of her voice. If he didn't act quickly he would lose her for good. "I don't want to give up, Raven."

She looked up at him. "I'm not sure I'm understanding you."

"I want to keep you and Julian safe." He stopped talking and shook his head. "It's not just that, sweetheart." I want the two of you in my life. I want you to be a part of my life."

Raven gave a bitter laugh. "You're something else, Andre. I won't give you my child, so now you're willing to—" She stopped short. Scanning his face, her expression changed. "No, that's not you at all. You wouldn't do something like that."

"No, I wouldn't. I mean it, Raven. I want to start over with you." Andre reached for her.

She fell into his embrace. "Do you think we can make it work this time?" she murmured against his chest.

Andre kissed her in response. He smothered her lips with demanding mastery. Raven quivered at the sweet tenderness of his kiss. When his mouth grazed her earlobe, she thought she might faint. Her thoughts spun out of control. . . .

STOLEN HEARTS

Jacquelin Thomas

BET Publications, LLC
http://www.bet.com
http://www.arabesquebooks.com

ARABESQUE BOOKS are puclished by

BET Publications, LLC
c/o BET BOOKS
One BET Plaza
1900 W Place NE
Washington, DC 20018-1211

All Kensington Titles, Imprints, and Distributed Lines are available at special quantity discounts for bulk purchases for sales promotions, premiums, fund-raising, and educationas or institutional use. Special book excerpts or customized printings can also be created to fit specific needs. For details, write or phone the office of the Kensington special sales manager: Kensington Publishing Corp., 850 Third Avenue, New York, NY 10022, attn: Special Sales Department, Phone: 1-800-221-2647.

First Printing: October 2002
10 9 8 7 6 5 4 3 2 1

Printed in the United States of America

DEDICATION

This book is dedicated to my readers.
I thank you and I cherish you all.

ACKNOWLEDGMENTS

Family, I just have to say thanks for your support thoughout this project. With the planning of RSJ 2002 and the researching and writing of this story—you all were especially patient. To my children, I am who I am because of all of you. Bernard, you proved to be a real Hero (although I've always thought of you that way) throughout this past year. I don't think any man could be a better father, husband, and friend than you. From wading through tons of research papers and drafts of this book, helping the committee plan the workshops, the menus for the conference, to giving monies—you were there for me. During the times I just wanted to quit, your smile was all I needed to motivate me to keep going.

JoAnne Turner, I can't even begin to tell you what a life-saver you are. There are no words to express the gratitude I feel towards you. I'm so blessed to have you in my life.

Mrs. Virginia Hobson-Hicks, I appreciate your never-ending support from my first book to present. You never fail to make sure I'm included in all the local literary events for my hometown of Brunswick, GA. It's a wonderful feeling to know that I can always come home.

Victoria Christopher Murray and Lolita Files, I miss you guys and I only have one word for you: WOLF!

Mikki Kornegay, my dear friend, I have to tell you that I never would have been able to finish this book without your CD. It truly inspired me. Thank you for sharing your musical talent with the world.

This list could go on and on. There are so many wonderful and beautiful people in my life and I feel so honored. Although you may not see your name anywhere on these pages—rest assured that it's etched on my heart forever.

One

"If you don't get me that painting, you will never see Julian again."

Raven Christopher swallowed her panic at the ominous sound of his voice. "Please keep my little boy out of this, Lucien," she begged. "I've started a new life and I don't want to be a part of your world anymore. All I want is to be a good mother to my son. Why can't you understand that?"

"It is you who do not understand, my dear sweet Raven. I must have that painting and you're the only one who can get it for me." His tone turned deadly. "You have one month."

The phone went dead, leaving behind a dark void in the pit of her stomach.

"Dear God, what am I going to do?" Raven bit her lip until it throbbed in an effort to stifle the sob that trembled to her lips. She had to find a way to save her son, even if it meant breaking her vow of silence and calling Andre Simone. Raven hastily dried her tears and mentally pulled herself together. This was definitely not the time to fall apart. She needed to remain calm and rational.

Her heart aching with pain, Raven picked up the phone and dialed. Tapping her fingers impatiently on a table made of polished oak, she hoped Andre could still be reached at that number. More so, she prayed he would talk to her if he answered.

When he picked up, Raven's heart raced at the sound of his deep, rich voice. "Andre, this is Raven," she said quickly. "Please don't hang—"

The slamming down of the phone in her ear halted further conversation.

Raven swallowed the despair in her throat and dialed his number once more. This time it rang until the answering machine picked up. Speaking as clearly as she could manage, Raven voiced her plea. "Andre, pick up the phone. I know you're there. Please pick up. Look, I really need your help." She paused for a moment listening. "Andre, please pick up the phone." She was begging now. "Please, I really need to talk to you."

Resigned, Raven hung up, tears spilling down her face. She closed her eyes, feeling utterly miserable. Andre hated her and he had every right to feel that way, but it didn't lessen her pain. Three years ago, she'd hurt Andre deeply by her deceit and he hadn't wanted more to do with her since. When Raven went to see him after she found out that she was pregnant with Julian, he threw her out before she had a chance to tell him about the baby. She never tried to contact him after that.

She cried for a long time. Then, as suddenly as they'd started, her tears tapered off. Raven took a tissue from her purse and wiped her eyes with it. Standing, she strolled over to the sliding glass doors, opening them. She walked outside.

Raven inhaled the salty air while watching the seagulls swooping and diving into the greenish waters of St. Simons Island, off the coast of Georgia. It was the Fourth of July weekend and the sandy beach was covered with bodies in dazzling shades of brown, symbolizing the rich, vibrant history of African Americans on the island. It was a beautiful sight to behold, and under normal circumstances, Raven would stroll the ribbons of sandy beaches, but not today. Her mind remained focused on her missing two and a half-year-old little boy. She had to find a way to get him back.

Raven couldn't do this alone. She needed Andre, but at the moment she couldn't even get him to talk to her, so how was she supposed to manage this? Turning, Raven headed back into the house still pondering the thought. She would just have to find a way to get through to him and make him understand that her plight was a desperate one.

Sneaking a peek at the clock, Raven made another call. This time she made reservations for the next available flight to New York. She was going to see Mr. Andre Simone in person. This time, he would hear her out because she would give him no other choice.

New York, NY

Saturday afternoon, Raven stepped out of the yellow taxi and paid its driver. Looking up, she stared at the imposing height of the building on West Seventy-eighth Street, where Andre had been living for the past six years. Seeing this place again brought on a rush of memories. The three-story town house was the only place where Raven had been truly happy.

Uneasiness filled her, but Raven refused to give in to her apprehension. Pausing outside Andre's door, Raven took a deep breath before knocking.

Andre answered almost immediately as if he had been expecting someone, but the venom-filled look he gave Raven clearly showed that it hadn't been her.

"Raven Christopher. Well, to what do I owe this great

pleasure?" He scoffed contemptuously. His expression was grim as he watched her.

Andre was still as handsome as she remembered. He was tall and muscular with warm brown dreadlocks that hung loosely past his shoulders, giving him an exotic look. His smooth skin was the color of burnt almond, which complimented his hazel eyes. Eyes that now looked upon Raven with disdain. Andre stood blocking the entrance and gave no sign of moving. Summoning up her courage, she asked softly, "Can I come in, please? I really need to talk to you."

Before Andre could reply, she heard movement behind him. Looking past him, Raven caught sight of a beautiful woman. She recognized her as the model of the latest issue of *Essence* magazine. Her face had also graced a recent issue of *Cosmopolitan*.

The woman joined him at the door. "I . . . I didn't know we had company. I thought lunch had arrived." She stared piercingly at Raven.

Not missing the intimate way the woman touched Andre's arm, it hadn't occurred to Raven that Andre might not be alone. She had no reason to be surprised, though. Their relationship ended years ago and Andre had moved on. Feeling awkward, she turned to leave. But even as she changed her mind about leaving, Andre reached out and grabbed Raven by the arm, his voice no less bitter.

"Oh no you don't. You're not going to walk away from me that easily," he stated coldly. "So, what is it you want, Raven? Why did you come here? Uninvited, I might add."

The spark of hope she felt quickly extinguished. Seeing him like this, Raven had a feeling she was going to have to find Julian on her own. There was no way Andre would help her. "I really think it was a mistake to come back here." Waving her hand in dismissal, she stated, "Just forget it. I'll take care of this myself."

His hand firmly clasped on her arm, Andre led her into the town house. He pointed to a chair in the living room. "Raven, have a seat." As soon as she sat down, he ordered, "Now start talking."

She glanced around him at the woman standing silently nearby. "Could I speak to you alone, please?"

Andre tossed a look over his shoulder. "Carol, could you leave us alone for a moment? This shouldn't take long."

The woman eyed Raven warily for a moment before climbing the stairs. "I'll be in the bedroom if you need me."

He nodded, then turned back around to face Raven. "Why are you here?"

She was actually trembling now. Raven licked her lips slowly, considering how best to answer his question. She decided on the truth. "Andre, you're the only person who can help me."

He sneered at the ridiculousness of that notion. *"Help you?* Do you really think I'd lend a hand to you after everything that happened between us?"

"You have every right to be angry with me." She hid her trembling hands beneath the folds of her long denim skirt.

"I don't need you to tell me that," Andre replied nastily.

"Could you please put aside your hatred long enough to listen to me? I really need your help. I'm in trouble."

Still standing, Andre acknowledged, "I'm not surprised. Being an art thief has its downside, I would imagine."

Raven ignored his sarcasm. "Andre, this concerns my son. Lucien kidnapped him."

After a moment's pause, he asked pointedly, "Have you called the police?"

"I can't involve the police. You know that."

Placing one arm on the mantle above the marble fireplace, Andre asked, "What is it you expect me to do, Raven? This really doesn't concern me."

"Yes, it does," she responded quickly.

His arms now folded across his chest, Andre eyed her with suspicion. "What are you up to, Raven? I'm in no mood for games."

With her hands clasped tightly in her lap, Raven took a deep breath. It was time to tell him about his son. "Andre, there's something I have to tell you. I should have told you this sooner, and I really did try, but you were so angry . . ."

Looming over her now, Andre demanded, "What are you talking about, Raven?"

This was her trump card. "Lucien has *our* son."

His chin jerked up in surprise and disbelief was evident in his eyes. *"Excuse me?"*

"We have a son, Andre. His name is Julian and he's two years old. Actually two and a half."

"You're lying." His voice hardened ruthlessly. "Raven, I'm sorry about your son, but I can't get involved. I want no part of whatever game you're playing."

"He's your son, too," she reiterated. "I know you don't believe it, but I'm telling the truth. Please Andre, you've got to believe me." This was not quite the reaction she'd envisioned. Raven had mistakenly assumed he would be happy about the news of a son.

In response to her plea, Andre strode briskly over to the door and held it open. "Get out of my house, Raven. Leave and don't come back. Don't bother calling me either because I'm not interested."

She rose to her feet and crossed the room in quick

strides. "Please Andre, don't do this. I desperately need your help."

"Did you hear me?" Andre's tone was velvet, yet edged with steel.

Raven looked away, nearly destroyed by his lack of sympathy. The swell of pain she felt went way beyond tears. Standing in the doorway, she paused long enough to say, "Before I leave, I want you to know something. We have a son and right now he needs you. I was hoping you would be able to put aside your anger long enough to help find him, but I can see I was wrong." She paused a heartbeat before adding, "If by some miracle you change your mind, I'll be staying at the Excelsior Hotel."

Andre's mouth took on an unpleasant twist. "Good-bye, Raven."

She opened her mouth to speak, but no words would come. Raven could actually feel her throat closing up. Her heart was filled with so much sorrow, she could hardly breathe.

She wasted no time in leaving his town house. Once outside, Raven hailed a taxi and instructed the driver to take her to the hotel on West Broadway.

Raven held her composure until she was inside her suite. In the middle of the king-size bed, she collapsed in tears. She had convinced herself that once Andre learned about his son, he would immediately jump to her assistance. But she was wrong. Without his help, how was she going to get Julian back now? Her question brought on another onslaught of tears.

She cried until no more tears would come. After a while, Raven got up and went into the bathroom. She turned on the faucet and ran a washcloth through warm water. She wrung it out with both hands before wiping her face with it.

Back in the bedroom, Raven removed her address

book from her purse. She reached for the phone. Lucien had given her his cellular phone number and she needed to talk to him. Maybe she could reason with him or simply beg, but deep down inside, Raven knew she only had one real choice. She would have to steal the *Danse Macabre* painting.

"It's me."

"Raven dear, it's good to hear your voice."

Just the sound of Lucien's voice made her skin crawl. Clawing at the brocade bedspread, shoulders slumped in defeat, she muttered, "You win. I'll do it."

"You have an invitation to attend a cocktail party tonight."

Lucien's announcement surprised her. "H—How did you know I'd be in New York?"

His laughter was coarse. "I know you, my dear. I raised you remember? By the way, where are you staying?"

"I'm at the Excelsior, but you probably already knew this."

Lucien chuckled in response. "Get some paper and a pen. I need to give you Michael's address."

Raven did as she was told. Lucien gave her the details and she wrote quickly. When she hung up, Raven was trembling. At this very moment she hated her godfather. *How could Lucien do this to her? Had he ever loved her as he'd claimed in the past?*

Raven had been on Andre's mind ever since she'd called, but he had not been prepared to see her again. At twenty-eight, she was five years younger than him and still a striking woman with large bedroom eyes that beckoned him. Raven still wore her glossy midnight black hair cut short in a very flattering style, and she still wore the gold bracelet he'd given her on her twenty-fourth birthday.

Until now, Andre had been able to push into the far recesses of his mind just how sweet her full lips tasted and how her skin, the color of nutmeg, was soft to the touch. Muttering a curse, he didn't want to remember her smell or the way her hands felt . . .

Carol touched his shoulder lightly, putting an end to his thoughts of Raven. "What did *she* want?"

"Nothing," he stated coldly. "Raven is still the deceitful witch she's always been. She's just up to her old tricks." Andre strode over to the window and stared out. He'd tried unsuccessfully to put Raven out of his mind for the past three years, so the last thing he needed was to see her again.

"What's wrong, sweetheart?"

He glanced over his shoulder. "I've got a lot on my mind, Carol."

"Andre, we're supposed to attend Michael's cocktail party tonight. He wants to show off his newest acquisitions, including the *Danse Macabre*. Do you still want to go?"

Much had been made of Pierre Delacroix's last painting. The *Danse Macabre*, translated into English meant "Dance of Death" and was rumored to be the late artist's best work and was valued at millions. Rubbing his chin thoughtfully, Andre murmured, "I'd forgotten about that."

Carol stroked his arm, bringing Andre's attention back to her. Giving him a sexy smile, she murmured, "Why don't we just stay here. Maybe finish what we started before we were interrupted by your . . . your guest." Her hands moved up to his face. "What do you say to that, darling?"

Andre shook his head. "No, I want to go." He had a

strong feeling that Raven's sudden appearance was tied to the painting.

The doorbell rang.

"Do you think she's back?"

"No. That's probably lunch." Andre headed to the door. "I'll get it." Silently, he hoped it wasn't Raven. He couldn't deal with her right now. He had listened to her story and found himself with mixed emotions, for Raven spoke with such obvious conviction that he'd almost forgotten how good of a liar she was. But what if she was telling the truth? If so, he had a son.

Relief swept through him at finding the deliveryman standing there. Andre quickly paid the man and sent him on his way.

Carol sat down at the table in the dining room and Andre joined her. He fixed plates for them both. Neither the beautiful woman sitting across from him nor the delicious food, all his favorites, provided a distraction for Andre. Raven's visit haunted him still. He had to find out if she was telling the truth. He was so caught up in his thoughts throughout lunch that he barely heard a word Carol was saying.

"Honey, are you listening to me?" she asked, her brow wrinkling in irritation.

Andre met her gaze. "Huh? Oh, I'm listening."

"I don't believe you."

Carol's tone was teasing, but Andre detected just the barest hint of frustration in her voice. "I'm listening. I am," he insisted. "You were talking about your next assignment."

From the pleased expression on her face, Andre knew he'd hit pay dirt. He'd guessed as much. It was all Carol seemed to ever talk about. Focusing his attention on her, he decided that it was time to make some changes in their relationship.

* * *

Dressed in a long black sheath she had purchased in haste a couple of hours earlier, Raven climbed out of a shimmering black Rolls and was escorted to the front door of the Garner Mansion. She swallowed hard while playing with the double strand of pearls draped around her neck. Tonight, she was here to case the four-story home located on West Ninety-second Street.

Inside, she stealthily surveyed her surroundings. Raven felt ill, knowing what she had to do. Her eyes landed on a man walking toward her and felt compelled to smile. She was pretty sure this man was the host and the owner of this palatial town house. He looked vaguely familiar to her, but Raven couldn't place him.

Holding out his hand to her, he announced, "Miss Christopher, I'm Michael Garner. It's so good to see you again. When Lucien told me you were going to be in town, I immediately issued an invitation for you to attend."

Shaking his hand, Raven glanced up at the man who towered over her. His firm features and the confident set of his shoulders spoke of power. Even in a crowd, his presence was compelling. His brows and blue eyes were startling against his fair skin and light hair. She searched her memory. "I'm sorry, but you have me at a disadvantage. When did we meet?"

Michael laughed. "Let's see . . . you were about fourteen then."

She made a face. "During my braces years. Why don't we start over? Please call me Raven. And thanks so much for including me. You have a beautiful home, Mr. Garner."

"I would be honored if you'd call me Michael. Would you like a tour?" He offered his arm to her.

"All right. Michael it is." Taking his arm, Raven murmured, "I would love a tour. Thank you."

They took the elevator to the fourth floor and started there. She could tell no expense had been spared to make this house one of New York City's outstanding residences. Back on the first floor, they entered a room filled with Michael's vast art collection. She observed, "I hope you have a good security system. The artwork in this room alone is worth millions." She admired a recent painting of Andre's. This was his best work, she decided.

Michael drew her attention back to him by saying, "I just had a new video surveillance system installed."

As she listened, Michael described how his security system worked. Raven came to the conclusion that there was no way she would be able to get in and out without getting caught. What could Lucien be thinking? she wondered. The hair on the back of her neck suddenly stood up. Raven searched around the room and found Andre standing silently nearby.

Michael followed her gaze. Breaking into a smile, Michael greeted him. "Andre, how are you? Come here, I'd like to introduce you to this beautiful lady here. I was just showing her my latest acquisition of your work."

Raven straightened her back and stared into the hazel eyes of the man who once loved her. He was gazing at her with a bland half smile. "Andre and I already know each other, Michael."

He looked from one to the other in surprise. "Really?" The two men shook hands.

"It's good to see you again, Michael," Andre confirmed. "I know Raven Christopher quite well."

Michael seemed to notice the tension between Andre and Raven. Clearing his throat loudly, Michael uttered, "Well, if you two will excuse me, I see someone is trying to get my attention. I'll leave you two to catch up."

He left them alone, staring at one another in silence, uneasy with being alone, just staring at the picture, side by side.

Raven spoke first. "I love the painting, Andre. I think it's your best work yet. It's a masterpiece. But then I've always been a big fan of your work . . ." Her voice died when she realized she was rambling.

Pulling her off to the side, Andre growled, "If you think to steal the *Danse Macabre*, then you've got another thought coming."

Two

Andre wanted to shake some sense into Raven. How could she even consider stealing such a valuable piece of artwork? His eyes met hers disparagingly.

As if Raven knew what he was thinking, she stated, "I asked you for help. You refused, so I have no choice, Andre."

"You do have a choice," he argued. "For once in your life—tell Lucien to go to hell! I don't understand why you let that man control your life."

Raven's eyes hastily bounced around the room. They were alone in the gallery, but people were gathered in the hallway in small groups. "Will you keep your voice down?"

"Why should I?" Andre demanded in a harsh whisper. "Give me one reason why I shouldn't tell Michael why you're really here and let him have the police haul you off to jail?"

"Because I don't think you'd be able to live with yourself if something happens to our son," Raven shot back. Her eyes clung to his, analyzing his reaction. "Look, Andre, there's no easy way I can steal the painting anyway. Michael has this room guarded like Fort Knox. Right now we're probably being captured by hidden cameras, and who knows what else. All I really want is to go back to the life I had with my little boy. Nothing else matters, do you hear? Nothing else is more important than my child and I'll do whatever I have to do to save him." She threw back her head and placed her hands on her hips. "Even if it means stealing that painting for Lucien."

"What about going to jail, Raven?" Andre questioned. "Aren't you the least bit worried about that? What happens to your son then?"

Raven boldly met his eyes. "If I'm lucky, I won't get caught." She refused to consider the frightening thought.

"For Christ sake, Michael's brother-in-law works for the Art and Jewelry Theft Bureau of New York City."

Raven couldn't let that deter her. "What choice do I really have, Andre? I've already told you that Lucien has my son."

"I'm warning you, Raven. I'm not going to have anything to do with this."

She didn't bother to hide her frustration. "All I want you to do is keep your mouth shut. Can you at least do that much for me?"

Andre stared down at her, but didn't utter a response.

"If you open your mouth to ruin this and something happens to my son—I'm coming after you and there won't be anything you can do to stop me." Raven uttered with cold fury. She waited a heartbeat before turning on her heel and storming off.

Andre watched her exit the room, leaving behind a trace of the pain he heard in her voice. Although he wasn't sure he could believe a word of her story, he knew her well enough to know that she was running scared. Perhaps she was telling the truth. But then again, this could be another ploy of Lucien's. It wouldn't be the first time Lucien had used Raven to get to him. Only now there was a child in the equation. A child she claimed was his son.

Wanting to find out more, Andre started after her, but was halted by Carol who stood in his path with her arms folded. "I've been looking all over for you. What are you doing in here?"

"I just wanted to get a look at the *Danse Macabre.*" He pointed to a painting encased in an antique gold frame. "It's beautiful, isn't it?"

Carol nodded. She cleared her throat softly before saying, "Andre, I think we should talk. There's something going on with you, and it didn't just start with Raven's sudden return. It's been there all along."

He knew exactly what she was talking about. Things had become strained between them lately. Andre decided it was best to be honest with her. He didn't want the same things Carol wanted. But that was not the whole of it. He didn't love her and never would. "There's something you should know. But this is not the time or the place. We'll talk when we get back to my place."

Carol nodded in agreement, but her expression showed that she wasn't happy about it.

Silently, they joined the other guests. Andre spoke to a few of the others in attendance, but he didn't linger long with anyone in particular. He glanced around the room looking for Raven, but she seemed to have disappeared. Maybe she'd taken his advice and had decided to leave. There was just no way she could steal that painting and get away with it. In spite of what had happened in the past, Andre didn't want to see her behind bars.

Carol slid up beside him. "Looking for Raven? I saw her earlier. She looked upset, so I figured you two must have talked. Am I right?"

"Don't do this." There was a critical tone to his voice.

Eyeing him defiantly, she stated, "It was a simple question."

"If you really want to know, then yes."

A shadow of annoyance crossed her face. "I'm going to get something to drink," Carol announced suddenly. "Would you like a glass of champagne?" Her voice was laced with anger.

He shook his head in response. Andre didn't even notice when Carol left. He strode purposely back into Michael's art gallery. He wanted another look at the *Danse Macabre*. The painting had been lost for a number of years and had suddenly resurfaced last month at an auction. On the canvas, dancers gyrated around a fire in which viewers could glimpse the image of what could only be described as the angel of death.

Studying the rendition closely, it looked to Andre as if it was sloshed together without any real sense of veracity and painted with minimal facial detail and an abuse of burnt umber almost as if it had been done in anger. Andre stared long and hard at the signature of Pierre Delacroix. He was still giving the picture a critical look when Carol rejoined him.

"Maybe we should join the others," she suggested. "People are going to think it's true about you being antisocial if you keep hiding in this room."

"What others think is of no concern to me. However, they just might assume that I have a real appreciation for fine art," Andre threw back sarcastically.

Her lips puckered with annoyance. "I really hate when you get like this."

His voice rose slightly. "I'm not being any particular way, Carol."

"You can lower your voice, Andre. You don't need to yell at me."

Sighing, he replied, "I didn't yell . . . look, let's just make it through the rest of the evening, okay?"

"Whatever!"

Andre and Carol returned to the ballroom, but he could feel the undercurrent of tension flowing between them. He released a deep sigh, causing Carol to send a sharp look his way.

It was going to be a long night, Andre thought.

Raven was heading to the front door when Michael stepped off the elevator. She waited, giving him a smile as he neared. "Michael, thanks for inviting me. I had a great time."

"You're not leaving, are you?" he asked.

Playing with her pearls, she replied, "I'm afraid so. I flew in today and I'm exhausted."

"Maybe a glass of champagne will relax you," Michael suggested. His eyes slid down her body. "I'd like a chance to sit down and have a conversation with you. It's been a long time."

Smiling, Raven murmured, "Another time. I'm going to be in town for a few days."

Michael laughed. "Will you at least stay until after the fireworks?"

"Sure. I'll stay until the fireworks, but after that I'm going to have to leave because I am really exhausted." Raven searched the room, but she didn't glimpse Andre anywhere.

"He left a short while ago," Michael announced.

Although Raven knew exactly who he was referring to, she asked, "Who?"

"Andre. He is the person you're looking for?"

She nodded.

"The two of you have a history, don't you?"

Raven nodded a second time. "Not a very pretty one, I'm afraid. We're barely on speaking terms."

Reaching out, Michael took her face and held it gently. "I hate seeing you look so sad. I would like to put a smile back on your beautiful face."

It was painfully clear to Raven that Michael was attracted to her. No doubt this was part of Lucien's plan. This was to be used to her advantage. He had to be at least fifteen years older than her, but Raven could feel the sexual magnetism that drew women to him. Michael Garner had been linked to several socialites and Hollywood actresses since the death of his wife.

"I'm fine, really."

Michael was staring at her.

Raven ran her fingers through her hair. "What is it? Why are you staring at me like that?"

"You've grown into a very beautiful woman."

She smiled again. "Thank you," she murmured softly.

"How long will you be staying in New York?"

"I'm . . . I'm not really sure."

Michael looked her over seductively. "I would like to spend some time with you. Is that possible?"

"I'd like that as well," she lied. Raven allowed Michael to escort her back into the ballroom where he introduced her to a United States congressman, two senators and a host of other celebrities.

Shortly after ten, Raven left the Garner estate after promising to have dinner with Michael the next day. Only then did she allow her true feelings to resurface. She was frustrated beyond tears by the time she made it to her hotel room.

Toying with Michael's affections made her feel dirty. In the shower, Raven scrubbed herself raw in an effort to feel clean once again. Fate had been cruel when it allowed Lucien to find her. For the past four years, she'd been free to live her life the way she wanted. Now, her godfather was once again in control. With Julian in his possession, Lucien held all the cards. Some independence day, she thought sadly.

Raven would forever be grateful to him and Beatrice for taking her in after her parents' deaths. She'd been eight years old at the time and alone in the world. Ten years later, after the death of Beatrice, she came to realize how her guardians had amassed their great fortune.

She dried off her throbbing skin and slipped into a nightgown. Raven climbed into bed and lay clutching her pillow. "Please forgive me, Lord for what I have to do, but I've got to save my son."

Andre waited for Carol to take a seat in the living room. They had been home for nearly two hours and neither one of them had said a word. Finally, he called for her to come downstairs. It was time to have that talk. Andre offered her a drink.

Carol refused his offer. Eyeing him expectedly, she asked, "What is it you have to tell me, Andre? It must not be good since you chose not to tell me in the bedroom."

He sat down facing her. "I think we should keep our relationship strictly friends."

Carol's expression never changed. "Is it because of her?"

He hadn't expected her question. "Who?"

"Raven Christopher. You're still very much in love with her, aren't you?" Carol accused. "That's why you haven't let anyone get close to you in all this time."

It took him a moment to respond. "This has nothing to do with Raven."

Carol gave a short laugh. "Your response is weak at best, Andre."

They sat in silence.

"Carol, I'm sorry," Andre said after a while. "You and I have been friends for a long time."

She rose to her feet gracefully. "You don't owe me any apologies, Andre. I think I've always known from the beginning that our time together would only be for a season." Carol walked over to where he was sitting. Stroking the side of his face, she added, "Raven's the only one who's ever been able to put light in those pretty eyes of yours."

Andre shook his head in denial. "Raven and I are over."

"Yet you still love her. Andre, honey, you've got yourself a situation. Raven owns your heart. She's a lucky woman." Carol kissed him lightly on the lips. "I'm going back to my place tonight."

"You don't have to do that, Carol. I can sleep in the other bedroom."

"I need to prepare for my next shoot anyway." She rose to her feet. "I'll go pack my things."

While Carol was upstairs packing, Andre fixed himself a second drink. He didn't want to consider that she was right about his feelings for Raven. He had never been able to get her out of his mind.

She came down the stairs carrying an overnight bag. "If I've left anything, just send it over to my place by messenger."

"You really don't have to leave tonight. It's late, Carol."

"It's best that I go." Pausing at the door, she said, "I'll call you when I get back from London."

"Have a safe trip, Carol. I hope you have a good time."

"I always do, Andre." As an afterthought, she added, "You know, you should try it sometime."

Carol was trying hard to be cheerful, but he noted the shadow behind her eyes. He knew she cared for him deeply. Andre hated hurting her, but he had to be honest. They would never have a future together.

He threw his glass against the wall in frustration. *How could Raven still get to him after all this time?*

Andre was furious with himself. Furious that she could still make his heart jolt and his pulse pound just by walking into a room. Raven could still make the air seem electrified whenever she was around.

He felt an unwelcome surge of excitement. She was back and looking even more beautiful than before, if that were possible. Andre's excitement waned. Yeah, Raven was back. Back in town to rip away the last shreds of happiness and contentment he had left. But this time, he vowed that history would not repeat itself. He would not listen to his heart. However, one question remained. Whether or not he had a son.

Tomorrow morning he was going to pay Raven a little visit. He was going to find out the truth.

Three

Raven jolted awake. Someone was knocking on her door. The heavy knock came again, resonating throughout the suite and bringing her to her feet.

Glancing over at the clock, Raven wrapped the belt of her robe tightly around her as she made her way across the room. "Who in the world is knocking on my door at this hour?" Hope welled up inside her at the thought that it could be Andre. With that in mind, she rushed to open it.

As soon as she did, Raven felt herself swell with anger. "Lucien, what are you doing here?" She kept her fingers wrapped around the edge of the doorknob, unwilling to let them enter.

"I came to see how things went last night." Lucien brushed past her and walked into the room followed by another man Raven recognized as Cal, his bodyguard.

Rolling her eyes heavenward, she shut the door. She didn't bother to secure the lock because her guests would soon be leaving if Raven had her way.

Without preamble, Lucien stated, "I trust you and Michael got reacquainted last night. I'd hoped I wouldn't find you here this morning." He rested both hands on his silver handled cane.

Glaring at him, Raven uttered, "You're a disgusting man." She turned away from him and strolled over to her bed. Raven sat down on the edge, crossing her legs and folding her arms across her chest. "What do you want, Lucien?"

He asked a question of his own. "When will you see Michael again?"

"Tonight. We're having dinner."

He didn't seem to notice the strained tone of her voice. Lucien was clearly pleased, much to Raven's dissatisfaction. The man was no better than a pimp.

"Everything is going according to your plan, so why this little visit from you?" she wondered aloud.

"I thought you might need a little incentive." He gestured to his bodyguard. "Cal . . ."

The man placed a tape in the VCR and turned on the television.

Raven burst into tears when Julian appeared on the screen. "My b—baby . . ." She wiped her eyes. "Look at him," she said, pointing to the television. "*He's scared, Lucien.* How could you be so cruel?"

Signaling for Cal to turn off the VCR, he replied, "The boy is being well cared for, Raven dear. Once I have the *Danse Macabre* in my possession, you and your son are free to return to your dull lives. I give you my word."

"Why, Lucien? Why is this painting so important to you? You certainly don't need the money."

"It's not about the money, Raven. I'm a collector. I love fine art."

"Michael has a state-of-the-art video surveillance system. This is not going to be an easy feat, Lucien. If I'm caught, I could go to jail for a very long time. What would happen to Julian then?"

"First-time offenders are rarely punished very severely. Long-term probation after a quick plea deal is the general rule. As for Julian, you don't have to worry about your son. I will raise him just as I did you."

"NO!" she shouted. "I don't want you anywhere near Julian. I will not have your influence on him." Pain rose up in her. Lucien never once cared for her. He fully expected her to go to prison willingly if caught.

"Raven dear, you seem a bit ungrateful. Have you forgotten that neither your black relatives nor your white relatives wanted you after your parents were killed in that accident. I saved you from being shifted from foster home to foster home. Beatrice and I treated you as if you were our own child. We sacrificed for you, Raven."

Lucien knew exactly how to wound her. Stiffening, Raven kept her voice even, trying not to reveal her fury. "I appreciate your raising me, Lucien. I just wish I could have led a normal life. I wish you could have loved me as if I were your own daughter. That's all I ever wanted. Someone to love me. Until now, I thought you did."

"Your life was one of privilege. Would you have rather lived poor? Fighting for food or clothes? Wearing hand-me-downs? Because of me, you attended some of the best schools—you had the best of everything, Raven. Very few people have had the opportunities afforded you."

Her lips thinned with anger. "You've turned me into a criminal and I hate you for it."

"Do this one thing for me and I will stay out of your life, Raven."

"You say that now," she snapped. "How do I know that you won't do this again? As long as you're alive, Julian will always be in danger."

Lucien made his way over to where she was sitting and eased down beside her. "I have given you my word."

"Your word means absolutely nothing," Raven sniped in response. "For all I know you're doing this just so that I can end up in prison and you can take my son away from me. I haven't forgotten how much you wanted a son." Silently, she vowed that if she went to jail—she would not be alone. Lucien would be joining her.

"Your imagination is running wild as usual, Raven. You're wrong and I can prove it. I've brought you some equipment to help you with this job."

"Like what?" She watched Cal open the briefcase he'd brought with him.

"A laptop computer and a disc containing the floor plan and everything you need to know about Michael Garner's security system, including the codes. I want you to study it until you know it like the back of your own hand."

"I'm not going to even ask how you acquired this information."

Cal handed her the computer.

"It's not going to be as difficult as you first thought," Lucien stated. "You are like a daughter to me, Raven. I don't want to see you behind bars. People like us could not possibly survive the harshness of prison life."

He reached out to touch her, but Raven moved away. Without thinking, she said, "Keep your hands off me. If you don't have anymore to say, please leave."

"We need to discuss our plan."

"Let's get one thing clear, Lucien. This is not *our* plan—it's yours."

For one moment he looked frustrated. "Must you always be so difficult?"

"Say what you have to say," Raven eyed the clock. "Then get out of my room. I can't stand the sight of you or your shadow."

"You mustn't let your temper get the best of you," he warned.

Raven's eyes turned deadly. "If anything happens to my son, I will make you pay. Do you hear me?" she screamed.

"Lower you voice, Raven," he ordered. "Don't tell me you're still prone to temper tantrums."

She didn't respond. Raven itched to wrap her fingers around Lucien's throat. She relished the thought of watching him take his last breath. Cal would stop her, she knew. But with Lucien sitting right next to her—perhaps she could take some small measure of delight in his struggle to breathe. Yes, the thought of strangling the life out of Lucien thrilled her.

Lucien cut into her silence, putting an end to her musings. "Talked to Andre Simone lately? Does he know that he fathered a son with you?"

Raven glared at him. "He still hates me. I'm sure this little piece of news makes you very happy."

Rising to his feet, Lucien gave a look of mock innocence. "You can't blame me for that. You made the mistake of falling in love on the job. Then you decided to confess all to him. What did you expect?"

Clenching her hands into fists, Raven was furious. "I hate you with all my body and soul."

Lucien ignored her comment. "Let's get started. This is the plan . . ."

Raven only half-listened to his words. In her mind, she tried to think of as many ways to make him pay for all he'd done to her as she could. Strangely, she didn't feel one ounce of guilt for wanting Lucien dead.

When he finished, she glared at him and said, "Get out. When this is over, I want you to stay out of my life. *I mean it, Lucien.*"

Lucien and Cal made their way over to the door. "The sooner you take care of our little business, the sooner I'll be out of your life."

"Now, I want you and your shadow to get out of my room." She spat out the words contemptuously while her dark eyes clawed him like talons. Once Julian was back with her, Raven intended to make sure Lucien stayed away permanently.

Andre stood outside of Raven's hotel room debating whether or not to knock. It wasn't quite eight o'clock yet, but he needed to find out the truth. He'd been up most of the night wondering if what Raven had said was true. *Did he really have a son?*

Just as he was about to knock, he heard voices. Andre recognized Lucien's voice immediately. He and Raven were arguing. She'd been telling the truth, he realized as he listened. He could hear the pain in Raven's voice as she told Lucien that he hated her. He didn't hate her, Andre admitted. He just didn't trust her. And trust was very important to him.

A sudden feeling of protectiveness filtered through Andre. His son had been kidnapped. He was filled with a sudden urge to break down the door, but decided against it. No doubt Lucien's bodyguard was with him. Besides, it wouldn't help them locate the child. In fact, it might even make matters worse.

The voices got louder and seemed to be coming toward him. Apparently, they were getting ready to leave. Andre stealthily made his way down the hall and hid in a storage room of some type.

He stayed out of sight until the voices died and he heard the sound of the elevator. Easing back up the hallway, Andre peeked around the corner to make sure the men had gotten on the elevator. He returned to Raven's door and knocked.

When she opened the door, he took note of her tearstained face as he strode briskly into the room. Andre waited until they were seated before he stated, "You look like hell."

Glaring at him, Raven responded, "What do you expect, Andre? I couldn't sleep because of all this craziness . . ." Her eyes filled with tears. "Lucien was just here and he showed me a tape of Julian. My little boy looked so scared. It made me sick to my stomach to see him like that."

"I heard the two of you arguing."

The silence between them grew until it was almost unbearable.

Finally Andre spoke. "Do you have pictures with you? Of the boy?" The words emerged quickly and quietly, as if he couldn't keep himself from saying them.

"Yes, I do." Raven walked over to the desk where she'd left her purse. Reaching into it, she pulled out a wallet. She handed a photograph to him.

Andre smiled. "He's beautiful. He looks just like you."

She pointed to the picture. "He has your eyes though. Andre, I'm sorry I kept Julian's existence from you. When I found out I was pregnant, I tried to see you but—"

"I practically threw you out of my house," he cut in. "I remember."

Raven's level gaze met his and held it. "You wouldn't return my phone calls either, so I stopped trying. I figured after everything that happened, you wouldn't believe me anyway. I'm not so sure you believe me even now."

Andre's expression froze. He returned his gaze to the photo, noting the hazel eyes that stared back at him.

"Right after we broke up, I moved to Georgia." Raven settled into the deep floral cushions of the sofa. "But I guess that wasn't far enough because somehow Lucien found me."

He wedged himself onto the seat next to her. "I saw

him leaving your room earlier. Any idea where Lucien was headed?"

Raven gave a slight shrug. "Who knows? He didn't tell me anything outside of what he wants me to do. He showed me this." She used the remote to turn on both the TV and the VCR. Andre's reaction was similar to hers.

"I'm going to call a friend of mine. If anybody can rescue Julian, A.C. can do it." Andre reached for the phone. "Mind if I use your telephone?"

"No. Go ahead." Raven gave him a grateful smile.

When Andre was done, he said, "I want you to stay put. There are some people I need to see, but I'll be back later." Looking down at the photo in his hand, he asked, "Can I keep the photo?"

Nodding, Raven murmured, "It's yours."

Memories of the past assailed him and Andre began to have second thoughts. Maybe this was just an elaborate trick. But then he recalled the arguing between Lucien and Raven. They couldn't have known he would be outside the suite. He stood in the doorway, watching her intently, and showing no emotion, added, "You'd better not be lying to me."

Andre closed the door behind him and was gone.

That Sunday evening, Raven climbed into the limousine Michael sent for her. During the drive to the restaurant on Barrow Street, she prayed for courage to go through with Lucien's plan. Somehow she was going to have to seduce Michael into trusting her long enough to get into the security system and shut it down, so that she could steal the painting.

Michael met her at the beautifully restored, eighteenth-century carriage house once owned by Aaron Burr and greeted her with a kiss on the cheek. He scanned her critically and beamed approval. "It's good to see you again."

"You, too." Michael had to be in his early forties, she estimated, but he was still a very handsome man.

In the candlelit dining room filled with the soothing sounds of piano music, he held out a chair for Raven. Glancing around the room, she murmured, "You've been talking to Lucien."

"Why would you say that?"

Her eyes met his. "That's the only way you could have known that this is one of my favorite restaurants. Lucien used to bring me here every time we came to New York."

Laying a napkin across his lap, he stated, "This happens to be my favorite eatery as well."

She gave him a tiny smile. "So we have something in common, I see."

"This is only the first." His eyes traveled her face then dropped downward.

Raven shifted in her chair, bringing Michael's attention back to her face. She met his gaze with a smile. "I had a great time last night. And your house . . . it's absolutely gorgeous. I truly loved the hand-painted furnishings in the ballroom."

"Ah . . . the Roma collection. Thank you. My wife spared no expense in decorating it before she died."

"I saw her picture in your library. She was a very beautiful woman. You must miss her a great deal."

Michael gave a slight nod. "It's been six years. I still miss Anne, but it's gotten better with time."

"I remember meeting her. Even back then I admired her beauty."

"But you don't remember me."

"I do. It came to me this morning. We met at one of Lucien's Christmas balls." Raven hadn't really remembered until Lucien reminded her that morning. "I haven't attended any of his parties for the past four years. You might as well know that he and I had a big falling out. We're just now on speaking terms."

"I thought it might be something like that." Michael gestured for the waiter. He ordered wine for them both. "I hope that you two will be able to patch things up. Lucien adores you."

"Surely you didn't invite me to lunch to discuss my relationship with my godfather."

The waiter arrived with their wine. After pouring each of them a glass, he took their orders.

While they waited for their meals, Michael and Raven discussed their mutual love of art.

"I've been teaching art history at Glynn Academy in Brunswick, Georgia. You've probably never heard of it."

"Actually, I have. I've vacationed on Jekyll Island a few times. Anne used to love it down there."

"St. Simons is my favorite of the Sea Islands. That's why I moved there."

"Wow. An art history teacher. So, tell me . . . what is your favorite style?"

"Hmmm . . . I guess I would say any classical art. Especially the classic romantic artists such as Eugène Delacroix. I truly adore his work."

"I've heard that Pierre Delacroix is a descendant of his," Michael commented.

"I believe it. Their styles are very similar. You find that common in family members."

"Andre Simone's work is often compared to that of Pierre's. Do you think they're related?"

"No. I'm sure he would've mentioned it, if it were true. But you're right. Like Pierre, Andre's work is reminiscent of Eugène Delacroix's. They all use vivid colors and strong, forceful brush strokes. Such use of color actually influenced impressionist painters. During my research on Eugène Delacroix, I found that it was his work that inspired Pablo Picasso."

"I had a chance to view some of Eugène Delacroix's work at the Museum of Fine Arts in Houston, Texas." Michael took a sip of his wine. *"The Andromeda."*

"One of my favorites." Raven nodded. "I love all of the old masterpieces. I love to paint, but I'll never come close to being considered one of the greats."

"I would love to see some of your work."

Shaking her head, Raven laughed. "I haven't painted anything in a long time. I only teach art now. Or at least I used to teach." As an afterthought, she added, "I'm taking some time off."

"Tell me, are you also a fan of Pierre Delacroix's work? You seemed very interested in the *Danse Macabre.*"

"I liked his *Parisian* series." Raven sipped her Chablis. *"Danse Macabre* is much different from his other works."

"I agree with you there. I never cared for his earlier works of art. They were too dark and depressing. Whatever happened in the last two years of his life was a good thing. His painting technique changed for the better."

She nodded in agreement. "His last painting was dark, but there was some maturity in his technique that wasn't there in his other works."

He agreed.

Their meals arrived. Raven attacked her food with relish.

Michael eyed her in amusement.

When she caught him watching her, she took her napkin and dabbed softly at the corners of her mouth. "I guess you can tell I'm hungry," she said sheepishly.

"I like a woman who enjoys food."

Raven laughed infectiously. "I would like to say that I'm usually more ladylike, but that wouldn't be the truth."

Michael released a soft chuckle. He took a bite of his own food and chewed. After swallowing, he asked, "Have you decided how long you're going to stay in New York?"

"Long enough to get to know you." She intended to give Michael the impression that she was flirting with him.

He seemed pleased with her response. "I could get you a job teaching here, if you'd like."

"We'll see." She stabbed another shrimp with her fork.

Michael reached over and took her hand. "Raven, I am very attracted to you. I would like a chance to explore that attraction."

Feeling awkward, Raven removed her hand from his. She knew he was waiting for a response from her and struggled to come up with the right words. "I'm flattered, Michael."

"I feel a 'but' coming . . ."

Raven broke into a smile. "There's no but. I was going to say that I think we should take time to get to know each other. Andre and I . . ." She paused for a moment. "We rushed into our relationship and it ended badly."

"How long ago did you two breakup?"

"It's been four years. But you should know that he was my last relationship."

"You've not dated in four years? I find that hard to believe." Michael shook his head. "A woman as beautiful as yourself."

"Michael, I have a son. Andre and I have a child. He's two and a half. Enough to keep me busy."

His brow raised in surprise. "I had no idea . . ."

"No one knew. Not even Andre," she confessed.

"Is that why you've come back to New York?"

"In part," she answered honestly. "I think Andre deserves to know he has a child."

Nodding, Michael replied, "I agree. Where is your son? Is he with you?"

"Julian . . . that's his name. He's with Lucien. They are spending some time together. Getting to know each other." The lie put a bitter taste in Raven's mouth.

"I hope to meet Julian. My sweet Anne and I were never blessed with children although we wanted them very badly." Michael's eyes darkened with pain. "Having wealth is nothing in comparison to the love of a child."

"I know," Raven murmured softly. "Julian has this way of looking at me—it's like I'm his entire world. He actually believes that I'm something great." *The same way I felt about Lucien*, she added silently. As a child, she adored Lucien and Beatrice Dupont. Her only desire was to please them.

"You are. It's obvious that you love him dearly. That's all children really want, you know. They just want to be loved. People who will look at them as if they're something great, to use your words." Michael leaned back in his chair. "My wife, she used to tell me all the time that I would make a good father. Anne even told me once that I could find another woman to give me a child. She didn't want to deprive me of the experience."

"She sounds like she was a wonderful woman."

"She was," Michael acknowledged. "In hopes of giving me a child, she endured several painful procedures and surgeries. Twice we were successful in Anne getting pregnant . . ." His voice broke. "Sh—She miscarried both times."

Reaching out, Raven covered Michael's hand with her own. "I'm so sorry. I can imagine how painful that was. There was a time when I thought I wouldn't be able to carry Julian to term. I ended up on bed rest for the last two months of my pregnancy. I was terrified."

"You were alone?" Michael wanted to know.

Shaking her head, Raven answered, "No. My neighbor literally moved into my house to care for me. She was one of the sweetest women I've ever known and very motherly."

Michael speared a green bean and stuck it into his mouth as he listened.

"Pansy was a good friend and I needed that support. I wouldn't have made it without her."

"I'm glad to hear you weren't alone. It saddens me when I hear about women having to experience motherhood without their partner."

"After Julian was born, I suffered a bad case of postpartum depression. Pansy was there and she took care of Julian. I made her his godmother."

"Where is your friend now?"

"She died a few weeks ago in a car accident." Although Raven hadn't considered it before, she now wondered if Lucien had something to do with Pansy's death. How else could he have known that she would need someone to look after Julian? The thought made her sick to her stomach.

Grabbing her purse, Raven rose to her feet quickly. "Please e—excuse me."

"Raven—"

"I'll be right back . . ." She rushed off before Michael could say another word.

The thought that Lucien could have killed Pansy was so horrifying. She made it to the bathroom and into a stall just as the bile rose to her throat.

Afterward, she pulled a compact toothbrush and miniature tube of toothpaste from her purse. Raven brushed her teeth quickly. After touching up her makeup and running her fingers through her short hair, she felt better.

When she stepped out of the bathroom, she found Michael waiting for her. "I'm so sorry," she began.

He embraced her. "You don't have to apologize, sweetheart. Losing someone close to you is never easy."

Raven relaxed in his arms. Michael assumed she'd run off because of her grief over Pansy's death. It was true in part, but mostly because she suspected the man she had loved unconditionally could be capable of murder.

Four

Andre paced back and forth in his third-floor studio. Every now and then he would stop and just stare at the photograph of his son. Julian was a beautiful little boy, resembling Raven only in the way he smiled. He had taken the rest of his features from Andre. His heart skipped a beat at that single acknowledgment. If anything happened to his son, he vowed to hunt Lucien down like a dog.

He glanced over at the clock. Andre had placed a call earlier to longtime friend, A.C. Richardson and was now waiting for her to call him back. He was becoming impatient with each passing moment.

"Come on, A.C. Call me back," he whispered. Andre stared at the phone, silently willing it to ring. If anybody could find Julian, it was A.C. She had connections all over the world.

His thoughts were pierced by the shrill ringing of the telephone.

Andre answered on the first ring, hoping and praying all the while that it was A.C.'s voice. His sigh of relief was audible when he heard her voice on the other end.

"What's the matter?" she asked almost immediately. "Your message sounded urgent. What's up?"

"It is urgent, A.C. I need your help. I need you to find someone for me."

"Who?"

"My son. He's been kidnapped."

She was silent for a moment. "Have there been any ransom demands?"

"No. He was taken by a family member, if you could call him that." The thought tore at Andre's insides. He hated Lucien Dupont. The man reminded him of someone from his past.

"There's a lot of that going around," she murmured.

"Excuse me?"

"Nothing. My sister recently finished another case with a missing child."

His stomach clenched tight. "She found the child?"

"Yeah. It wasn't easy, but she found him."

Andre's relief was evident. "That's good to hear."

"Why don't you talk to Onyx—"

He interrupted her. "No. I would feel better having you handle this case yourself, A.C."

"What's going on, Andre?"

"I told you already. I have a son and he's been kidnapped." Andre tried to hide his growing irritation. Right now he didn't want to be bothered with a lot of questions. Anxiety spurted through him. "We have to find him, A.C."

"Was he taken by the mother?"

"No. He was taken from her."

"I'll catch the next plane to New York."

The tense lines on Andre's face relaxed. "Thanks, A.C."

"No problem. Oh, Andre, I'm going to need to talk to the mother. Is she in New York?"

"Yes. I'll pick you up from LaGuardia and then take you to meet Raven."

"Sounds good. Try not to worry, Andre. I'll find your son."

"I know. That's why I called you . . ."

Andre ended the call a few minutes later. He felt relief at the thought of A.C. taking the case, but the fear did not completely dissipate. It was there hidden in the deep recesses of his mind. Every now and then it would slither out like a snake, threatening to choke his thoughts.

He wanted a chance to hold the son he had never known. "Please let me hold my son in my arms," he prayed. "Let me have the chance to get to know him."

His eyes grew wet with unshed tears. Andre couldn't remember ever feeling this helpless. He took a deep breath and tried to relax.

A.C. hung up her phone and glanced around her Los Angeles office. Richardson and Associates started out as a two-person PI agency, with A.C. and her sister, Onyx as partners. In the beginning, they worked primarily for corporations researching personnel.

Now, almost two years later, the agency had expanded to eight operatives, using former law enforcement officers. A.C. focused mainly on international crimes such as terrorism and takeovers, while Onyx concentrated mainly on missing persons and industrial espionage.

When they were approached by one of the world's richest men to find his son, A.C. initially declined, but Onyx convinced her to take the case. Her sister even insisted on handling the case herself. A.C. wasn't surprised, however. The thought of a child being held hostage really bothered Onyx. Her sister had always loved children and wanted to have a couple of her own one day.

Her phone rang. Thinking it might be her travel agent, A.C. answered it. "Richardson and Associates."

"Hey, it's me," a baritone voice boomed. "Since when do you answer the phones?"

Smiling, she leaned back in her chair and crossed her legs, relaxing. "My receptionist left early to pick up her sick child. Preacher, how are you?"

"Fine. And you?"

"I'm okay." She and Preacher were longtime friends beginning from her agency days. Now they both owned private detective agencies and spoke almost weekly. A.C. gave him a quick update of the goings on in her life and he did the same.

"I thought you stayed away from cases involving cheating spouses," A.C. was saying.

"Normally, I do. This one's different though."

"If you say so," she mumbled.

"Winston called me this morning," Preacher announced.

Hearing Winston's name prompted memories from A.C.'s CIA days. "What did he want?"

"Looking for some drug dealer. Kenison Moore."

"Why do I know that name?" she wondered aloud.

Onyx peeked into the office and waved. A.C. ended her call. "I've gotta go, Preacher. I'll call you next week." Hanging up the phone, she broke into a smile. "Hey Sis."

Leaning with her back against the door, Onyx asked, "When did you blow back into town?"

"Last night, but this is only a pit stop. I've got to leave for New York. I'm taking a red-eye later tonight."

"What?" Onyx shook her head in dismay. "A.C., why don't you let me take over for you? You're going to run yourself into the ground."

"This is a favor for a friend. You remember Andre Simone, don't you?"

Nodding, Onyx answered, "The artist. I definitely remember him. He's a handsome man." She sat down in one of the chairs facing A.C.

"Well, his son has been kidnapped and I've got to find him." Playing with a pencil, she added, "I didn't even know he had a child."

Onyx shifted her position in the uncomfortable chair. "Well, you have to remember that while you were deep undercover in Mexico for all those years—life continued." She moved again. "Girl, we need to get some better chairs."

A.C. agreed. "Sometimes I wonder if I changed or just everyone around me."

"I'd say it's a little of both."

"Onyx, what made you leave the DEA?" she asked, wanting to put all the pieces together. Her sister hadn't been herself since she showed up in Los Angeles two years ago. "I know how much you loved your job."

Her sister's expression suddenly became guarded. "Burn out," Onyx stated evenly. "It happens sooner or later. You know that."

A.C. surveyed her sister's face. "That's it?" Her instincts told her it was something more.

Onyx nodded.

"I don't believe you. It's more than burn out, but I'm not going to push. Just know that if you want to talk about it . . ."

"I know." Onyx stood. "I have a meeting in two hours, so I'd better get out of here."

A.C. stood, too. She moved from around her desk to walk Onyx to the door. "I'll call you when I get to New York."

Tilting her head to one side, Onyx stole a slanted look at her. "I'm the missing persons expert. Why don't you let me handle the case?"

"I was going to do that initially, but Andre wants me to

handle this one personally." A.C. met her sister's gaze. "I told him I would do it."

"If you need any help, I'm just a phone call away."

"I know." A.C. embraced her sister. "I'm pretty sure I'm going to need some assistance."

Onyx murmured, "Stay safe."

A.C. nodded woodenly. "I'll give it my best shot. You do the same."

The phone rang again.

"That's probably the travel agent. I'd better get it."

"Would you tell June that I need a flight to San Francisco, leaving day after tomorrow."

"When do you plan to return?"

"Next Monday. I shouldn't be gone any more than four days."

"I'll tell her." A.C. picked up the phone on the fourth ring. After giving the agent her sister's request, she had June fax over her confirmation.

Grabbing her leather backpack, she left the office and headed home.

Although she wasn't crazy about her assignment, A.C. loved New York. Maybe she would filter in some time to do a little shopping while she was there. Looking down at her black T-shirt and jeans, she frowned. It was time to buy some new clothes.

Michael whisked Raven from her suite shortly after ten that morning. He took her to Fifth Avenue where she browsed through Ann Taylor, Hermes and Tiffany & Co.

From there, Raven requested that they go to Bloomingdales where she purchased a couple of outfits for herself and for Julian.

"They have the cutest clothes for children," she explained.

"I hope you're having a good time."

Grinning, she replied, "The time of my life, Michael."

He laughed. "Good."

Michael offered to pay for her purchase, but Raven staunchly refused.

"And this time I'm taking you to lunch," she announced.

"You don't have to do that."

"I want to," she insisted. "So don't offend me by refusing. I want to do something for you for a change."

He relented. "Okay, I won't."

Raven instructed the driver to take them to Chanterelle in the TriBeCa area after calling for reservations. Smiling, she settled back against the leather seats.

"Have you ever been to Chanterelle?"

His whole face spread into a smile. "No, I haven't. Heard about it though."

"It's a beautiful place, Michael." Raven's face became animated in her excitement. "The dining room seems to glitter beneath the soft lights and they have these charming window alcoves. You can never get bored with the food because the menu changes monthly, I think."

"I'm sure I'll love it."

"You will," she assured him. "The food is delicious."

They made small talk as they rode to the restaurant. Once there, Raven and Michael didn't have long to wait before they were seated.

He allowed her to order for him. Raven chose the seafood sausage with a beurre blanc sauce.

"You're going to love it," she told him.

A faint light twinkled in the depths of his blue eyes. "I'm sure I will."

Michael told her about his upcoming business trip to Washington D.C. "You're welcome to come with me, if you'd like."

"It sounds inviting, but I'm afraid I'm going to have to decline. I need to stay in New York." Her mind was already searching for a plan to get into Michael's home while he was away.

"For your son?"

"Yes. For Julian." Raven reached for her wine glass. "How long will you be gone?"

"For about a week."

"I'll miss you."

"I won't be leaving for another couple of weeks."

"Oh." She tried not to let her disappointment show. Raven enjoyed Michael's company, but she was beginning to get vibes that he was ready to take their relationship further. She was going to have to work quickly.

After lunch, Raven talked Michael into going to the Metropolitan Museum of Art. "It's been a while since my last visit," she explained. "I want to see some of the new acquisitions."

It was after eight P.M. when Michael returned her to the hotel. He escorted her up to her suite.

"I hope I didn't wear you out. We've had a full day," she stated.

"I can't remember when I've had such a wonderful time. I have you to thank for that, Raven." Michael sat her shopping bags on the floor near the sofa.

"I had a great time, too."

His hand suddenly came down over hers possessively. "I don't want you to leave. I need someone in my life like you."

"Michael . . ." His declaration didn't come as a surprise, yet Raven had no idea how to respond. She didn't want to lie outright.

"I mean it, sweetheart."

She gently drew her hand away. "I don't want to rush things between us. I've not had much success in my relationships."

"I understand and I promise not to push."

She smiled in gratitude. "I appreciate that."

Raven allowed him to kiss her on the cheek. When she opened the door to let Michael leave, they found Lucien and Cal standing outside the room.

Her mouth tightened as she glared at them. "What are you doing here?" she demanded.

Lucien's dark eyebrows arched mischievously. "Hello, dear."

"How are you, Lucien?" Michael inquired.

"I'm fine. You don't know how much it thrills me to see you here with my goddaughter." His eyes strayed toward Raven. "Were you two on your way out?"

"No."

Michael stole a glance at Raven. "I was leaving actually. Raven and I spent the day together."

"Surely you don't have to leave right now. Cal and I came to see if Raven would have dinner with us. Why don't you join us?"

"We had a late lunch, so I'm not hungry," she stated dryly. "Right now all I want to do is take a long hot bath and catch up on my reading." Her eyes issued a silent challenge to Lucien. She dared him to push the issue.

Raven was well aware that Michael was silently observing them. Pasting a smile on her face, she said, "If *all* of you will excuse me . . ."

Lucien chuckled. "I get the distinct impression that you're trying to get rid of us."

Raven clamped her jaw tight and set her chin in a stubborn line.

It was Michael who broke the tension-filled silence by saying, "I get the hint. I'm going to say good night. Raven, I'll call you tomorrow."

She nodded. "Thanks, Michael."

Lucien waited until Michael disappeared around the corner before his mouth took on an unpleasant twist. "I don't believe you want to continue this conversation in the hall."

"Where is my son?"

"Julian's fine, Raven dear." He glanced at a couple coming toward them. "I think we should finish talking inside your suite."

Raven debated a moment before giving them entry. "What is it now, Lucien? Why are you here checking up on me?"

"I merely came to see how things are progressing."

"As you can see, things are fine," Raven snapped. "Now go away!"

His distinguished face had become brooding. "You really need to improve your attitude."

Raven held up a hand to silence him. "I'm tired, Lucien. Why don't you have your shadow take you back to wherever you're hiding."

"Hiding? Dear, I'm not hiding." Lucien rubbed his hand over the curved top of his silver-tipped cane. "I don't have to hide."

Raven ran her hands over her face in frustration. "I'm not going to argue with you. I'm doing everything I'm supposed to be doing. You just make sure nothing happens to my son."

"Get *Danse Macabre* for me. You and Julian can then live happily ever after. Involve the police or anyone else

. . . well, lets just say Julian and I will disappear. You'll never find us."

"Get out, Lucien!" she yelled.

He pretended to be hurt. "What happened to us, Raven? We used to be so close. You let Andre Simone turn you against me, but look what happened. He dropped you, dear. Without so much as a second thought, he dropped you. I hope you realize now that Andre never loved you."

Lucien's words hurt. Raven turned her back to him so he wouldn't see her pain. "I want you to leave."

She sensed his nearness. Raven moved out of his reach and turned around.

"Don't you dare try to comfort me, Lucien. You're the last person I would seek comfort from. *I hate you.*"

Giving her a smug look, Cal opened the door and held it for Lucien to exit. "I'll be in touch, Raven."

Shaking with fury, Raven picked up a vase without thinking and threw it. It crashed against the closed door, shattering into millions of pieces.

Andre couldn't reach Raven. He tried a fourth time. Then a fifth. Frustration mingled with distrust and he threw a pillow across the room. "Where are you?"

His question was met with silence in the empty room. The clock on the mantle read 8:30 P.M. He'd told Raven to stay in her suite, but obviously she hadn't listened to him.

Andre stared at his latest project, a painting of a seascape. He felt guilty because he hadn't bothered to pick up a paintbrush in the last couple of days. He was usually very disciplined. Andre tried to rationalize it by saying he didn't paint during holiday weekends, but it really wasn't true. He painted whenever the mood struck.

His stomach was in knots right now, so Andre didn't feel like painting. Raven dominated his thoughts—something he vowed would never happen again.

Andre made a conscious effort to relax his hands which were balled into fists.

A thought occurred when Andre noticed the blinking light on his answering machine. He hadn't bothered to check his messages before now. When he did, he found that Raven had called earlier to say she was spending the day with a friend.

"What friend?" he wondered aloud. Surely, she wasn't with Lucien. Andre shook his head. "Nooo. I know you're not with him."

He resisted the urge to call her a sixth time. He was pretty sure Raven hadn't returned home in the short span of fifteen minutes since his last call.

The phone rang and Andre answered it on the first ring.

"It's me," A.C. announced. "I'm at the airport. My plane leaves in forty-five minutes. I'll get in around eleven."

"Do you want me to pick you up?"

"No. I'll take a taxi to the hotel. I'll see you in the morning, okay?"

"A.C., thanks. I really owe you this time."

"That's what friends are for, Andre. I don't mind doing this for you."

"Just don't forget to send me the bill," Andre said matter-of-factly. "This is not a freebie."

She laughed. "I'll see you in the morning."

"Have a safe trip, A.C."

Andre was grateful for her call. He'd known she would

come as quickly as she could. A.C. always kept her word. He trusted her with his life.

He'd once felt that way about Raven. Blind trust—it could cause a person a lot of heartache.

Andre stole another look at the clock. He thought about trying to reach Raven one more time. Again he changed his mind.

There wasn't any news, so what did they really have to talk about? Andre had to finally break down and admit to himself that he merely wanted to hear her voice.

That admission haunted him for the rest of the evening.

Five

Raven sprang up from a deep sleep as if she'd been tapped on the shoulder. She glanced around the room, half expecting to find someone there, but the suite was empty.

Shaken and disoriented, Raven climbed out of bed and made her way to the bathroom. She had finally died from pure exhaustion around six that morning only to be resurrected at ten-fifteen.

Lucien's surprise visit disturbed her more than she realized. Raven cursed him for putting her in this situation, but she tried to console herself with the reminder that once this was all over, she would have Julian back.

She felt somewhat better after her shower and first cup of coffee. She ordered breakfast, but didn't eat it. Raven wasn't hungry. Still wearing her robe, she brushed her teeth and ruffled her short hair with her fingers.

Around noon, Raven got dressed and was ready to face what was left of the day. Raven located her cell phone and placed a call to Andre. She was disappointed when there was no answer. She hadn't heard from him at all in the last day. He hadn't even bothered to return her call after she'd left a message.

Maybe Andre had changed his mind and decided he

didn't want to be involved after all. Raven didn't want to believe it, but she had to face facts.

She had just hung up the phone when someone knocked on her door.

"Yes?"

"It's me."

Raven threw open the door.

"Andre . . ." Her voice died when she realized he was not alone. The woman with him was dressed in a pair of black jeans, a white T-shirt and wore her long black hair in a thick braid. Like Raven, she was also of mixed race. Her dark sunglasses successfully hid her eyes from view, but Raven could tell the woman was studying her as well.

Andre made the introductions. "This is A.C. Richardson. She's the person I told you about."

"She's going to help us get Julian?" Raven questioned. Looking at the beautiful woman, she couldn't imagine what A.C.'s part in all of this could be. "Are you a detective?"

"Yes," was the firm response. A.C. entered the suite and strolled around the room as if she were searching for something. She peered at lamps, taking the shades off and inspecting them closely. A.C. took the phone receiver apart and meticulously put it back together again.

"What is she doing?" Raven whispered.

"She's making sure there are no listening devices anywhere."

"Bugs?" Raven had never considered that Lucien could have someone listening to her. It shouldn't surprise her, she thought. *He's proven that he's capable of anything.*

"Is something wrong?" Andre inquired.

She shook her head. "No. I was just thinking that Lucien's capable of anything so I really shouldn't be shocked by any of this."

A.C. joined them. "Looks like we can talk safely here."

Raven gestured toward the wet bar. "Before we start, would either of you like something to drink? I have soda, tea and coffee."

"No," they answered in unison.

Dressed in a black knit dress with a fish motif, Raven sank down onto the sofa, half in anticipation and half in dread. Stealing a peek at Andre, she found him watching her and she became increasingly uneasy under his scrutiny. She didn't even want to venture a guess as to what he was thinking. He finally took a seat on the arm of the love seat.

Seated on the matching chair across from her, A.C. reached for the floral centerpiece and moved it down to the floor beside her. She pulled out a small notebook and a pen from her leather backpack. Leaning forward, she removed her sunglasses and said, "Raven, I'd like for you to start from the beginning and tell me what happened."

"Well, I hired a nanny for my son about three weeks ago. She told me her name was Marie Ducette. Three days ago, they left for the park and never returned. When I discovered she and my son were missing, I called the agency and no one there had heard of her."

"Marie Ducette? Did this Marie Ducette tell you specifically that she was from the agency?" A.C. questioned.

"Yes, she did and I'm afraid I believed her." With the admission came guilt. Raven was angry with herself for being duped by Miss Ducette. She should have been more careful.

"Did she ever tell you anything of her background?"

She relaxed a little when she didn't find judgment in A.C.'s eyes. "Only that she grew up in France. Marie told me that she'd moved here with her family about five years ago. I don't know if any of it is true." Raven could feel Andre's eyes boring into her and she refused to look his way.

A.C. wrote quickly. "What did the police say?"

"Before I could call them, my godfather contacted me. He told me that Julian was safe—as long as I did what he wanted and the police remained out of the loop."

Andre had been silent until now. "How could you be so careless as to hire someone without thoroughly checking them out, Raven?"

"The agency has a reputation of thoroughly screening their applicants. It's why I used them in the first place." Raven swallowed her tears. She wanted to shout that it wasn't her fault. But even she didn't believe that. She blamed herself.

Andre appeared to be studying her thoughtfully for a moment. "I'm sorry. I shouldn't have said that."

"I wouldn't have intentionally placed Julian in danger."

A.C. nodded in understanding before glaring at Andre. "Raven, I have to ask you this. Do you know anything more? And I'm going to need your godfather's name."

"Lucien Dupont." Raven spat the name out like it was poison.

A.C.'s face registered her surprise. "The Lucien Dupont? As in one of the richest men in the world?"

Raven nodded. "The same. He hired Marie Ducette to take my son."

"Why does he want the child?"

"He's using Julian as a pawn to force Raven to do something she doesn't want to do," Andre answered.

"What's that?"

"We'd rather not say, but it's something that could get her into a lot of trouble."

"I really wish I could figure out how he found me," Raven murmured more to herself.

A.C. laid her notebook on the table. "I can answer that for you. He hired my firm to find you."

Raven gasped. "You! You found me?" Her voice was shakier than she would have liked. "Why?"

"Are you serious, A.C.?" Andre cut in. "Why didn't you say something sooner?"

"I didn't make the connection until Raven mentioned Lucien's name. My sister actually worked the case," she explained.

"Please tell me you know where to find him?" Raven pleaded softly.

"I don't have any idea where he is right now, I'm afraid. After my sister located you, that was the end of our business with Lucien Dupont." Looking from one person to the other, A.C. continued, "The man is very wealthy and has homes all over the world, but I'll find him."

"I read that he recently purchased an island somewhere," Andre offered.

Raven's heart jumped in her chest. *"What?* Lucien has an island? If that's true, then we may never find Julian."

"I don't know anything about an island, but I have a feeling that's where we'll find the boy. He may figure that's the safest place to hide Julian," A.C. explained. "If he bought an island, I'll be able to find it."

"How are we going to be able to rescue my son if he's on some island somewhere? We don't have a clue where to look." It was becoming hard to breathe and Raven's chest began to tighten. Her stomach was churning with anxiety and frustration and her pulse began to beat erratically. Raven rushed to her feet and began to wander restlessly around the room.

"It's important that you remain calm, Raven," Andre told her. "A.C. knows what she's doing."

"The challenge is in pinpointing the child's location," A.C. admitted. "But once we find him—the rest is easy."

"Lucien's here in New York," Raven announced. "He's come to see me twice."

"Twice?" Andre questioned.

She nodded. "He was here last night."

"Will you be seeing him again?" A.C. questioned.

"I don't know," Raven responded honestly. "You never can tell with Lucien. He just seems to pop out of nowhere."

"If you do hear from him, be sure and call me." A.C. closed her notebook. "I'll check everything out and see what I can find. In the meantime, I'll need copies of your phone records. Maybe if we're lucky, your girl used the telephone to call friends or family. I'll also need the contact person and the name of the agency you used."

"A.C., I need you to do me a favor and keep this quiet. We can't involve the police. I don't want any harm to come to Julian. He's just a little boy." Raven decided to keep quiet about Pansy's death for now. She didn't know anything about A.C. and she didn't want to risk involving the police. If Lucien did kill Pansy as she suspected, then he wouldn't hesitate to kill Julian.

"I'll do what I can, Raven." A.C. rose to her feet. "Here is my card. If you remember anything, please give me a call day or night."

Andre stood and approached A.C., embracing her. "Thanks so much for your help."

"We're going to find them. I won't quit until I do." She glanced over her shoulder to where Raven was standing. "I promise."

Walking her to the door, Raven shook her hand. "Thank you, A.C."

When she looked at Andre, his expression darkened with an unreadable emotion. Raven felt a terrible tenseness in her body. "This is not my fault," she practically whispered. "I'm a good mother." Her voice started to grow in strength. "How dare you presume to blame me for what happened."

"You should know Lucien better than anyone. How could you believe that he would just let you slip away? You got careless, Raven."

The thought that he actually blamed her, stunned Raven into silence. Turning away from him, Raven walked away. Raven couldn't bear the look of disapproval on his face.

Tears threatened to spill forth, but Raven fought the urge to cry. She would not give Andre the satisfaction of seeing how deeply his comments hurt her. She was suddenly anxious to escape from his disturbing presence. "I think you should leave."

"I'm trying to talk to you."

"No, you're not, Andre. You're accusing me of being a terrible mother." Raven dropped down onto a chair, her fingers tensed in her lap. "Just get out."

Andre sat down beside Raven. Her features were contorted with anguish and he regretted his comments. "I'm sorry. I didn't mean to imply that you weren't a good mother."

"That's the second time tonight you've said that. However, you're absolutely right, Andre. You shouldn't have. *I am a very good mother,*" she replied in a low voice taut with anger.

He thought it best to change the subject before they found themselves arguing. Raven's mothering skills were still questionable as far as Andre was concerned, but he would let it rest for now. "Where were you yesterday? I called you at least five times, and I distinctly remember telling you to stay put."

"I spent the day with Michael." The insolence in her voice was ill-concealed. "I left you a message."

"But you never mentioned that the friend was Michael."

"I wasn't aware that I had to identify my friends to you." Raven's eyes met his. "Lucien showed up just as Michael was leaving."

"They saw each other?"

"Yes. I know Michael suspects something. I was barely civil to Lucien. I'm sure I can find a way to explain it to him."

Andre's face was marked with loathing. "You're going through with this, aren't you? You're going to steal that painting."

Raven lifted her chin and boldly met his gaze. "Don't you dare look at me in that way, Andre. I have to pretend to go through the motions until we find Julian. Lucien's not going to believe me otherwise. Hopefully, we'll find my son before I have to go that far, but we don't have much time."

Although Andre didn't like it, he had to agree with her. "You mentioned earlier that you'd moved to Georgia. Why Georgia?"

"Like you, I fell in love with St. Simons Island."

"So you moved there?" Andre's steady gaze bore into Raven in silent expectation. He was surprised to hear that she'd moved to St. Simons.

Nodding, Raven explained, "Lucien never knew of the time we spent there so I felt safe. It's where we . . . it's where Julian was conceived, so I thought it fitting that I raise him there as well." She chewed on her lower lip and stole a look at him.

"St. Simons was always a place I could wind down and just enjoy my surroundings. It inspired most of my paintings." He didn't add that his inspiration lacked its original luster after he and Raven split up. She had even taken that from him.

"But you hadn't been there in three years. Why not?"

A probing query came into his eyes. "How do you know that?"

"I just assumed because I never ran into you on the island. I used to visit your favorite spots quite frequently, hoping to see you."

Andre's eyes darkened with emotion. "I couldn't go back there. Not after we were . . ." He couldn't find the right words.

"So happy there," Raven finished for him. "Shortly after that, I decided to tell you the truth about everything."

Andre didn't want to rehash their final day together. It was one of the most painful days in his life. "I will always have my memories of St. Simons. Bittersweet memories. Going back now . . . well, it wouldn't be the same," Andre confessed.

"I'm sorry if I ruined your paradise for you." Raven said then.

Those were the words he avoided saying. Andre had a feeling she was waiting for a response but none was forthcoming.

Raven's eyes grew bright and she chose her words carefully. "I needed some part of you. St. Simons was all I had."

Andre's eyes grew wide, as if guarding a secret. "You can live wherever you choose. It's a free country."

There was a spark of some indefinable emotion in his eyes. Raven wasn't sure how to take his comment so she decided to change the subject. "What happens when we find Julian?"

He turned around to look directly at her. "We take him somewhere safe. Someplace where Lucien will not be able to touch him."

Raven sat slumped over with a worried expression. "I have to wonder if such a place exists. I'd thought so until he got his claws into my son." Her voice was resigned. She was restless and couldn't keep still. Pushing to her feet, Raven went to the wet bar and poured herself a cup of coffee. Looking over her shoulder at Andre, she said, "I have some herbal tea. Would you like a cup?"

Andre shook his head, drawing attention to the soft sway of his dreadlocks. "I'm fine, thanks."

Raven returned to the sitting area with her coffee and sat down.

"What exactly is this plan of Lucien's?" Andre questioned. "How are you going to steal a painting without Michael knowing?"

"I'm supposed to replace it with a copy."

"It's not going to work, you know," Andre said with quiet emphasis. "Michael would know if it were missing for even one night."

"Lucien intends to invite him to Martinique for a little R&R. I would join them a day later."

"So, you would stay behind to steal the painting and replace it with the copy."

"Yes . . . Michael locks up his gallery whenever he's traveling and there's only one person working around the clock. The others go home daily. I only have to drug that person—get into the gallery, steal the painting, replace it with the copy and get out."

Andre's voice hardened ruthlessly. "You've got things all figured out, don't you."

"This is Lucien's doing, Andre," Raven said in her defense.

"I'm not going to copy—" he started.

"You don't have to," Raven cut in. "He knows you won't have anything to do with something like this. Lucien already has that taken care of. As far as I know, he has no idea that you're even talking to me."

A frightening thought occurred to Andre. "Do you think he's having you followed?"

Shrugging, Raven answered, "I don't know."

"It's something else to consider. From now on, maybe we should be more careful. Being seen together could make this situation a lot worse. Do you have a cell phone?"

"Yes."

Andre pulled a piece of paper out of his shirt pocket. "Give me the number and I want you to write mine down as well."

Raven recited her phone number and then wrote his down. "So what do we do now?"

"We wait to hear from A.C." Andre ran his fingers through his dreadlocks. "That's all we can do for now."

"I've never been good at just sitting and waiting."

An uncertainty crept into his expression. "Raven, you're going to have to be patient this time. Any impulsive actions could result in failure."

"I won't do anything to jeopardize Julian's safety."

"When we find Julian, I want you to know that I intend to get to know him."

Raven detected a thawing in his tone. "I'm relieved to hear you say that. I've always wanted you to be a part of his life, Andre."

His hazel eyes searched Raven's delicate features

slowly, but Andre could detect no trace of deceit in her expression. However, he was still wary of her. Raven had perfected her look of innocence.

It was going to be a struggle for him to maintain the wall he'd erected around him where she was concerned. Even now, he ached to touch her. Each time Andre saw her, the pull was stronger, harder to resist. Her nearness made his senses spin. Unconsciously, he withdrew from her, deliberately trying to shut out any awareness of her.

Raven looked as if she was about to cry.

"What is it?" he asked out of genuine concern.

Tears stung her eyes. "I think Lucien killed my friend."

Andre was momentarily speechless in his surprise. "What are you talking about? What friend?" He wondered why she hadn't said anything before.

"Pansy. She was Julian's godmother and she was killed a couple of weeks before I hired Marie Ducette. Pansy used to take care of Julian while I worked."

"How did she die?"

"It was a car accident, but Lucien could have had the brakes tampered with."

"Why haven't you mentioned this before?"

"It just recently occurred to me. Besides, I don't have any proof, but how else could he have anticipated my needing a nanny?"

"Raven, why didn't you tell A.C.? She needs to know."

"I just said I don't have any real proof," Raven snapped. Restlessly, her hand stroked the arm of the chair. "I don't know if I'm going to make it, Andre. This is driving me crazy. I just want to hold my baby in my arms. What if we never find him? I—" Her voice broke.

"We're going to find him," he interjected quickly. "I

promise." Andre wrapped an arm around her. "Raven, don't you fall apart on me. I need you to stay strong."

Wiping away her tears, she nodded.

Andre was afraid to voice his biggest fear. If Lucien had her friend killed, then he wouldn't hesitate to bring harm to their son as a way of hurting Raven. Lucien was no doubt furious over the way she'd escaped him and the life of crime and deception he'd planned for her future. This was his way of keeping her under his control. Raven was right. They had to find Julian.

The feel of Andre's arms around her brought back familiar stirrings within Raven. She'd missed him so much over the past four years. When she met Andre, he gave her a taste of what a loving relationship could be like. He made her feel normal. When she fell in love with Andre, Raven went to Lucien and pleaded with him to give up his plan. In an effort to keep her under his thumb, he threatened to make sure Andre knew the truth about her and their relationship.

Raven went to Andre herself and confessed all to him. She thought it better that it come from her than to chance having Lucien put his spin on it.

Angry and hurt, Andre had thrown her out of the town house they shared and out of his life. It was then she formulated a plan to get Lucien out of her life for good. She'd erased all traces of herself and disappeared, or so she thought, while Lucien was away in Paris.

Raven got up and poured herself a fresh cup of coffee.

Silently, she prayed that God would return Julian to her. Raven wanted to watch him departing for school each morning with his backpack wagging as he rushed for the school bus. She wanted to listen to the sound of his voice and his laughter forever. Raven went back over to the sofa and sat down. She managed to sip the hot coffee, despite her shaking hand. Her eyes met Andre's over the rim of the cup.

The coffee jostled precariously as Raven set the cup and saucer down on the table. She leaned back against the plump cushions, her chin lowered against her chest in despair.

She wasn't aware she'd fallen asleep until she felt Andre gently nudging her. Sitting up groggily, she murmured. "I'm sorry. I didn't mean to fall asleep."

"It's okay. I'm sure you're tired. You look as if you haven't slept in weeks."

Her mouth turned downward. "Thanks, Andre. I really wanted to hear how terrible I look."

"You know I didn't mean it that way."

His gaze was riveted on her face, then moved slowly over her body. She felt a lurch of excitement within her at the realization that Andre still found her attractive. Raven moved toward him, impelled involuntarily by her own needs. She kissed him, lingering, savoring every moment.

The touch of his lips was a delicious sensation. Blood pounded in her brain, leapt from her heart, and made her knees tremble. Andre's hands moved gently down the length of her back. His lips seared a path down her neck and before Andre realized what he was doing, he was kissing her shoulders.

Caught up in the heat of passion, Raven pulled his face upwards. She pressed her lips against his. Her body responded to his touch, coming alive after all that time. She wanted him and knew Andre felt the same way.

He groaned softly, then pulled away from her, breaking their kiss. Andre rose to his feet abruptly, saying, "I'd better get out of here."

Her lips were still warm and moist from his kisses. "Do you have to leave right now?"

He nodded.

The mood had somehow shifted, she realized sadly. Andre had become guarded once more. Raven stood up and followed him to the door. "When will I hear from you?"

Andre refused to look at her. "I'll call you later. Leave your cell phone on."

Raven wrapped her arms around herself, below her bosom. "I will," she promised. There was so much more she wanted to say to Andre, but decided it was better left unsaid. At least for now.

"We are going to get Julian back, so try not to worry," he reassured her before leaving.

The suite suddenly felt lonely without Andre's presence. Raven stole a peek through the window at the picturesque skyline highlighted by the sun.

It was good to be back, but New York no longer felt like home. She didn't belong here in this busy panorama of asphalt and skyscrapers anymore. Home was wherever she and Julian would be safe.

How she missed him! The waiting was the worse part of all this. Raven felt like she was coming apart at the seams. She had to put a hand to her mouth just to keep from screaming.

Her body was filled with so much anxiety that Raven found she couldn't concentrate on reading or watching television. She finally gave up and picked up the laptop computer, carrying it over to the desk.

After she was seated, she opened it up and turned it on. Raven slipped the CD inside.

She made notes as she studied the floor plan of

Michael's house and the security system. Raven took pains to note the trigger attached to each painting.

Michael had invested top dollar to protect his collection, which was a wise thing to do. Without the help from someone on the inside, what Lucien wanted her to do would be an impossible feat.

You can't give up. The words echoed inside her. Her son's life was in her hands and Raven couldn't fail him. With renewed vigor, she turned her attention back to the computer screen.

Michael called her an hour later.

Raven wasn't really in the mood for conversation, but she managed to remain pleasant. "I'm glad you called." She shut down the computer. "I was just thinking about you."

Somehow she knew he was smiling on the other end.

"If you're not busy tomorrow night, I'd like to have dinner with you again. Afterwards, we can attend a Broadway show if you like."

"Sounds wonderful."

After Michael arranged a time to pick her up, they chatted for a little bit longer. Raven was relieved when he received another call that he needed to take. She hung up, feeling more depressed and distraught than before. Raven left the desk and strode over to the bed where she dropped down on the edge.

"Please hurry up, A.C.," she whispered. "I can't take much more of this. I don't want to hurt Michael."

As the day wore on, Raven spent the rest of the afternoon memorizing everything on the CD.

For the briefest of moments, she thought about going to Michael and telling him the truth. But would he believe her? He and Lucien were close friends and had been for years. Raven had no doubt that Lucien would turn everything around on her and she would be the one behind bars.

She wasn't willing to chance it. Not without any real proof.

Six

The next morning, Andre met with his attorney. As soon as they found Julian, he planned to sue for full custody of his son. He intended to give Raven reasonable visitation rights because he wasn't without a heart, but this wasn't the life for Julian.

As he rode home in the taxi, Andre refused to contemplate his feelings for Raven. He knew they could never have a future together because he would never be able to trust her completely. He allowed that she was not totally at fault. Lucien shouldered a lot of the blame. He'd raised her in an environment of lies and deceit. Frankly, Andre wasn't sure Raven even had a clear sense of right and wrong.

Family and surroundings helped to shape a person. Andre knew this from his own personal experiences. It was part of the reason he detested such dishonesty. His own family had been caught up in a web of lies and the results had been tragic.

Andre shook off the memories. He didn't want to think about that right now. Like Raven, all he wanted to do was find the son he never knew and hold on to him as tightly as he could.

He'd missed out on the first two and a half years of Julian's life, but Andre was determined to rectify that. From now on, he intended to be a permanent fixture in his son's life. He couldn't forget that Raven was also a part of that package. That simple truth caused his heart to hammer foolishly. The warmth spread from his stomach to the rest of his body. Since Raven had come back, Andre practically had to wrench himself away from this ridiculous preoccupation of her. She dominated his thoughts of late.

He decided to focus on Julian and exactly what he planned to say to his son once they were face-to-face.

Andre made a sandwich and poured himself a glass of soda. He sat down to eat alone, grateful for the silence.

A.C. muttered a string of curses. If Raven was telling the truth, then her sister had unknowingly participated in a kidnapping. A.C. didn't like the direction in which this case was going. Maybe there was another explanation. After all, Andre and Raven both had been very vague about some things. Maybe Raven hadn't been totally honest with either one of them.

She recalled the day Lucien had shown up at the office offering a large sum of money to locate his son. She and Onyx had been thrilled with the money, but if what Raven said was true, then it made A.C. feel like a fool. Worse yet, she felt guilty. A.C. wanted to get to the bottom of this puzzle. Holding her leather backpack close, she threw up her hand to hail a taxi. She was going to visit Andre. Until she found out the truth, A.C. decided to not say anything to Onyx.

By mid afternoon, Andre began to feel the strain of getting up before the sun ascended to the heavens. He'd lain awake most of the night thinking about Julian and

Raven. Although he would never let her know it—he was just as afraid as she was.

He had a lot of trust in A.C., but Andre had to admit that even she couldn't create a miracle. When Lucien dared to enter his thoughts, Andre curled his hands into fists. "If anything happens to my son, I'll hunt you for the rest of my life and I'll kill you," he vowed.

He wandered aimlessly throughout his town house, pacing back and forth. Walking did nothing to calm his agitated nerves, so Andre went upstairs to his studio.

He found he had no desire to paint either. He was tired and sleepy. Getting up early and then spending most of the morning at his attorney's office—Andre was more than ready for a nap.

He stretched himself out on the leather couch in his studio, propping a pillow underneath his head.

He has barely shut his eyes when the doorbell sounded. Andre tried to ignore it, but his visitor was persistent.

Andre rose to his full height, grumbling. He stomped down two flights of stairs, heading to the front door. His demeanor changed when he saw his visitor.

He kissed A.C. on the cheek. "I didn't expect to see you so soon, but I hope you've come with some good news."

"Nothing definite yet." She laid her backpack on his sofa. "Before things get crazy, I need you to be straight with me, Andre. What am I really getting into?"

He sensed that she was trying to draw answers from him. "Raven and I just want our son back."

A.C. clearly wasn't satisfied with his answer. "Does Lucien have custody of this child?"

"Custody? No. It's nothing like that."

"Are you sure?"

"I'm positive," came his dry response. Andre had a

feeling that she was on to something, or so she thought. He considered telling her what Lucien wanted of Raven.

"My instincts tell me there's more to this story." A.C.'s eyes met his. "I can't help you if you don't trust me, Andre."

"It's too complicated right now. But as soon as I can, I'll tell you everything."

"Don't wait too long, Andre," A.C. warned. "I don't like surprises."

"Trust me, A.C.," he urged.

"I do trust you. The question is whether Raven can be trusted. Is she telling the truth about everything?"

Lifting his chin, he answered, "Yes."

"Are you sure? Andre, I won't be a partner to a kidnapping. Are you positive Raven has told you the truth about everything?"

Confused, he wandered restlessly around the room. "What's going on with you, A.C.? Why all the questions?"

"I just want to make sure this time around. We believed him, Andre. There was no reason to do otherwise. Lucien had custody papers in his possession. I made a few phone calls on the way over and found out that there is no case file, so the papers Lucien has are fake."

"Then why don't you believe us?" Andre demanded.

Pacing slowly, A.C. played with a gold bracelet on her arm. "Something else is bothering me. Andre, you told me this was your child and that you've only recently found out. Are you sure?"

"Sure about what?" he asked.

"That the child is yours." She stared point blank at him.

"Yes," he answered with quiet emphasis. "Why do you ask?" Andre wondered where A.C.'s questions were leading.

"There's no way this child can be Lucien's?"

"No. That much I know is true. Raven never would have willingly gone to bed with that man. He's family to her. She sees him as a father figure."

"Children can also be conceived out of rape," A.C. murmured.

"Julian is my son. Of that I have no doubt." His voice was calm, his gaze steady.

"Good. I'm just trying to make sense of all this."

"A.C., when all this over, I'll tell you everything, I promise. I just can't get into it right now. I just need you to trust me on this."

"As I said earlier, I do trust you, but I have to make sure this is done the right way, Andre. My company's reputation is at stake. Not to mention that Onyx and I are involved."

"All I can tell you at this point is that Lucien took our son to force Raven into doing something illegal."

"Does it have something to do with art theft?" A.C. asked, her eyes narrowing.

Andre met her gaze straight on. "Why would you ask something like that?"

"Lucien's name came up in connection with a stolen painting. A Picasso was stolen a couple of years ago. He was in France at the time and also a guest on the owner's private yacht. Nothing was ever proven, however."

He abruptly changed the subject. "Were you able to find out anything about the island?"

"Nothing yet. I'll let you know as soon as I find out anything." A.C. stood. "I need to get going. Don't forget. If you or Raven hear anything, let me know."

"We will," Andre promised. "I can't tell you how much I appreciate your help."

"We're friends. But don't think that I didn't notice how you suddenly changed the subject." She picked up her backpack and slung it across her shoulder.

"Where are you going now?" Andre asked.

"To check on recent island purchases. Then I need to update my sister." A.C. shook her head sadly. "She's not going to take this well at all. Onyx hates being played for a fool."

Nodding in agreement, Andre said, "I know the feeling and I don't like it myself. That's the main reason Raven and I are not together now. She lied to me."

A.C. strode to the front door. "Do you still love her?"

Following her, Andre pondered, "Why does everyone keep asking me that?"

"Maybe that's a question you should seriously consider." A.C. turned to face him and placed a kiss on his cheek. "I'll be in touch."

Locking the door, Andre made his way back upstairs to his studio. He stared for a moment at his latest project. He picked up a brush and dipped it in red paint. He worked furiously, sloshing paint everywhere. Next, he assaulted the canvas with a bright orange, blending it into the red.

Andre worked with a vengeance. He painted for the next four hours straight before finally putting down his brush. He stepped back to admire his handiwork.

From his viewpoint, he eyed the house burning on canvas, flames spewing everywhere. Andre just stood there, caught up in the past. If he stared long enough, he could almost see the golden, red-orange flames dancing throughout the two-story house.

The painting seemed to take on a life of its own and Andre could almost feel the hot rage of the fire ripping at him.

"The flames of deceit," he mumbled. Andre stayed in his studio throughout the evening touching up his painting before succumbing to exhaustion. He didn't even make it out of the studio, opting to stretch out on the sofa and sleep there.

In his dreams, he heard a woman's scream warring with the loud ravings of a man. Together, their voices drowned in the flames.

Andre catapulted out of his sleep, drenched in sweat.

Raven decided to wear a platinum-colored dress for her date with Michael. She stared at her reflection in the mirror and whispered, "I'm doing this for Julian. When this is over, Julian and I will disappear again. Only this time, Lucien will never find us."

She applied her makeup, than ran her fingers through her short dark curls. Raven examined her reflection once more because she wanted to look her best. In a few short weeks, she was to make Michael fall in love with her and then betray his trust by stealing his prized possession. The whole idea of it made her sick to her stomach. But if she was lucky, he would never find out she was involved. Raven planned to be long gone before the robbery was ever discovered.

Truth of the matter was that Raven was beginning to have a genuine affection for him. She couldn't understand how Lucien could be so callous. Her godfather didn't care who he hurt as long as he got what he wanted in the end. She lived for the day Lucien would get what he truly deserved and Raven prayed fervently that she wouldn't have to pay the price along with him.

Michael arrived promptly at seven.

He did a double take when she opened the door to let him in. "You look beautiful as always, Raven."

Raven smiled at the compliment. "Thank you, Michael."

This time Michael took her to Layla, another favorite

haunt of his. Michael ordered for them both shortly after they were seated. This was Raven's first time trying Middle Eastern cuisine. She sat back and watched the belly dancers swaying through the maze of tables with little interest.

Raven wanted to relax and enjoy the evening, but it wasn't easy. She couldn't erase the tension running rampant through her.

"Why are you so quiet this evening?" he inquired. "Is everything okay?"

"It's fine," she lied. Michael was really a nice man and didn't deserve this duplicity. "I was just thinking about my son."

"I would like to meet him one day soon. Maybe we could take him to Coney Island. I used to go there often as a child."

Raven awarded him a warm smile. "He would love it. I'll keep that in mind."

"I was beginning to wonder what it would take to put a smile on that pretty face of yours?"

Raven gave a small laugh. "I'm sorry, Michael. My day was sort of rough, so why don't we talk about you? Why don't you tell me how your day was?"

Giving a slight wave of dismissal, he replied, "I don't want to bore you with talk of business meetings. Outside of that, I thought of tonight. I couldn't wait to see you."

She broke into another smile. "You are so sweet. I thought of you as well." She was grateful that he hadn't brought up the subject of Lucien showing up at the hotel the other night.

"You flatter an old man."

"You're not old, Michael," she countered. "I certainly don't think of you that way."

A waiter returned with their dinner.

"So you don't mind being seen with me?" he teased.

Her mouth twitched with amusement. "I don't mind at all. Spending time with you has truly been the highlight of my stay in New York."

Michael laughed richly. "I don't believe that for one minute."

"Well, it's true." Raven took a sip of her wine. The golden liquid slid down her throat, warming her insides. She felt the tension slowly evaporating with each sip.

Throughout their meal, Raven and Michael discussed their favorite subject—art.

When they had finished eating, neither one of them wanted dessert, so Michael paid the bill. Raven insisted on leaving the tip. They left the restaurant holding hands and laughing like children. From there, they went to see a play on Broadway.

Afterwards, Michael had his driver take them to the Excelsior Hotel.

"Would you like to come up and have a drink?" Raven offered. She didn't want Michael getting suspicious, so she decided she'd better act as if she had a growing interest in him.

"I'll take a cup of coffee, if you have it."

"French Roast okay?"

He nodded.

They took the elevator to her suite.

As soon as they were inside her room, Raven strolled over to the wet bar and washed her hands. While she prepared the coffee, Michael made himself comfortable on the couch.

Every now and then, Raven would glance over at him. Michael was one of the good guys. Handsome too. And so attentive and caring. He would make some woman a good husband, she knew. But none of it mattered to her because Andre was the only man she would ever love.

All Raven could aspire to was accepting that she and

Andre had no future together, but she would never stop loving him.

She poured two cups of coffee and carried them into the living room. She handed one to Michael.

"Thank you."

Taking her by the hand, he gently pulled her toward him. Raven sat her coffee on the table before easing down beside him. She looked over at him with effort and smiled.

Raven barely touched her coffee while they talked. When she felt Michael's arm slip around her waist, she mentally tried to prepare herself for what was about to happen next. He was going to kiss her.

Michael's mouth swooped down to capture hers. Although she kissed him back, Raven felt nothing. She kept her eyes shut to hide her tears. Raven wished it were Andre that she was sharing this moment with. She wished fervently that it were his arms around her.

Michael must have sensed her hesitation because he pulled away from her, whispering, "I guess I should say good night."

She nodded, unable to speak.

He stood up, straightening the custom made suit he wore. "Will I see you again, Raven?"

She forced a smile on her face as she rose to her feet. "Most definitely." Raven escorted him to the door. "Good night Michael."

He kissed her a second time before leaving.

Fighting tears of frustration and of guilt, Raven locked up behind Michael and headed straight to the shower. She doubted if she would ever feel clean again.

Afterwards, she slipped into a comfortable nightgown with matching robe in a vivid purple.

Raven turned down her bed and was about to climb inside when an incessant knocking on her door stopped her. She hurried to the door and looked through the peephole. It was Andre. She noted the fatigue and pain etched on his face. Something was terribly wrong.

Fear knotting inside her, Raven opened the door to let Andre enter. "What's wrong? Has something happened to Julian?"

"No. Everything's fine."

She was like a volcano on the verge of erupting. "Then why do you look so troubled?"

He looked as if he were weighing the question. "I . . ." Andre suddenly looked embarrassed. "I woke up from this dream." He put both hands to his face. "I'm sorry. I don't even know how I ended up here."

Raven recalled Andre's nightmares from before. But they had stopped after a while. "I thought the dreams had gone away."

His clothes were disheveled and his expression tortured. "Why don't you sit down, Andre? I'll fix you a cup of tea."

He did as he was told.

Andre would never talk about his dreams, but Raven knew it had something to do with a fire. She'd heard him talking in his sleep one night. Whatever happened to him had left him deathly afraid of fire. He wouldn't even strike a match.

"Did they just recently start up again?" she asked.

He nodded.

Raven handed him the cup. "Drink this, Andre."

"Thank you."

They sat in silence while he drank his tea. Raven could tell he had really been affected by this last dream. Even now, something disturbing replaced his smoldering look.

When he finished, Raven took the cup and saucer from him and placed them on the coffee table.

They sat there, not talking to each other. Raven played with the lace on the sleeve of her robe.

After a moment, he stood up. "I don't know why I came here. I should go."

She rushed to her feet pleading, "Please, Andre, don't leave."

He was shaking his head slowly. "Raven, I don't think this is a good idea."

Large, dark brown eyes took in his turbulent expression. Andre was hurting. But why didn't he understand that what he was feeling at the moment she also felt? "You need a friend, Andre. I need one too." Her voice trembled slightly.

Andre appeared to be thinking it over. Finally, he said, "I'll stay for a little while longer." Having said that, he made himself comfortable on the couch.

"Have you heard anything from A.C.?" she asked.

"Not since she came by my place earlier."

"Did she have any news?"

"Nothing yet."

Raven felt a little irritated. "She has to move quickly on this, Andre. Lucien's a very clever man. He could hide Julian someplace remote and we'd never be able to find him."

"A.C. will find him. I have a lot of confidence in her abilities."

"I'm glad to hear that." Raven had to look away because she wanted to crush Andre to her, comforting him, but she knew it wouldn't end there. She hungered for the sweetness of his kiss and she yearned to feel his touch . . .

He cut into her thoughts. "What are you thinking about?"

Raven glanced over at him. "I wasn't thinking about

anything in particular," she lied. "Actually, that's not true. I was thinking about the past."

Andre hesitated, measuring her for a moment. "The past? Why?"

She fingered the bracelet he'd given her. It had been on her arm since the moment he'd placed it there. "You don't ever think about it?"

"Sometimes it's all I think about," he admitted. His expression was guarded.

"Ever wish you could go back and change the past?"

"What would be the point?"

Disregarding the warnings of her heart, Raven asked, "Just answer the question, Andre. Do you ever think about us?" She was opening herself to heartache, but she couldn't stop herself. Raven had to know.

Her question hung in the air.

Seeing Raven in that nightgown was doing things to Andre. Having a child had not harmed her hourglass figure at all. Her stomach was toned and flat, her breasts . . . He glanced around the room, looking for something other than her body to focus on. "The past is the past," Andre stated. His mind floundered, as memories of the life they once shared floated through his head.

"There's such a wide gulf between us. Can't we call some kind of truce? I would like for us to put the past behind us—at least for now."

Andre's breath caught in his throat as he felt his heart pounding. "Raven, I think you're trying to make something out of nothing. This is not about us—it's about our son."

"I know that, Andre. Believe me, I know. However, there is something else going on. You treat me as if I'm nothing more than a stranger."

"You're overreacting," he accused.

"I don't think so." Raven regarded him with somber curiosity. "Andre, does this have something to do with Michael? Are you jealous?"

He wouldn't admit it, but it really bothered him that she was seeing Michael. He wasn't jealous though, Andre rationalized. He was simply worried that the man would be made a fool of and his affections wasted on Raven. *But that wasn't the whole of it,* his heart reasoned. "He's a good man."

"I know Michael doesn't deserve this, Andre. But it's either him or Julian."

Raven always seemed to know what he was thinking. "I still say you don't have to pull him into this craziness," he argued. "All you need to do is remain patient and give A.C. a chance to find Julian."

"This is my son you're talking about," Raven shot back. "I can't just sit still and do nothing."

"It may be asking a lot of you, but I need you to have some faith in me."

Her voice shook with raw emotion. "I do have faith in you, Andre. I've always had faith in you."

Her tone was not accusing, but Andre felt the sting of blame anyway stabbing at him. "Then give A.C. a chance. Let's keep everybody else out."

"In other words, you don't want me seeing Michael again. Am I right?"

He didn't dare respond or even glance her way. Instead, Andre reached for the remote control, asking, "Mind if I turn on the TV?"

Cold silence engulfed the room.

"You win, Andre. I'll give A.C. a few days, but if she doesn't come up with something soon . . ."

He looked at her then. "Does that mean you'll end things with Michael?"

"What if I happen to care about him?"

"Do you?"

"I do, but not in the way you think. I care too much for Michael to hurt him, so I'll do it. I'll stop seeing him. I have to do it gradually or Michael will get suspicious. I just hope my son isn't the one who has to pay."

"A.C. is good at what she does, Raven. She's one of the best."

The affection she heard in his voice prompted her to ask, "How long have you known A.C.?"

"A long time. About ten or eleven years."

"Really?"

"Yeah." Andre gave her a sidelong glance. "Why do you sound so surprised?"

"I've never seen or heard of her in all the time we were together. I'm just curious as to why you never mentioned her."

"She was out of the country. She only came back about two years ago."

Raven couldn't stop herself from asking, "Were you two ever lovers?"

Andre didn't respond, but just kept his expression blank.

When she realized he wasn't going to answer, she sighed and said, "Okay, I won't push." Raven leaned back against the cushions of the couch. "I hope you're feeling better."

He was. She could always make him feel better just by being around her.

"Andre, can I ask you something?"

He cut off the television and turned to face her. "What is it, Raven?"

"Did the nightmares come back because of me? I need to know."

"I already told you that they have nothing to do with you, Raven," he replied without inflection.

"Do you think you'll ever stop hating me?" she whispered.

"I don't hate you." Andre's eyebrows rose inquiringly. "Where are you getting this from?"

"You seem so cold toward me. If I haven't said it already—I'm sorry."

Waving off her apology, Andre said, "There's no point in dwelling on the past, Raven. Let's just move on."

"I can't stand all the disappointment I see in your face whenever you look at me." She paused before adding, "Mostly, you just don't look at me."

He couldn't tell her that it was torture looking at her, but not being able to touch her. Instead he responded, "I'm sorry, Raven. It's going to take some time."

She looked so sad and vulnerable. It really bothered Andre seeing her that way, but he couldn't let her get to him—he could never survive the heartache a second time. He had to get out of there.

This time when Andre readied to leave, Raven didn't stop him.

"The nightmares stopped for a while after we were together. Now they've started up again, but it has nothing to do with you. It's something I have to work out on my own."

"You still don't want to talk about them?"

"No." Andre stood by the door. "Thanks again."

"I hope you'll be able to sleep tonight."

"I want the same for you." Surprising himself, Andre pulled Raven into his arms. He stood there holding her, feeling the trembling in her body. Time stopped for them as they tried to give comfort to one another.

It was Raven who broke their embrace. "Please let me know as soon as you hear anything."

"I will," Andre promised. It was too easy to get lost in the way she looked at him.

He tried to shut out any awareness of her body so close to his. His mind burned with the memories of times better left forgotten.

"Are you going to be okay?"

Her words were like tepid water; drowning the fire that was slowly building and drawing his attention back to the present. "Huh?"

"Andre, are you okay?" She asked a second time.

"I'm just tired," he replied. Andre cleared his throat, pretending not to be affected by Raven.

She stood there, watching him intently. Her gaze was as soft as a caress. Without a word, Andre reached out, taking her face in his hand and holding it gently. The mere feel of her skin sent a warming shiver through him. Bending his head, his mouth covered hers hungrily. The touch of her lips was a delicious sensation. Andre took her mouth with savage intensity, leaving them both feeling weak and confused.

At last, reluctantly, they parted a few inches. "I'll call you tomorrow," Andre whispered hoarsely.

On the way back to his town house, he sat in the backseat of the taxi, staring off in a daze. Andre had no idea why he'd acted so impulsively. He was angry with himself over his actions. He acted as if he had no control over his own emotions.

After starting the shower in his bathroom, Andre ripped off his clothes and stepped inside the tub. Warm water sprayed over his body, giving him little relief.

Andre readied for bed. The phone rang and he picked up the receiver. "Hello."

"I've found something. Lucien recently purchased property in Tennessee. It's an island," A.C. announced.

"That's great news. I can't wait to tell Rav—" Andre

stopped short. "Do you know whether or not Julian's there?"

"I won't be able to confirm that until I actually go to Tennessee. I'm leaving first thing tomorrow morning."

"Maybe I should go with you?"

"No. I want you to stay here with Raven. She's going to need you. I'll call you as soon as I find out anything."

Relief and gratitude poured out of every pore. "Thanks again, A.C."

"I'll call you when I get to Tennessee."

Andre hung up. He then called Raven on her cell phone. It was late, but he knew she wouldn't mind his disturbing her.

She answered on the first ring almost as if she'd been expecting his call. "Andre?"

"A.C. found the island Lucien purchased. It's in Tennessee."

"Thank God!"

"Raven, she doesn't know for sure whether Julian's on the island, but she's leaving tomorrow morning to find out."

"I want to go with her."

"She's not going to allow that. A.C. wants to go alone. She said she'll call us as soon as she finds out anything."

He could hear the joy in Raven's voice. "I know he's there, Andre. Julian's on that island. I can feel it."

"If he is—A.C. will find him, sweetheart. *She will.*"

"I believe you. I can't wait to see my baby."

"I can't wait to meet him."

"He's a sweet little boy, Andre. You're going to love him."

"I know." He could hardly wait to see his son. Andre was looking forward to fatherhood. However, he wasn't thrilled with having to hurt Raven.

* * *

Raven rejoiced in the news that Julian would soon be back in her arms. She turned on the radio and danced around the suite.

Breathless, she dropped to the floor. Raven felt exhilarated to the point of shouting. Julian was finally coming home.

Tears of joy streamed down her face. She wiped them away in haste. It was too soon to get so emotional. Although she felt strongly about Julian being on the island—no one really knew for sure.

What if he isn't there? The question hammered at her, trying to shake loose her hope. Raven refused to accept any negative thoughts. She would not allow herself to believe that Julian would never be found.

Raven was too excited to sleep. Instead, she immersed herself in memories of the night Julian was born, and of the promises she'd made to him. "Once I get you back, I'm never going to let you go."

Seven

On Friday, A.C. flew to Asheville, North Carolina where she rented a car and drove to Douglas Lake. She hadn't called Andre yet because she wanted to verify her findings first.

Situated just thirty-five minutes from Gatlinburg on the north side of the Smoky Mountains, she enjoyed the gorgeous view of the shoreline.

"The perfect place to hide a child," A.C. murmured softly as she put away high-powered binoculars and wrote her notes in a small notebook that she carried everywhere with her. She'd spent the last three days observing the Dupont estate. She laid the binoculars beside a camera with a telephoto lens.

The island was accessible only by boat, seaplane, or helicopter. She noted that once on the island, there were several walking paths along the groves of cedar trees leading up to the house.

A.C. checked her watch. She was due to meet with her sister in a short while. Onyx had gotten a lead she wanted to follow-up. Gathering up her things, A.C. put them in her car and drove back to Asheville.

Onyx was already seated in the hotel lobby by the time she arrived.

"You're late," she complained.

"I know." A.C. laid down her backpack. "What happened?"

"I got a job. And you're not gonna believe what I'll be doing."

"Well, don't keep me in the dark. What?"

"I'm going to be a clown."

A devilish look came into A.C.'s eyes. "You're kidding."

"No. It's the perfect disguise, don't you think?"

A.C. burst into laughter. The image of Onyx made up as a clown was hysterical.

"Lucien's hired a circus for the child's entertainment. It's going to be there for the next three or four days. He requested four clowns. I'm going to bring Davies in as one of the other three. He's interviewing as we speak."

"This is crazy. Are you sure this is going to work?"

Onyx grew serious. "This is my fault and I'm going to set this right. I'm going to get that little boy back to his mother where he belongs. This is not going to happen to me again."

"Again?" To her knowledge, Onyx had successfully located all of the missing children in their caseload. "What are you talking about, Onyx?"

"Nothing. Look, I'm hungry. Can we get something to eat?"

A.C. eyed her sister. Onyx was hiding something. But what? She had a strong feeling that whatever it was, it had something to do with her leaving the DEA.

There was sadness in Onyx's eyes. It was never there before. Her sister had delved into all of her assignments with gusto and A.C. recognized the reason why—it was the same for her. They were both trying to stay busy to forget the pain.

For A.C., it was Gennai Li's death. A man she loved,

but before they could start a life together, he was killed right before her eyes.

Who or what was the cause behind her sister's heartache? A.C. was determined to find out.

Andre didn't call Raven until noon the next day. "I just heard from A.C. She's on her way back to New York. She's going straight to the Excelsior. She should be there in a couple of hours."

"Has she found—" Raven began.

"Yes, we'll talk when I get there."

"Andre . . ."

He hung up.

She shut down the laptop and put it away before going into her bathroom to shower.

Her heart sang with joy. Julian had been found. But Andre had hung up before she could find out if A.C. was bringing him with her.

Hopeful, she slipped on her clothes, a pair of navy pants and a white silk sleeveless shirt. She ran her fingers through her hair, fluffing her dark curls. After applying a light touch of makeup, she was ready.

A.C. arrived before Andre. This time she was dressed in a stylish black pantsuit and her hair was pulled into a bun at the nape of her neck.

"Hello A.C." Raven glanced around. "Where's Julian? Isn't he with you?"

"No, but I do know where he is."

Raven was disappointed.

"Raven, Andre told me that you suspect Lucien Dupont may have killed your friend. Why didn't you ever mention this to me?"

"I don't know for sure if he is responsible, but that's

the only way he could have known that I would need a nanny."

"Is there anything else you haven't told me?" A.C. pulled out her cell phone. "I'm going to make some calls and see if I can find out more about her accident. What was her name?"

"Pansy. Pansy Taylor-Ellis." Raven's throat felt tight and she tried to swallow. "If it's true, then it's all my fault and I'll never be able to forgive myself. Pansy would still be alive if she hadn't befriended me."

A.C. patted her hand. "You shouldn't blame yourself."

Andre arrived ten minutes later. He and Raven both settled down to hear what A.C. had to say.

"I found your son. Lucien has him on an island in Tennessee. It's not under heavy guard, but there are a few men patrolling the grounds. However, that won't stop me. I'm going to go in and rescue Julian."

"How do you know all this?"

"I haven't actually been on the island, but I have some people on the inside. Two, in fact. There are two docks, one of which is located in front of the main house. There are also three coves cut into the island, providing sheltered boat access. None of them have been used. The third one actually leads up to a hidden room in the house. My sister discovered it quite by accident."

"Have you seen Julian?" Raven wanted to know.

"Yes, from a distance though. Onyx has seen him up close and he's healthy and happy. He's with the nanny you hired. She appears to be taking very good care of him, Raven. She takes him for walks on the estate daily. For the last couple of days, there have been clowns and other cartoon characters on the grounds to entertain him. Lucien has arranged for a mini-circus, it seems."

"Julian loves the circus," Raven murmured.

"He calls Lucien grandpapa."

Pain ripped through Raven.

"My sister is there masquerading as one of the clowns along with one of our other operatives."

"How on earth are you going to get on the island long enough to rescue Julian?" Andre asked. "And when? Can't Onyx and this other person just take him off the island?"

"They could," A.C. admitted. "But I don't want to risk blowing their cover. The circus will be there two more days. I'll go in and get him day after tomorrow. Lucien will be leaving Monday morning on business."

"I'm going with you."

"Andre, I don't think that'll be a good idea. We're trained for this type of assignment."

"I'm going, A.C.," he said more firmly.

"Me, too," Raven announced. "I need to be there. Julian doesn't know any of you. He's been frightened enough already."

"You will have to remain in a hotel, Raven. *Both of you.*" A.C.'s tone brooked no argument. "We're going to have to charter a boat to get on the island. The only way on and off is by boat or plane. This is going to have to be done very quickly."

"Why can't we just wait in the boat?" Raven asked.

"I can't guarantee your safety," A.C. explained. "Besides, it going to be something small. One of the coves leads directly to the house. We're going to hide the boat there."

"I need to go in with you," Raven insisted. "For this to work, I have to go with you. Julian will be scared. This could even traumatize him. Besides, I can keep him quiet."

Andre took her by the hand. "I have to agree with Raven."

"We could give him a sedative," A.C. suggested.

"No! That's absolutely out of the question."

"I won't lie to you. This could get dangerous, Raven."

"Julian is my son. He needs to see my face. That's the only way this is going to work. I'm not faint at heart, A.C. I'm also pretty good with a gun. Some might even consider me a crack shot."

A.C. tried to hide her amusement. "I see."

Andre was just as determined. "We're going with you, A.C."

Shrugging in resignation, she said, "Okay, but you're going to have to listen to everything I say. It's imperative that you follow my directions to the letter. If you don't, you could lose your son forever."

"I won't let that happen," Raven stated.

"We'll do whatever you say," Andre agreed.

Nodding, A.C. said, "Good. Why don't we get started?"

Raven glanced over at Andre. For the time being, they were a team. After they found Julian, she was sure they would go back to being strangers, and Raven tried to prepare herself mentally and emotionally. It would be like losing him all over again.

While going over her plan, A.C.'s phone started to vibrate. She looked down at the caller ID. "I'd better take this call."

A.C. reached for her pen and started to write. Raven could tell from her end of the conversation that it concerned them. She tried to hide her trembling hands within the folds of her jacket.

"Everything's going to be fine, Raven," Andre said in a low whisper.

"I know," she whispered back.

A.C. ended her call. "That was Onyx. Everything is set." She went back over the details of their plan.

"Are you sure that the coves are safe?" Raven inquired.

"Onyx is pretty sure that they don't know about the one we're going to use."

"You said that it leads to the house."

"Yes. She only found it by accident. She says that part of the island isn't guarded." A.C. rose to her feet. "I need to get going. I still have a lot to do."

They escorted A.C. to the door. "Thanks again," Raven murmured.

"Be ready," she advised. "We leave first thing tomorrow morning."

"We will," Andre vowed.

"Raven, you'll fly out with me," A.C. stated. "Andre will be on a separate flight."

Raven knew A.C. still had doubts about her coming along, but it was important that Julian see her face instead of strangers.

"What's on your mind, Raven?" Andre inquired after A.C. was gone.

She looked up. "Julian."

"It's almost over." He took her hand and led her over to the sofa.

"I know. Andre, I can't thank you enough."

"He's my son, too."

They sat down beside each other in silence for a moment.

"I appreciate you telling me about Julian. You didn't have to—especially after I treated you so badly."

"I guess I deserved it."

"What are you going to do when this is over?"

Raven turned to face him. "I haven't given it much thought," she admitted. "But I've been thinking about going to Holland for a while. I have some relatives there. An aunt and a host of cousins."

Andre didn't say a word. He appeared to be deep in thought.

"After Holland, I don't know where we'll end up. At some point, I'll have to get a job because I don't have enough saved to allow me to retire."

"I'll give you money—"

Raven cut him off. "I'm not after your money, Andre. We've been doing fine without it." She knew she sounded defensive, but she couldn't help it. She didn't want Andre to think this had been part of her plan all along.

"Julian's my son and I'm not going to abandon my responsibility. I want to help you."

Giving him a tight smile, she said, "Let's just get him back first."

"We have to have a plan though. You have to take Julian someplace safe."

Raven nodded in understanding. She really didn't have anywhere to go. Suddenly, she felt alone.

"Have you ever met them? Your relatives in Holland?"

"My aunts came to visit us a couple of times while my parents were alive. After the deaths of my parents, one of my aunts contacted Lucien about seeing me, but he refused."

"Wouldn't that be the first place Lucien would look for you?"

Raven shook her head "no." "I've never had a relationship with any of those people. They didn't want me after my parents died."

"You never thought he would find you in Georgia, but he did."

"You're right about that. This time I'll have to be more careful. I guess Julian and I will have to assume new identities or something. I used my mother's maiden name the last time."

"Do you think going to Holland is best? You've said yourself that you hardly know those people."

"I don't know what else to do, Andre. I . . . I really don't have anywhere else to go and I'm tired of being alone. Julian needs to get to know some of his family."

"You're sure about this?"

She nodded. "As soon as I get Julian back—we're on the first plane to Holland. Lucien would never think of looking for us there. "

Andre didn't like the idea of Raven taking his son all the way to Holland. He wanted a chance to get to know him, but with Lucien on the loose, it would be difficult. Unless. . . .

He didn't like where his thoughts were headed, but there didn't seem to be another solution. Andre would just have to go with them. They wouldn't have to go to Holland, however. He knew exactly where they could go and be safe. Andre had always known he would have to return one day to face the tragedy of the past. Maybe now, the nightmares would finally end.

Eight

The next morning Raven and A.C. left for the airport. They flew to Washington, D.C. where they met up with Andre. The trio then headed along the busy corridor toward their departure gate.

Raven sat watching the clock as they waited for the boarding to begin on the flight that would take them to North Carolina. In a surprise move, Andre took her hand in his. He didn't say a word nor did he glance her way. Perhaps it was simply her own uneasiness, but he seemed as restless and worried as she.

She spied a tall, dark man with a bald head coming toward them. Raven stole a peek at A.C., who did not seem at all alarmed.

"This is Preacher Watson, a very good friend of mine," A.C. announced. "Now the gang's all here."

Half an hour later, they boarded the plane that would take them to Asheville.

Raven couldn't stop her trembling. She was scared, but never once considered backing out. She wanted Julian back with her and would go through the depths of hell to make that happen. She was grateful for the way things had turned out. Michael was leaving today for business. When he returned, she would be long gone.

Andre glanced over at her. "You okay?"

She nodded.

"Are you sure?"

"I'm okay."

"You seem like you're a thousand miles away. You haven't said much since you arrived."

"I was just thinking of the moment when this nightmare is over. I just want to hold my baby in my arms. I'm not ever going to let him go."

Andre's expression changed and he looked away, prompting her to ask, "What about you? Are you doing okay?"

"I'm fine. No, that's not exactly true. I am a little anxious," he admitted.

Raven had no idea why, but his confession made her feel better.

A.C. heard him. She turned and said, "Andre, it's not too late. You and Raven can still back out."

He shook his head. "No, we can't. We have to go through with this. It'll be over tonight."

Deep down, Raven didn't believe that for a minute. She knew it would never really end for her until Lucien was dead. The last thing she wanted to do was walk away from Andre, but she had no choice in the matter and it saddened her. Raven hated the thought of losing him all over again. She wasn't sure she would ever see Andre again but then there wasn't anything between them, outside of Julian.

A.C. turned around to face them. "If either one of you is not comfortable with any phase of this mission, I need you to tell me now."

Raven spoke first. "I'm ready to get my son."

"Everything's fine, A.C.," Andre stated. "We're ready."

She watched them a minute before turning back to the front.

Andre took Raven's hand and squeezed it in assurance. She smiled and leaned back into the seat, closing her eyes. It was going to be so hard leaving him again. Only this time, it would be final. Raven found herself wishing that that time would never come.

Everyone had dinner together that evening. Andre looked up and found Raven staring off into space. She'd been so quiet on the plane and even earlier after checking into the hotel in Asheville.

Preacher and A.C. were engaged in conversation and appeared to be having the time of their lives. Andre sliced off a piece of chicken and stuck it into his mouth.

He chewed thoughtfully. His eyes traveled to Raven, who was now playing with her food. She moved around the artichokes from one side of the plate to the other. She hadn't even taken more than a couple of bites from the looks of it.

Raven caught him watching her.

"You should eat," Andre advised.

"I'm not real hungry."

"You're worried about your son, but he's fine."

Raven turned to look at A.C. "He may look fine on the outside, but who knows what he's feeling inside. The thought of him being along and scared really kills me, you know."

"Your son most likely thinks he's on a vacation or something. Only you know the truth. Lucien is very good to the child according to Onyx."

"I know you mean well, but that, really gives me little comfort, A.C. I can't bear the thought of my baby in Lucien's clutches. It pains me to even think about it."

She nodded in understanding. A.C. returned her attention to her food.

Raven glanced over at Preacher. "I really want to thank you for helping us."

He awarded her a rare smile. "The pleasure's all mine."

Andre prompted her a second time. "Try and eat something, Raven." He didn't want her passing out on them tomorrow night.

She sampled her fish, but ignored the rest of the food on her plate. Andre was about to push again, but A.C. shook her head. He backed off.

After dinner, Preacher and A.C. went for a walk. They'd invited Raven and Andre along, but both declined.

They stepped off the elevator.

"Would you like some company?" Andre asked.

Raven shook her head "no." "I think I'm just going to call it a night."

Scanning her face, he asked, "You okay?"

"Just a little scared."

Andre embraced her. "I'm here if you need me."

Raven looked up at him. "Thank you for saying that."

"I mean it."

She nodded. "I know."

He walked her to her room. "I'm right next door. Just call me."

"I will," she mumbled softly. Raven unlocked her door and stepped inside. She turned around. "I'll see you in the morning."

"Sleep well, Raven."

"You too."

Andre smiled. "It's almost over. Just keep telling yourself that."

He stayed outside her door until he heard all the locks in place. Andre entered his own room, deeply relieved that Raven had turned down his invitation. Right now they were both very vulnerable. In this state, they could easily end up in bed together, and to do so would be a big mistake. There could be no future together—Raven destroyed that chance a long time ago.

After spending the entire day going over their plans, the time for action had finally arrived.

The sky was illuminated by the brightness of the full moon. Raven sat in the boat chewing on her bottom lip. The silence was nerve wracking and it was driving her crazy. She tugged at the neck of her black sweater.

"You shouldn't worry, Miss Christopher," Preacher reassured her. "A.C. will be back shortly. When she returns, we're going to have to move quickly."

She nodded.

Andre wrapped his arms around her. "It's not going to be much longer."

"A.C.'s been gone awhile. Maybe something happened," Raven worried.

"Here she comes," Andre interrupted. He pulled his dreadlocks back into a ponytail and slipped a rubber band around them.

"Are you two ready to get your son?" A.C. asked when she returned.

"Yes," they said in unison.

"Let's go."

Andre helped Raven out of the boat and into the water.

"We're going to have to tread water, but it's not much."

Raven held onto Andre's hand as if her life depended on it. "Please don't let them catch us," she prayed softly. "Keep us safe from harm." She hid behind a huge rock and waited for A.C.'s signal. Then she followed Andre along the dark path leading to Lucien's house.

They were careful to stay close to the bushes and the cedar trees. She followed A.C.'s instructions to the letter. The house was huge and looked ominous in the moonlight. On the grounds was a huge tent. Julian's circus. *Where are the people?* she wondered.

They entered the house through a hidden room. Stealthily they took the stairs to the first floor. A.C. checked to make sure the coast was clear before they entered a room that Raven assumed was the library. The first floor consisted of a large living room, dining room, library and kitchen.

Onyx met them in the hallway. "Lucien left earlier today for Los Angeles," Onyx whispered. "He took four men with him and the other four are sleeping like babies in the servants' quarters behind the house, thanks to this." She held up a bottle with clear liquid in it.

"Where are the circus employees?" A.C. asked.

"Everyone leaves the island everyday at five. Davies and I charted a small boat and came back."

"What about the nanny?"

"She's a sound sleeper. Besides that, she's harmless."

Raven stealthily ascended the stairs. The house was quiet and seemed empty. Spotting one of the security cameras, she stopped. Turning to Andre, she pointed and mouthed the word, "camera."

"Onyx's already taken care of that," A.C. whispered. "Keep moving. We only have a few minutes to get the child and get off this island."

Pulling out his gun, Preacher said, "I'll stay down here. A.C. will stay with me. Onyx, you take them to the boy."

Leading the way, Onyx led them to the room where Julian lay sleeping. Gesturing for Raven and Andre to stay back, she peeked into the room first and then motioned for her and Andre to enter. Raven headed straight for the bed.

With tears in her eyes, she stroked her son's cheek. He woke up immediately and reached for her whimpering, "Mommy. Mommy."

"Ssssh . . ." Raven cuddled him to her chest. "It's okay, baby. These are Mommy's friends. Don't be scared. Mommy's here now."

Julian stuck his thumb in his mouth.

"He's never sucked his thumb." Tears filled her eyes. "Oh baby . . . I'm so sorry."

The little boy whimpered in response.

"We've got to get out of here," Onyx whispered.

Fear gripped Raven as they headed to the door. It opened and they were face-to-face with Marie Ducette.

"He's missed you," she whispered fearfully. "I kept telling him you were coming to get him."

Pointing her gun at Marie, Onyx uttered, "Move out of the way."

Holding her hands up, Marie replied, "I won't make any trouble. He should be with his mother. I was going to try to leave the island with him . . . I have a bag already packed for Julian." She pointed toward the bed. "It's hidden under there."

Andre knelt down to check. He pulled out a backpack and said, "She's telling the truth."

"Can I go with you? Please. I just want to go home."

Raven heard the fear in her voice. "Onyx?"

Aiming her gun toward the girl, Onyx said in a low voice. "If this is some ploy, I will kill you."

The girl gasped and then began to cry. "I didn't want to do any of this. I didn't."

"Let's get out of here," Onyx ordered. To Marie, she

said, "There's no time to pack. If you're coming—we have to leave now."

Marie nodded. "I don't need anything. I just want to leave this place. I am ready."

When they met up with Preacher and A.C., he took one look at Marie and asked, "Who's this?"

"The nanny," Onyx announced. "We're booking her on the first plane to Paris."

He nodded in response. They then left quickly and headed down to the cove.

"Do you know what you're doing?" A.C. asked.

"Yeah, I do. She got caught up in a bad situation and I'm giving her a way out," Onyx announced.

Raven could see a strong resemblance in the two women.

"This is my sister," A.C. confirmed.

Onyx shook hands with Raven. "I'm so sorry about all of this. I really thought Lucien Dupont was telling the truth. A.C. never really wanted to take the case in the first place. I should have listened to her. "

Now that she had her son back, Raven was in a forgiving mood. "It's over. Julian's back with me and that's all that matters."

In the boat, Raven eyed Marie. She looked no older than twenty-four. Forgiveness vanishing, she demanded, "Why did you do it?"

Marie looked ashamed. "My family needed money. Monsieur Dupont said you were not a good mother."

"He lied to you, Marie."

"I believed him."

Raven scanned the young woman's face. "You are afraid of Lucien. Why?"

"I don't like the way he looks at me. There have been times when I've woken up and he was in my room. He would stand there and just stare at me."

"Did he ever touch you?"

"No. I was just afraid that . . ."

"That it would come to that," Raven finished for her. "I'm so sorry."

"I have no one to blame but myself. I was greedy."

"Preacher's chartered a couple of planes for us," A.C. announced. "Andre, you and your family will be on one. The rest of us will be on the other. Once you arrive to your destination, I'll be in touch."

He nodded. "Thanks for all you've done."

"This was easy compared to what I've had to do in the past."

Raven glanced down and caught sight of A.C.'s ankle holster. She knew her strength wasn't hidden behind the guns she carried and Raven admired her. She wanted to be in control of her own life like that.

"What is going to happen to me?" Marie asked no one in particular. "Am I going to jail?"

"You are returning to France. If I were you, I'd marry some nice Frenchman, have a couple of babies of my own and settle down," A.C. advised. "I wouldn't even come back to America. Not even for a visit. *Understand?*"

Marie nodded. "I just want to go home. What about my parents? They are here in America."

"We can arrange for them to join you," Preacher announced. "We'll need to move quickly on that. Lucien will probably start with them when he begins looking for Marie."

"What if he finds me?" She started to tremble. "Monsieur Dupont is a very wealthy man. He will kill me." Marie broke into tears.

"You will be under the protection of a friend of mine. You and your family will be safe," Preacher assured her.

"Preacher is our relocation expert. He can make anybody disappear."

"Can he make us disappear?" Raven asked. She was conscious of Julian picking at the buttons on her sweater.

A.C. nodded. "If it's what you truly want."

Raven glanced over at Andre. "I don't think I have any other choice."

"Why don't you think about this some more?" A.C. suggested.

Kissing Julian on his forehead, Raven decided to do just that.

"He's a beautiful little boy," Onyx murmured.

"Thank you."

Leaning forward, Onyx inquired, "Julian, would you mind if I asked you for a hug. Just a little one?"

The toddler held open his arms.

She hugged him close. "Oooh, you feel so good. . . ."

"You sister really loves children," Raven whispered.

"Yeah, she does," A.C. replied.

Rubbing Julian's back, Raven held him close to her. She would die before she let him be taken from her again.

The plane landed in a remote location. Raven had no idea where they were and she didn't really care as long as Lucien couldn't find them. Standing outside one of the airport hangars, she thanked A.C. and Preacher once again. She turned to Andre and said, "I guess this is it. We're off to Holland."

"You're not going to Holland," Andre announced.

She looked surprised, "Where are we going?"

"I'll tell you once we're on the plane." He pointed to the next hangar. "This is our plane."

"You're going with us?"

Andre nodded. "Would you rather I didn't?"

"No," she responded quickly. "I'd feel much safer if

you did. I'm just kind of surprised, that's all. Never in a million years would I have imagined that you'd be coming with us."

Staring at his son, Andre stated, "I have my reasons for coming along."

He wanted to get to know his son and the thought thrilled Raven. She'd always believed that children needed both parents.

She settled back, feeling much better now that she and her son were reunited. Raven placed a gentle kiss on Julian's forehead. She was aware of Andre watching her every move, but pretended not to notice.

He puzzled her. There were times she sensed that he was fighting some war within himself. It was almost as if he wanted to keep his feelings hidden. Was it possible that he still cared for her? Raven wondered. Hope rose within her, followed by doubt. No, Andre didn't trust her. He had been hurt by her and would never grant her a second chance.

One hour later, Raven and Andre were in the air en route to Chicago. From there, they took another plane to New Orleans, Louisiana. A.C. had explained that they would be taking several chartered planes under assumed identities to cover their trail.

"Why are we going to New Orleans?" Raven questioned.

"My mother lives there."

This came as a complete surprise to Raven. "I thought she lived in Boston."

"She did. She moved to New Orleans about three years ago."

"Does she know we're coming?"

"No," he replied. "I thought it best just to surprise her. She won't mind though. My mother's been after me to visit for a while now. It's long overdue."

"Oh."

"It's going to be fine. My mother will be thrilled to see us, I assure you." Looking over at Julian, he added, "She feared she would never become a grandmother. She's going to be delighted."

"I'm relieved to hear that," Raven confessed. "Although I'm sure she's going to have some questions."

"I'll explain everything to her. Don't worry."

But Raven did. She worried if Andre's mother would take one look at her, and then slam the door in her face.

A.C. was still pondering her sister's reaction over Julian. She couldn't remember ever seeing Onyx so emotional over a child. Especially one who was a complete stranger to her. *What was going on with her?*

"Well, it's time Marie and I boarded our plane," Onyx announced. She embraced her sister. "I'll see you in a few days."

Gesturing toward Marie, A.C. said, "Keep her safe."

Onyx smiled. "As always, I'll give it my best shot."

A.C. watched her sister's departure, worry creasing her brow. She felt strong hands on her shoulder.

Turning around to face Preacher, she said, "Well, the children are off. I guess we can go home now." She hugged him. "I'm really gonna miss you. It's too bad we don't get to work together much."

He nodded. "It's been fun, A.C., but I can't wait to get back to my wife," he stated. "Sabrina's pregnant again."

A.C. beamed with joy. "Congratulations! I'm so happy for you both. How are Matt and Kaitlin? I haven't spoken to them in a while."

"They're doing okay. Travaile is growing like a weed."

"I'm sure."

They walked toward the airport terminal. "All of the Ransoms ask about you," Preacher announced. "You missed the last big barbeque."

"I know. I just couldn't go . . . they're all so mushy, you know. Seeing all that love and happiness flowing around just kind of makes me sick."

"You still miss him a lot, don't you?"

A.C. nodded. "I do. Gennai and I never had a real chance. I think back on all the time I wasted with Matt—"

"I don't know if he would see it that way," Preacher cut in.

She smiled. "You know what I mean. I always thought Matt was the one for me. We cared about each other and I'll never forget the time he and I spent together, but Gennai and I . . . we really clicked, you know."

"Gennai wouldn't want you going around all alone. He would want you to move on with your life. Are you dating?"

"With the business, I really don't have any time for dating." She fingered the strap of her leather backpack. This was not a topic she enjoyed discussing.

"You're the boss, A.C. Make time. Your company is doing well."

"Maybe in a few months. Right now I want to focus on work."

Preacher shook his head. "I think my wife might be dead wrong on this one."

A.C. frowned. "What are you talking about?"

"Sabrina had a vision right before I left. It was about you. She saw you wearing a wedding dress."

She burst into laughter. "You're kidding me, right?"

Preacher shook his head "no." "I'm not a kidder."

"Well, I agree with you. Sabrina's off on this one." A.C. broke into more laughter. "She couldn't be more wrong.

Must be those pregnancy hormones throwing her off."
She embraced Preacher. "I really appreciate your help."

"Anything for a friend."

"I hate to see you leave. Give Sabrina and that cute little boy of yours a big hug and kiss for me."

"Will do." Preacher gave her a slight nod and disappeared into the crowd.

A.C. watched him until she couldn't see him anymore. He was a man going home to his family. She would never know what that felt like. She put on her sunglasses and headed in the opposite direction.

It was a sad, dismal thought at best.

Nine

Tuesday morning, the New Orleans sun embraced Andre and Raven with rays of warmth as the weary couple climbed out of the cab and slowly made their way up the steps of the corner house on Royal Street. Raven shifted a sleeping Julian in her arms to a more comfortable position.

The housekeeper met them at the door. Her mouth opened in surprise, but she recovered quickly and wrapped her arms around Andre, saying, "It's so nice to see you again. I had no idea you were coming."

He smiled. "It was a last minute decision, Anna."

The plump woman escorted them into a huge two-story house with an imposing Greek Revival entrance. After seeing that they were comfortable, Anna offered to put Julian to bed.

"Anna has been with the family for years. She'll take good care of him," Andre assured Raven who stared back at him.

"I can't bear losing him again," she stated.

"He'll be safe here. You have my word."

Raven relinquished her son to the housekeeper. She watched as the woman carried him up the stairs until she couldn't see them anymore.

"He's in good hands," Andre assured her. "Anna

would die before she allowed something to happen to Julian."

She gave a slight nod.

"Andre . . . my goodness, it's so good to have you home," a woman called out as she rushed into the room. "I never thought you would come *here.*"

Andre stood up and embraced the petite woman tightly. After giving her a kiss, he made the introductions. "This is my mother, Serene Simone."

Rising to her feet, Raven held out her hand. "It's very nice to meet you."

"I've heard a lot about you, Raven."

Heat rose to her face. "I hope some of it was good."

"It was interesting," Serene admitted. Gesturing toward the sofa, she said, "Please have a seat. I'm sure you must be tired after your trip."

Raven smiled in gratitude and sat down. She could feel Serene's gaze on her. Her hands started to tremble slightly, so she hid them in the folds of her skirt.

Serene threw her arms around Andre once more. "Son, I'm so glad to see you. I've missed you so much."

"I missed you too, Mom."

Raven watched their reunion in silence. It was obvious that they were close. When she and Andre were together, he used to talk about his mother all the time and she'd been touched by his obvious devotion. They'd broken up a week before his mother was due to visit them, so she hadn't met her before now.

Raven didn't want to imagine all the horrible things Andre must have said about her to Serene.

Andre was watching her, so Raven was careful to keep her face devoid of emotion. She would not let him see her crumble even now. He looked as if he wanted to say something to her, but remained silent.

"I'm going to the kitchen and make something special

for you both," Serene announced brightly. Laying her hand over her heart, she beamed. "Andre, I just can't believe you're here."

He gave her an indulgent smile and another hug. "Mom, you don't have to go to any trouble."

She gave a slight wave of dismissal. "It's no trouble. Make yourselves comfortable."

Serene disappeared through a door, leaving them alone. Raven turned to Andre. "Why did you bring me here of all places?"

"We lived in New Orleans when I was a small child."

She glanced around the room. "So this is where you grew up?"

"For a while. We moved to Boston when I was six years old."

"I see." Raven glanced in the direction of the stairs. "Do you have any idea which room Anna put Julian in?"

"He's asleep in the nursery. You don't have to worry, Raven. Our son is safe."

"Andre, I'd like to know something. What did you tell your mother about me?"

"I told her the truth."

"About everything?"

"Yes."

Raven suddenly felt miserable. "I guess she thinks I'm just horrible."

"Nobody thinks you're a horrible person, Raven. I certainly don't think so. I do believe that you've made some bad choices—"

"Do you have to keep throwing it up in my face?" Raven cut in. "I know that already."

"I was trying to explain—"

She wouldn't let him finish. "Don't bother, Andre. I know exactly how you feel about me. None of that matters right now. All I want to do is keep Julian safe. Do you think you can just help me with that? I'm not asking for anything more."

"I'm sorry."

Raven's mouth dropped open in surprise. "What did you just say?"

"I said I'm sorry. I know that I've been hard on you, but I thought this was another ploy of Lucien's. I'm sorry I didn't believe you at first."

"Your apology means a lot to me. I just want to get along with you, that's all. I don't have a hidden agenda."

"You wouldn't be here if I thought you were running a game, Raven."

Serene strolled back into the room carrying a tray of food. Andre jumped up immediately to assist her. "Let me take that."

She allowed Andre to take the tray from her. "I'll be back with your tea."

Putting the tray down on the coffee table, Andre stated, "Sit down, Mom. I'll get the tea."

He left the room.

Serene turned her attention to Raven when they were alone. "I want you to feel comfortable here. If you need anything, don't hesitate to let me or Anna know."

"Thank you for your kindness, Mrs. Simone. I really appreciate it."

"I know that my son wouldn't have brought you here unless he felt you were in danger. You're safe here, Raven."

Andre joined them. He sat down beside his mother.

"We need to stay here for a while."

Serene nodded in understanding. "No one will know that you're here."

Andre awarded his mother a grateful smile.

Raven ate in silence. She sat listening to Andre and his mother catch-up. He looked a lot like her, she noticed.

They had the same hazel eyes and the same burnt almond complexion.

Every now and then, Andre would get this vacant look on his face. He seemed . . . Raven searched for the right word. *Haunted.* That was it. Andre seemed haunted by something. But what? If only she could get him to confide in her. *Stop dreaming,* her heart warned.

After they ate, Andre asked, "Would you like to go upstairs and rest? You didn't get much rest on the plane."

"Yes, I'd like that," Raven confessed. "I also want to check on Julian." She stood up and headed toward the stairs.

"Raven . . ."

She stopped and turned around. "Yes?"

"You were wrong before."

"About what?"

"You don't know exactly how I feel about you."

Raven gave Andre a tiny smile before climbing the steps to the second floor. She was exhausted, but would not rest until she knew that Julian was out of danger.

She found him sound asleep in the nursery. Raven stared lovingly at her son. She had failed him once, but vowed that she would never do so again.

He was back. Back at the very place that was the root of his nightmares. Andre's eyes scanned the spacious living room. He wasn't sure what he was feeling at the moment. He was thrilled seeing his mother and Anna, but this house . . .

This house with all its splendid furnishings was filled with terrible memories of the past. A past that had shaped Andre's future. He moved around the room slowly, running his fingers across the sofa, the club chair and the love seat.

He was around Julian's age when he had lived in this house. Andre vaguely remembered all the happy times he and his family shared here. His memories had been tarnished by the tragedy of long ago.

His mother was right, though. It was time for him to come back. The only way he would ever get rid of the nightmares was to face what had happened. The trouble was that Andre didn't know if he could. He sighed heavily, shoved his hands in his pockets and stared out the window.

Andre had no idea how long he stood at the window. Finally, he turned around and made his way to the stairs. He was going to check on Raven and Julian.

He found her sitting beside Julian's bed in the nursery. She'd fallen asleep in the rocking chair.

His eyes strayed to the sleeping child. His son. Andre's heart soared at the thought of getting to know his little boy. Raven had not yet told the boy about him, but he determined that Julian would know soon enough. They'd been kept apart far too long.

As he neared the bed, Andre saw that Julian was wide-awake. He just lay there watching his mother and sucking his thumb.

His eyes strayed off her and found Andre.

He gave the boy a smile and a tiny wave and was rewarded a tentative smile in return.

Raven stirred and slowly opened her eyes. Spying Andre, she sat up straight. "Hi."

"Hi yourself."

Raven glanced at her son and broke out into a grin. "How long have you been awake, Sweetie?"

He took his thumb out of his mouth long enough to say, "I'm hungry. Want a p'nut budder sanwish."

Backing out of the room, Andre said, "I'll have Anna

prepare lunch for him. Mom loves peanut butter sandwiches, too."

Raven smiled at him. "Thanks. In the meantime, I'll give this little guy a bath."

"The bathroom is just down the hall. You can't miss it." Andre's eyes strayed back to Julian. "He's going to be all right, Raven. He just missed his mommy, that's all."

"You really think so?"

"I do."

"I'm so glad to have him back." Raven hugged her son to her. "I love him so much."

Andre believed her. It made what he had to do that much harder.

Raven and Julian walked hand in hand. Suddenly, he broke away and took off running to the far end of the hallway, stopping at the last door. He was just about to turn the knob.

"Honey, this is the bathroom," Raven said in a loud whisper. "Come here." She bent down and held her arms outstretched. "Come on, let's get you cleaned up. Don't you want to put on some clean clothes?"

Grinning, Julian ran back down the hall toward her. Wrapping his arms around her, he planted a wet kiss on her cheek. "I wuv you, Mommy."

"I love you, too." Raven held onto him as if he were her lifeline.

They sat like that, just holding on to each other until Julian pulled away and asked, "Where's Ree, Mommy?"

"Ree?"

He nodded. "Ree. She was with us when we left Grandpapa's house. Where is she?"

Comprehension dawned. "Honey, Marie went home. She went back to her own country."

"She missed her mommy. Her daddy too," she told me.

Raven nodded. "I know. They're going to be together real soon."

"Just like us?"

"Yes, baby. Just like us."

"Only I don't have a daddy."

Oh honey, your daddy's right here in this house with you, she yearned to tell him. "You do have a daddy, sweetness. And you know what? I have a feeling that you're going to meet him very soon."

Julian grinned. "I want a daddy."

His plea touched Raven to the core of her being. "I know you do." Raven prayed that Andre would soon take on an active role in Julian's life. She hadn't wanted to push the issue with him because she knew he was still somewhat leery where she was concerned. The last thing Raven wanted was for Andre to assume she was using Julian to get next to him. The only way he would ever be a part of her life would have to be on Andre's own terms.

After lunch, Raven spent the rest of the afternoon in the nursery playing with Julian. That's where Andre found her.

He broke into a smile as he watched them crawling around on the floor. Raven seemed nothing more than an overgrown kid. Andre had never seen this side of her before, but then, Julian hadn't been born at the time.

Squealing with delight, Julian climbed on top of his mother. Raven burst into laughter. Her laugh dissipated when she spotted Andre in the doorway. She struggled to sit up.

"We were just playing around," she said sheepishly.

Andre smiled. "I see. Looks like you two were having a lot of fun."

She ran a hand through her short hair. "We were."

The room grew silent for a moment.

"This house . . . it's nice."

Andre's eyes bounced around the room, taking in the blue and yellow wallpaper with tiny teddy bears printed all over. The comforter on the bed matched the pattern. When he lived here, this was his room. Near the window sat the white rocking chair that his mother and grandmother used when they read to him or told him stories. He had shared some special moments with his family in this very room. That was until . . .

Raven sensed a change in his mood. "What is it, Andre?"

"It's just strange being back here after all these years. It's the same house, but yet so different."

"Different in what way?"

He shrugged. "It's not as dark . . . I don't know, Raven. It was a long time ago."

She was dying of curiosity. Andre seemed so uncomfortable being here in this house and she wanted to know why. This was once his home, but the expression on his face was something akin to dread.

"It was a long time ago," Andre repeated softly.

"You were a small boy. Everything looks different in the eyes of a child."

"Maybe you're right." Pulling his dreadlocks into a rubber band, he said, "I'm going to go out for a little while, but I'll be back shortly."

"What are you going to do?"

"Take a walk . . . I don't know." He stood up. "I need to do some thinking."

"Are you okay?"

He nodded. "I'm fine. Just need to clear my head a little."

Raven surveyed Andre. Something was troubling him deeply. In her heart, she wanted to help him, but he'd managed to build a wall around him so thick—she doubt she could penetrate through.

She would just have to sit by silently until Andre decided to give her entrance. It wasn't easy to stand by and watch someone you love hurting. Raven doubt she could ignore his pain. If she could find a way to help him through whatever this was—maybe it would atone for the heartache she had caused him.

Shortly after Andre left for his walk, Raven took Julian by the hand and went to her room.

She turned away from the wrought iron bed with the dappled ivory finish and pulled open a drawer on the dresser. It was empty except for the fragrant, floral paper lining the bottom.

She unpacked the one suitcase she'd brought with her, putting underwear in the drawer. Everything else, Raven hung in the closet. She had no idea how long they would be staying in New Orleans, but she suspected she was going to have to do some shopping.

Julian's clothes lay in the bottom of her suitcase, so she took them out and carried them to the nursery. Anna was there with Julian, reading him a story. Raven listened for a moment before returning to her own room.

For the next minute or so, she just stood in the doorway, surveying the bedroom. Andre's mother had a talent for decorating. She'd selected a cornflower blue and ivory color scheme for this guestroom.

"Is everything okay?" Serene asked from behind her.

Raven turned around. "Yes, ma'am. I was just admiring your decorating. This room is absolutely gorgeous."

"Thank you. Decorating is a favorite pastime of mine. I find it comforting."

Raven strolled forward into the room. She picked up a mantel clock made of solid aged brass. Her finger traced the decorative rim of cornflower blue encircling the antique face of the clock. "This looks like the one on Boulevard Etienne in Paris."

Serene smiled. "It's a reproduction. I love Paris and wanted to bring that French flavor into the house."

"I noticed you have a lot of antiques. Are they family heirlooms?"

"Most are, but not all of them. I love estate sales and auctions."

"Have you ever given any thought to being an interior decorator?"

Nodding, Serene replied, "I've decorated a few houses . . . just for friends, you know."

Raven ran her hand along the bed coverings. "This is a such a beautiful room and it feels so . . ." she searched for the right word. "Peaceful."

"I'm glad you feel this way. I want you to be comfortable during your stay."

"I'm sure I will, Mrs. Simone. I really appreciate the way you've opened your home to us."

"If you need anything, my room is two doors down."

"Thank you."

Serene left and went back downstairs.

Raven returned to the nursery. Anna had changed Julian and was reading him another story. She looked up and smiled.

"Your mama's here, little one. I'll finish this tomorrow night, okay? Make sure you give Mama a big hug and kiss."

"What about Miss Anna? Doesn't she get a hug and kiss, too?" Raven asked.

Julian reached out. He embraced Anna tightly and screwed up his face as he puckered his tiny lips.

Raven hid her smile behind her hand.

When Anna left, Raven picked up her son and placed him on her lap. "I love you so much. Do you know that?"

"I wuv you too." Julian puckered up once again, this time to kiss her.

He laid his head on her chest and closed his eyes.

They stayed in that position until he was asleep. Raven gently laid him in bed and covered him. She eyed him lovingly one more time and left before she could give into the urge to crawl into the twin bed beside him.

Raven returned to her room and found that someone had folded back her sheets and duvet cover. The pillows looked as if they'd been plumped until they were standing proud against the headboard.

She closed the door and moved to stand in the middle of the room, listening.

There was only silence.

She walked over to the bed and climbed in. Raven wondered briefly if Andre had returned from his walk. Or even if he was awake. She'd thought he would've come by her room, if only to say good night. Disappointed, she plumped up her pillows and lay down.

Andre checked on his son when he returned from his walk. Julian was sleeping. On his face, he wore a tiny smile. Some of the tension he'd felt earlier had evaporated and he was starting to relax.

He stayed in the nursery for almost an hour just watching his son sleep. Andre propelled himself to his feet and eased out of the room as quietly as he'd come. He didn't want to frighten Julian.

He neared Raven's room and slowed his pace. Andre

leaned over, placing his ear to the door. There was a light on under the door, but he didn't hear a sound in the room. She was probably sleeping, he decided.

Andre moved on to his room. But before going inside, he gazed long and hard at the closed door to Raven's room. He felt like talking to her. Andre missed their conversations. In truth, he missed everything about her.

Ten

Two days later, Raven grew tired of being cooped up
and took a stroll around the estate. Built in 1845, the Simone's atypical Vieux Carre styled house was one of two
others that remained in the French Quarter. This was
her first trip to New Orleans and it was everything she'd
ever read about it. To Raven, it was the most delicious
city her eyes had ever tasted. During the ride over, she'd
glimpsed ornate mansions encrusted with carved
Mediterranean acanthus leaves, Greek Cornices, Moor-
ish domes, French doors, Spanish fanlight transoms and
Italianate balustrades.

It was a beautiful city where the past was not left behind, but intricately woven into the lacy iron balconies
from Spanish colonial times and in the handmade
benches of the oldest running streetcar in America.

New Orleans was an international gumbo of customs,
music, festivals and foods. Raven wanted to explore the
richness of the Crescent City, but Andre felt it was much
too soon to venture beyond the property. For now, she
had to settle for little walks around the estate.

The grounds were fertile with rose bushes, picturesque magnolia trees and towering oaks with moss
hanging from them. Raven could hear the steady buzz of
a motorized garden trimmer and she glanced in the di-

rection of the sound. It was the gardener. She smiled and waved.

He waved back, then continued his work, chopping off weeds. Every now and then, he would cut the engine, wipe his brow with a dingy towel, then return back to his work.

Raven heard Julian's peal of laughter. He was playing hide and seek with Anna.

Her hand folded across her brow to shield her eyes as she watched them for a while. Raven broke into a round of laughter as she reveled in the sight of her son playing. She was grateful that Julian had escaped unharmed.

Nearly twenty minutes passed, but Raven was unaware. It had been a long time since she'd felt such a sense of peace. But it didn't last long.

A frisson of fear ran up her spine when the hair on the back of her neck stood up. Raven had an eerie sensation that someone was watching her. Glancing around, she caught sight of what appeared to be a woman looking out of a window upstairs. Anna was outside showing Julian the flowers and Andre's mother had left earlier to do some shopping, so who could it be?

Raven knew that voodoo was once practiced in New Orleans and she'd heard the ghost stories . . . She stifled her scream when she felt an arm on her shoulder. It was Andre.

"I didn't mean to scare you."

Her breathing slowly returned to normal. "I'm sorry. I'm just a little jumpy." She gave an embarrassed laugh. "I thought I saw someone upstairs in the window."

"You probably did. This is my grandmother's house. In fact, she still lives here."

Raven released an audible sigh of relief. "I thought I was losing my mind for a minute there."

Andre burst into laughter.

Raven socked him in the arm. "It's not funny. I was really scared. I've heard about the ghosts of New Orleans, but I'm certainly not prepared to see any."

He laughed even harder. Raven's sense of humor took over and she joined in the laughter.

Sobering, Raven peered back up at the window. This time, she detected no movement in the curtains. "If your grandmother's here, then why haven't we seen her?"

His expression was suddenly guarded. "She doesn't leave her room much."

Tilting her head back, Raven peered at his face. "Why not?"

Andre abruptly changed the subject. "What were you doing?"

"Nothing. Just taking a walk." Raven glanced around. She didn't see her son anywhere. "Where are Anna and Julian? They were outside a short while ago." She insisted on knowing where he was every minute of the day.

"I just passed them on my way out here." His eyes grew openly amused. "They're getting ready to bake cookies."

"Really?" Raven burst into laughter. "I can just imagine the mess."

"It'll be all right. Anna loves children. She's never been able to have her own."

"She's not going to run off with mine, is she?"

Andre's eyes blazed down into hers. "No. She's not like that, Raven. In case you haven't noticed, Anna's up in age."

"I hate feeling so paranoid."

Reaching out, Andre massaged her shoulders. "You've been through a lot. It's understandable."

"I could hardly sleep last night. I kept seeing Lucien in my sleep."

"Eventually the nightmares will end, Raven."

"You really think so?" She was now facing him. "Yours haven't."

"My situation is different, Raven."

Andre turned to leave, prompting her to ask, "Where are you going?"

"Upstairs. I have a few phone calls to make."

Walking alongside him, Raven said, "I'll go inside with you. I'm sure I'm going to have to help poor Anna clean up the kitchen."

Andre laughed.

Raven loved the sound of his laughter. She had to admit she loved everything about Andre. The fact that his nightmares had returned, really bother her. She still wondered if she was the cause.

She still loved him, but if being a part of his life caused him pain, then Raven would move on. She didn't want to hurt him like she had before—even though it had been unintentional.

Raven wanted a chance to make up for the heartache she had caused him, but Andre would never give her the chance. He detested her, she knew. If it were not for Julian . . .

She was not going to stoop so low as to use her son to get to Andre. If by some miracle he came to accept her back into his life, it would be on his own accord.

After his phone calls, Andre left his room and walked down to the door located on the far end of the hall. He stood there a long moment, trying to summon up the courage to go inside. He hadn't seen his grandmother in years, he thought guiltily.

It was long past time, his heart whispered. Without knocking, Andre slipped into the room. His eyes bounced around the room, stopping briefly to admire

some of the paintings that adorned the walls before settling on the small frame of a woman standing near a
window peering out.

Without turning around, she said, "I wondered when
you would finally make your way up here to see me. I
didn't know if I would ever see you again. It's been such
a long time since your last visit."

He wrapped his arms around her and kissed her
weathered cheek. "Hello, Grandmother." The material
of the black dress she wore tickled the hair on his arms.
"I've missed you, but you know how I feel about this
place. How can you stay here?"

"Your grandfather bought this house for me. This is
the place where you were born. I won't let bad memories
chase me from my home."

Andre glanced around the room. This part of the
house had been completely rebuilt after being ravaged
by a fire long ago.

"Who is the woman?"

"Her name is Raven Christopher."

"And the boy?"

"He's my son," Andre announced proudly. "His name
is Julian. They're in trouble, Grandmother, so I brought
them here. To keep them safe."

She nodded. After a while, she said, "The woman. She
is very beautiful."

"She is," Andre agreed.

"Do you love her?"

"I used to," Andre replied.

"Humph," she muttered under her breath.

Hiding his amusement, Andre questioned, "What was
that for, Grandmother?"

She turned around slowly. Andre smiled at her, but inside his heart ached. One side of her body was badly
scarred because of the fire that had almost robbed her

of life. Antonia Savoy was once revered as one of New Orleans's great beauties. Now she hid herself away not only from the world, but also from her family with the exception of Andre, his mother and Anna.

"I would like to bring Julian up here to meet you."

"My great-grandson. Who would have thought that I would live long enough to see a great-grandchild?"

"I had no doubt whatsoever."

She touched his cheek. "You were such a sweet little boy and you have grown into a wonderful man. I love you so much my dear grandson. I would have died for you."

His eyes grew wet. "Grandmother, I'm sorry. If I hadn't come up here . . ."

"It's not your fault, child. How can I make you believe that it was never your fault."

"It is because of me that you . . ." his voice died. "If I could make it up to you, I would."

Taking Andre by the hand, she led him over to a nearby couch. "Come. Let's not talk of the past. Tell me about this woman, the mother of your child."

After putting Julian down for the evening, Raven glanced down at the other end of the hallway. Andre's grandmother was behind that door. She had to be because the other rooms were empty. She'd been here two days and there had been no sign that another person lived in this house. If she hadn't seen her in the window earlier, Raven would have assumed Serene and Anna lived here alone.

She walked along the hallway, debating whether or not to venture to the end of the hall, when Andre's voiced boomed behind her. "Where do you think you're going?"

Raven turned around to face him. "N—Nowhere in particular. I was just looking around, that's all."

"My grandmother does not like visitors," he stated flatly. "Especially without invitation. With the exception of my mother, Anna and myself."

"Why doesn't she ever come downstairs?" Raven wanted to know. She couldn't imagine why anyone would hide within the confines of their own house.

"She prefers the solitude of her own suite."

"Seems a bit lonely to me."

"Regardless of what we feel, we respect my grandmother's wishes."

"Will I ever get to meet her?"

"I don't know. My grandmother is a bit of a recluse."

"How long has she been that way?"

"As long as I can remember. Look, Raven, I need you to promise me that you will not bother my grandmother."

"I just wanted to say hello. After all, I am staying in her house."

"Grandmother will come to you if and when she's ready. It's important that you understand that, Raven."

She was beginning to feel a little defensive. "I heard you. You don't have to worry, Andre. I'm not going to burst into your grandmother's room. You know, you really think the worst of me."

"When did you become so argumentative?"

"I'm not. It's just that you're treating me as if I'm not to be trusted . . . but then, that's because you don't trust me, right?"

"I'm not going to argue with you, Raven."

"I'm not looking for an argument. One thing you should remember, Andre. Even the biggest liar tells the truth once in a while."

In a huff, she turned on her heel and rushed to her

room. Raven wiped away an escaping tear. She and Andre would never be able to patch things up. He would never even consider it.

A.C. went over her schedule for that day. Noting the July seventeenth date, she went through her tickler file, jotting notes on her To Do list.

The receptionist buzzed her. "John Simmons is on the line. Onyx isn't here yet, so can you take the call?"

"Sure."

After A.C. hung up the phone, she went in search of the Simmons file. When she had no success in the records room, she asked her receptionist about it.

"Your sister had me pull it for her a couple of weeks ago. Maybe she still has it."

"Thanks." She headed to Onyx's office.

There was a stack of files on her sister's desk. Going through them, a name caught her eye. *Kenison Moore.* She scratched her head using her ink pen. The name struck a familiar chord in her, but she couldn't place it at the moment. Her hand hovered over the file for a few seconds before moving on.

A.C. searched through a second stack of files.

Onyx strolled into her office and found A.C. sitting at her desk. "What are you doing in here?"

Looking up from her task, A.C. asked, "When did you get back?"

"Last night. Now answer me," Onyx demanded. "What are you doing in here?"

"I was looking for the Simmons case. He called this morning." A.C. eyed her. "What's up with you?"

"Nothing. Do I have any messages?"

She pointed to a small stack of paper's lying near the

corner of the desk. "Right there. Don't worry. I didn't look at any of them."

"I'm sorry, A.C. The flight from France was a long one. I'm tired and cranky."

"Onyx, why don't you tell me what's really going on with you? You know you can trust me. I was always the one who covered for you, remember?"

"I know. A.C., I wish I could . . ." Onyx shook her head sadly. "You can't help me. Nobody can."

"What about Dad or Turquoise? Can they help you?"

She shook her head no. "I'll get the file and bring it to your office. I need to work in mine."

"Onyx . . ." A.C.'s voice died. It was no use. Her sister wouldn't open up until she was ready. "Okay, I get the message. I'll leave."

"Thanks."

She went back to her own office. A.C. needed some advice. She decided it was time to pay a visit to Pearl, their older sister. As soon as she could clear her schedule, A.C. was going to New Orleans. While she was there, she would check in on Andre and Raven.

Lucien Dupont had people looking for them both. She had originally planned to give Andre a call, but this way was better, A.C. decided.

Eleven

A week later, on July twenty-fourth, A.C. showed up at the house. Raven was caught off guard when she found A.C. sitting in the living room, admiring a painting when Raven walked by.

Spotting her, Raven retreated a step. "A.C.? What are you doing here? Does Andre know you're here?"

She nodded. "The housekeeper went to get him for me. I expect he'll be down in a few minutes. But I didn't just come to see Andre. I came to check on you and Julian as well. How's he doing?"

"He's adjusted well. Marie kept telling him that I would be there to pick him up, so he just kept looking for me. He even asked me what took me so long."

Andre strolled into the room and embraced A.C. "Anna just told me you were here. I didn't think I'd see you again until after I returned to New York."

"There's something you both need to know." A.C.'s gaze met Raven's. "Lucien has feelers out. He's looking all over New York for you. I think he may even have someone watching Andre's town house."

A soft gasp escaped her. "Can he trace us to New Orleans?" Raven asked in fear.

"No. I instructed Andre to destroy any links to New Orleans before he left. You all should be safe here." As an afterthought, A.C. asked, "Have you already canceled service for both cell phones?"

"Yes," they answered in unison.

"Good. I'm going to hang around New Orleans for a few days to make sure all is clear. But I'm not here just for business. I have a sister who lives here."

There was a knock on the front door. Anna rushed to answer it.

Fear siphoned the blood from Reven's face. She glanced nervously over at Andre. They listened to an exchange of words, and then Andre suddenly broke into a smile. "I don't believe it. It's my cousin, Paul. I haven't seen him in such a long time."

Andre strode to the door. "What in the world are you doing here?"

The two men embraced.

"I haven't seen *or* heard from you in years," Paul stated. "Andre, it's good to see you, man."

A.C. and Raven sat quietly watching the men as they talked. Andre turned around after a while to introduce his cousin to them. "This is Paul Robichaux. Paul, this is A.C. Richardson and Raven Christopher."

"Two extremely beautiful women . . . how did you get so lucky?" The warmth of his smile echoed in his voice.

A.C.'s expression never changed while Raven granted him a smile.

"Have a seat, Paul," Andre offered.

Anna brought in drinks for all of them. She left as quickly and as quietly as she arrived.

Paul couldn't seem to take his eyes off A.C. Raven bit back her smile. When she glanced Andre's way, she could tell he'd noticed too.

Andre gave Paul a brief overview of what had transpired. ". . . so it's important that you tell no one that we're here."

"Don't worry, cousin. I won't say a word."

A.C. stood up and announced that she had to leave.

"I hope you're not leaving on my account," Paul stated. An easy smile played at the corners of his mouth.

"No. I . . . I'm meeting someone. My sister."

Before she left, A.C. made plans to have lunch with Raven for the next day.

"Is she married?" Paul inquired after A.C. had gone.

"No. A.C. isn't married," Andre replied. "She's quite single for the time being."

Paul smiled. "This is turning out to be a great day."

"Are you still living here in New Orleans?" Andre asked.

"For now." Paul finished off his ice tea.

"You're planning to move?"

He nodded. "I'm thinking about it. I've been offered a job in Los Angeles with a major cosmetic company. I would head the research and development department."

"That's great. Congratulations." Andre and Raven exchanged an amused look.

Looking from one to the other, Paul inquired, "What's that look for? I haven't decided if I'm going to take the job."

"A.C. lives in Los Angeles."

Paul was speechless for a moment. "You're kidding me. I may have to consider taking this promotion. So much for my original plan."

"What was that?"

"I was thinking about just staying here in New Orleans."

"Why?"

"I guess I'm just not sure I'm ready for L.A. I'm a small town man."

Raven smiled. "New Orleans is not that small of a town."

"It's a far cry from Los Angeles though."

Andre and Paul then launched into tales of their teenage years.

"Paul used to spend his summers with us in Boston," Andre explained.

Standing, Raven excused herself to give them some time alone.

"You don't have to leave," Andre stated as he stood up.

"I don't mind. Besides, it sounds like you two have a lot of catching up to do."

Rising up, Paul said, "It was nice meeting you, Raven."

"You too." They shared a smile.

Raven ascended the stairs. She wanted to check on her son. She stopped at the top of the stairs when she heard Andre's deep laughter. She hadn't heard that sound in a long time.

Her one wish in the world was to be able to glimpse the old Andre again.

"So what do you think is going on with Onyx?" Pearl asked as she poured sugar into her coffee. She and A.C. were seated in *The Court of Two Sisters* and had just finished dining on lobster etouffee and shrimp Toulouse.

Shrugging, A.C. answered, "I don't know. I just have this strong feeling that she's in a lot of pain."

"Hmmmm . . . the last time I spoke to her, Onyx did sound a bit depressed. Maybe it's a man. She was under deep cover—not as long as you, but it had to be just as grueling. Leading a double life is hard."

A.C. agreed. "Yeah, I know. Pearl, you may be on to something. I think it does have something to do with a man, but my intuition tells me that it runs much deeper."

"Like maybe she started to believe the lie?"

A.C. nodded. "It can happen."

"Maybe that's why they pulled her out."

"I still have some contacts with the DEA. Maybe I should—"

Pearl was shaking her head. "Don't do that, Amethyst."

She was the only one of her siblings who insisted on calling A.C. by her birth name. Even their father called her A.C.

"We have always promised one another that we would stay out of each other's business, unless invited."

"Onyx needs us," A.C. countered. "Maybe she doesn't know how to ask for help."

Pearl disagreed. "She'll come to us whenever she's ready."

"I'm worried about her, Pearl. I really am."

"Onyx is strong. She'll get through this—whatever it is."

"She's in trouble, Pearl. I can feel it. We can't just stand by and do nothing about it."

"We have no choice, Amethyst," she reminded her. "We can't intrude in Onyx's life like that."

A.C. had to admit Pearl was right, but she didn't like it though. A.C. didn't like it at all. There had to be a way to help Onyx.

Saturday afternoon, Raven and A.C. met for lunch as planned. A.C. took her to a café three blocks from the house. When they were seated, A.C. stated, "I sensed you needed to get out of the house."

Stirring her chicory coffee, Raven admitted, "I did. I was going stir crazy. Thank you, A.C." Wearing a smile, Raven inquired, "So what do you think of Paul?"

"He's handsome." A.C.'s tone was noncommittal. She pretended to be interested in the menu.

"He's also single and very interested in you."

A.C. peeked over her menu. "Yeah, right."

"He is," Raven insisted. "Paul asked a lot of questions about you yesterday." She scanned the offerings, trying to decide what she wanted to eat.

A.C.'s interest peaked. "Really?"

Laughing, Raven nodded. "He's hoping to see you again."

Laying down the menu, A.C. muttered, "I doubt that will ever happen."

"Why do you say that?"

"Well for one thing, I don't live here in New Orleans. I live in Los Angeles."

"That could make things difficult," Raven agreed.

"For another, I'm not one for long distance relationships."

"It won't hurt to spend some time with him while you're in town though."

The waitress came to take their order.

They made small talk while they waited for their food to arrive. Raven and A.C. didn't have long to wait.

"How are things going between you and Andre?" A.C. asked while dipping a French fry in ketchup.

"He's tolerating me."

"I think it's much more than that, Raven."

"Sometimes I feel that way too, but then again, I'm not sure if I'm imagining things or not. It's almost as if he's built this wall around himself. Sometimes he'll let it down just a little, but once he realizes it—it's back up again." Raven bit into her sandwich.

"You still love him," A.C. accused. "I can see it in the way you look at him."

"I will always love him, A.C."

"Andre is a good man."

Raven agreed. "I just hope that he'll come around soon. There's all this tension between us and I hate it. I want things to be like they used to be—even if we never get back together. We used to be friends."

"Give Andre some time."

"I'm not going to push. The only reason I came here with him is so that he and Julian would have a chance to get to know each other."

"He adores his son."

"Yes, I think he does." A thoughtful smile curved her mouth. "I'm thrilled about that. I just wish we could at least be friends. Julian is eventually going to pick up on the tension between us."

"Have you tried talking to Andre?"

"A little. I don't want to push him."

"I think in time every thing will work itself out. You'll see." A.C. finished off her fries and drank the last of her tea. She signaled the waitress to bring her another one.

"I hope so." Raven picked up her pickle and took a bite. "Mmm . . . this is good. I love pickles."

A.C. sampled hers. "You're right. It is delicious. I don't usually care for them."

Leaning forward, Raven asked, "A.C., how can I protect myself?"

"You seemed to handle yourself well enough. What exactly are you talking about?"

"Can you please teach me some self-defense techniques? I can't stand being a victim and I don't like feeling so helpless. Although, I'm not afraid to use a gun—I just don't want to keep one in the house."

"Promise you won't use whatever I teach you on Andre?" A.C. teased.

Raven burst into laughter. "I really wish you were going to be around for a while."

"I'll be here for another day or so for sure. After that, we'll just have to take it one day at a time. My sister is trying to convince me to take a couple of weeks off from work. I'm considering it, but haven't made up my mind."

Just as they were about to leave, Paul showed up and pulled up a chair at their table without invitation. "Hello, ladies. Mind if I join you?"

Raven and A.C. shared a look of surprise.

He looked from one to the other. "What's wrong?"

"We were just talking about you," Raven answered. She patted the chair beside her. "Please have a seat."

Paul broke into a smile as he dropped down into the chair. "Really? Good things, I hope."

"Only good things," she replied. "Right A.C.?"

A.C. gave a slight nod.

"It's good seeing you again, A.C." He offered her a sudden, arresting smile.

This time she smiled. "You too, Paul," she said softly.

"This really is a surprise seeing you here," Raven pointed out.

"I had a taste for crawfish remoulade. This is the best place to come."

Raven gave him a knowing smile.

Picking up a menu, he stated, "Andre tells me you're from Los Angeles."

A.C. nodded. "I've lived there for a couple of years now."

"Do you like California?"

A.C.'s seemed more at ease when she responded. "Yes, I do. I love being near the ocean and I love the weather. Have you ever been there?"

"Just once."

Raven stood up after a while. It was apparent that Paul wanted to spend some time alone with A.C.

A.C. stood up abruptly. "Wait, Raven!"

Waving her hand in dismissal, Raven stated, "Don't worry about me. I don't mind taking a taxi home. I'll be fine."

A.C. sat back down.

"She'll be fine," Paul assured her. "The house is right down the street."

She reached for her tea. A.C. took a couple of sips before putting it down. Nervously, she glanced around, eyeing the people strolling past, the cars passing by—she looked everywhere, but directly at Paul. For some reason, he made her nervous.

When she finally looked his way, she found he was sitting there eyeing her. "Why are you looking at me like that? Is there something you want to say to me?" A.C. asked boldly. She didn't care for the way he was staring at her. It was almost as if she were a piece of meat. She didn't miss the lustful gleam in Paul's eyes either.

"Yes, actually there is. One year from today, you're going to become my wife." Paul signaled for the waitress. "I'm going to have dessert. How about you?"

A.C. was stunned into silence.

July Twenty-fifth was stored away in her memory bank. She had no idea why she was even considering his ludicrous remark. There was no way she and Paul would be getting married this time next year. The very thought was ridiculous.

Andre was outside beneath one of the towering oaks with a sketchpad in one hand and an oil pastel in the other. He glanced up from his drawing and saw Raven walking toward him. "Where's A.C.?"

"I left her and Paul at the café. I got the impression they wanted to be alone. At least Paul wanted to be alone with A.C."

"I see." He returned to his drawing without further comment.

Standing with her hands folded across her chest, Raven asked, "How did Paul know where to find us?"

Andre exchanged the black oil pastel for one in gray. "I might have mentioned it to him."

She burst into laughter. "I can't believe you're playing matchmaker."

He glanced up at her. "I'm not."

"Then what do you call it, Andre?"

"I simply told the man where you two were having lunch." Andre wasn't about to admit to anything more.

She dropped down on the grass beside him. Playing with a leaf, she said, "I've asked A.C. to show me how to protect myself."

Andre lay his pad down. "Excuse me?"

"I'm going to learn to fight."

He chuckled. "Okay . . ."

"It may be funny to you, Andre, but I need this for me."

He hadn't meant to hurt her feelings. "I'm sorry. I shouldn't have laughed."

"It's okay." Raven continued to play with the leaf.

Andre touched her hand. "Hey, I'm really sorry. If taking a self-defense class will help you feel more secure, then I'm all for it."

Her head came up quickly. "Thank you." Her voice was a breathless whisper, lulling and pulling him to her. Andre's face was only inches from hers before he realized what was happening.

He leaned back, fumbling around for his pad of paper and the oil pastels.

"I . . . I think I'll go check on Julian," Raven murmured.

Feeling awkward, Andre nodded. "He was with my mother playing the piano."

Raven managed to rise up by placing her hand on the tree to support her. Straightening her clothes, she crossed the yard in quick strides.

He released a heavy sigh. Raven was like an addiction for him. He didn't know how much longer he could keep from making a fool of himself. Andre muttered a curse. Why was it so hard to get this woman out of his system?

Twelve

They always seemed to take two steps forward and three steps back. The thought made Raven groan in frustration. She and Andre just never seemed to be in sync.

She tried to console herself with the fact that it was because they'd been apart for so long. Raven fingered the edge of her novel while in deep thought. *Stop thinking about this man,* her heart warned. "But he's fighting his feelings for me," she whispered to the empty room. "I can see it in his eyes every time he looks at me."

Feeling a little silly for talking to herself, Raven returned her attention to her book.

Raven laid down the book she'd been reading when Andre knocked on her door and peeked in. She gestured for him to enter. "What is it?"

He stood with his back against the door. "Are you okay, Raven? You were so quiet during dinner."

"I'm fine. Just had a lot on my mind." She drank in his finely chiseled face, the complexion she knew was smooth as silk and the well-kept dreads hanging around his shoulders. His appeal was devastating and Raven was powerless to resist.

She wanted him badly. Blushing, Raven tried to channel her thoughts into another direction.

"You're not scared, are you? I promise that you and Julian are safe." He gave her a tender smile, but it disappeared as quickly as it had come.

Maybe it was time to really clear the air, Raven thought. Clearing her throat, Raven said, "Andre, I want you to know something. I'm really sorry about everything. I never meant to hurt you. If I could do this all over again, I would. I would—"

"It's over," he interjected. "Not even worth talking about. We can't go back to the past, Raven."

"I know that, but it doesn't stop me from wishing we could," she confessed. "I would do things so differently."

Andre was still not willing to talk. "It doesn't matter now."

"Could you come in and sit down, Andre? It's uncomfortable talking to you while you're standing in the doorway. It looks like you're about to take off running."

He laughed. Andre strode into the room and dropped down on the edge of the bed.

"Before we can move forward, I think we need to talk about the past. Get everything out in the open."

He sighed heavily, his voice filled with anguish. "I don't want to rehash it, Raven. Why can't you understand this?"

"I don't know," she admitted honestly. "I guess it's because there were things I've wanted to say to you, but never got the chance."

His amber eyes darkened as Andre held her gaze. "I thought we'd said all we needed to say on that last day. There—"

Raven interrupted him vehemently. "You said all *you* wanted to say. I wasn't afforded that opportunity. You kicked me out of the town house, remember?" A sudden chill hung on the edge of her words.

Andre looked sheepish. "I was angry and hurt," he muttered.

"*Hurt?*" Raven permitted herself a withering stare. "You think I didn't suffer in any of this? That my heart wasn't broken?"

His nostrils flared with fury. "*I loved you, Raven.* Hell, I wanted to marry you. All you wanted was to convince me into copying a painting. Everything between us was a lie. You made me fall in love with you just to get me to commit a crime." Andre flashed her a look of disdain. "Something like that leaves a bad taste in your mouth."

"I loved you," Raven countered. "That's why I told you the truth. You changed my life, Andre. I wish I could make you understand how much you meant to me. That's why I told you the truth."

"I understand all too well. You were using me, Raven. You may have fallen in love in the end, but up until that point, you weren't planning to tell me the truth until Lucien threatened to expose you."

"I never wanted to hurt you, Andre. For what it's worth, I was never willing to do any of those things. Lucien forced me."

"How? You sought me out. You could have told me the truth from the beginning, but you didn't, Raven. You seduced me as Lucien wished. If you really didn't want to, then why do it? That's what I don't understand."

"I was in love with you, Andre. I wanted you. That's why I seduced you."

"Why are you so willing to break the law for that man?"

"You know that I'm the product of a mixed marriage. Well, after my parents were killed, none of my relatives wanted me. My white family thought I was much too black and well . . . my black family—they just didn't want anything to do with me." Raven stared down at her hands. "Lucien and Beatrice were my parents' best friends and my godparents, so they took me in. I had no idea what they did for a living until after Beatrice's death. I loved them both so much that I would do just about anything to please them. When Beatrice died, Lucien was all I had left."

"Beatrice Dupont was an extraordinary artist. I studied her works in school."

Raven agreed. "What the world didn't know was that Beatrice was an expert at copying masterpieces. Quite convincingly, it seems. There are quite a few collectors displaying her work as the original. Lucien had hoped I would follow in her footsteps, but my own painting never measured up. He was so disappointed in me."

"So he decided to have you steal fine works of art instead?"

Raven nodded in agreement. "It was a family business. He lorded it over my head how he came to my rescue when nobody else would. He and Beatrice were my family, Andre. All I ever wanted was his love in return." She paused for a heartbeat. "Lucien even told me that this was my heritage. He said the night my parents were killed, they had been driving away from a job they'd done for him."

Andre's brows rose in surprise. "Your parents were art thieves?"

"According to Lucien. I was too young to know if he was telling me the truth, but according to him, they were the best." Raven gave a heavy sigh. "All I wanted was someone to love me. I wanted a family and Lucien and Beatrice were good to me, Andre. They really were."

"He was grooming you to follow in your parents' footsteps."

"I know that now, but the fact remains that he was a good father to me. I won't take that away from him."

Andre glared at her, frowning. "I don't know how you can separate it like that. He raised you to be deceitful.

What values did he instill in you? What did he teach you about right and wrong?"

"I had nothing to compare it to," Raven countered. "He and Beatrice were my parents. I didn't know anything was wrong—at least not initially. It wasn't until I was older and by then it was too late, Andre."

"He took advantage of you, Raven. You do realize that, don't you?"

She nodded. "I guess that's what hurts so much." Raven raised her eyes to meet his gaze. "That's why I tried to disappear. I want nothing else to do with him."

"Yet Lucien always seems to find a way to get to you. This time it was through Julian." Andre's straight glance seemed to be accusing her coldly.

"We have our son back and I don't intend to let that happen again."

"Neither do I, Raven. I assure you that I'm not going to ever let Lucien near my son again."

"I'm going to take Julian out of the country."

"Lucien's money stretches worldwide, Raven."

Raven's lips thinned with irritation. "Then what do you think we should do?"

"For now—just stay here."

"But your work, Andre. What about your work?"

He sat down on the edge of the bed. "I'm going to have to go back to New York."

Worried, Raven asked, "Do you really think it's wise for you to go back to New York right now?" She would never forgive herself if anything happened to Andre. She didn't think it was a good idea for him to return home and told him so.

"We have to make sure Lucien doesn't connect you to me, Raven. This is the only way."

"But how are we going to pull this off?"

"Don't worry. A.C.'s going to take care of everything."

Taking her hand in his, Andre added, "She'll fix everything."

"How long will you be gone?"

"Right now, I don't know."

Their eyes met and held. Once again, she read the truth. *Andre wanted her.*

For Raven, it was a dream come true. She glimpsed that tiny shred of hope; the one thing she needed to keep her from giving up on Andre.

A.C. was having dinner with Paul. She decided she probably should have her head examined. The man was arrogant, had an ego the size of Texas and . . . Her sister's entrance into the room interrupted her silent tirade.

Pearl assessed her from head to toe. "You look nice, Amethyst. I can't wait to tell Onyx and Turquoise that you're finally going on a date."

Frowning, A.C. questioned, "What possessed our parents to give us these names?"

Popping her on the arm, Pearl explained, "Mama used to say that we were her precious stones. She said she valued us more than anything in life and so she named us after our birthstones."

A.C. made a gagging sound.

Pearl popped her again. "Stop that! We were very blessed to have such loving parents."

Rubbing her arm, A.C. replied, "I know." She paused for a second before continuing. "Mama was taken away much too soon. I didn't have much time with her."

"Onyx was only a few months old when she died. You and Turquoise were toddlers. I'm the only one who really remembers her."

"It must be especially hard for you, Pearl. You've had

to keep Mama alive for the rest of us. Then when you finally decide to get married and live your own life, Tom dies during that shoot-out in Miami."

"Death is very much a part of life. We can't escape it."

"That's the shrink in you talking."

Pearl broke into laughter.

A.C. pulled her hair loose from the braid and began to brush it, using long, brisk strokes. Gazing at her sister's reflection in the mirror, she asked, "Do you have a curling iron?"

"Yes. Do you happen to know how to use one?"

"Not really. I was hoping you'd take pity on me and curl my hair."

"Sure."

"Don't you dare laugh," A.C. ordered. She dropped down on the padded bench and faced the vanity mirror. Crossing her legs, she said, "I'm ready."

Pearl had A.C.'s ebony hair curled and gleaming by the time Paul arrived.

"You look beautiful," he complimented as soon as he had laid eyes on her.

She smiled. "Thank you."

Paul had made reservations at Victors'. When they pulled into the parking lot of the Ritz Carlton, A.C. was assisted out of the car by a valet. Paul came around the car and escorted her into the elegant hotel. Once they were seated, Paul ordered a bottle of wine.

While they waited for it to arrive, he asked, "So are you going to tell me what A.C. stands for? I'm sure your parents didn't give you initials for a name."

"Everybody calls me A.C."

Staring into her eyes, Paul responded, "I'm not everybody."

She was too stunned to reply. A.C. reached for her

water glass. She took several small sips, stalling for what—she had no idea.

"Well?" Paul prompted.

Putting down her glass, she said, "Amethyst. Amethyst Christina."

"It's a beautiful name. It suits you."

She laughed. "Really? Are you an expert on names or something?"

He shook his head. "No. Just making an assumption."

"It's my birthstone," she explained. "My parents named all of us after our birthstones."

"How many brothers and sisters?" he asked.

"Three sisters and no brothers. How about you?"

"I have a brother and two sisters."

A.C. glanced around the room. Paul really unnerved her. She couldn't figure out why one man could shake her up so easily. It was effortless where he was concerned. No man had ever made her feel this way.

"What do you do for a living?"

She took a sip of water. "I'm a private detective."

Paul seemed surprised by this. "Really?"

A.C. nodded. "My sister Onyx and I run an agency in Los Angeles."

"I never would have figured you for something like that."

"Why not?"

"You're so beautiful and so feminine—"

She jumped all over him. "You think women who look like I do can't kick butt?"

"That's not at all what I meant." Paul laughed. "Maybe I should just quit while I'm ahead."

A.C. murmured her agreement.

"It's not going to work, you know."

Inclining her head, she inquired, "What are you talking about?"

"This tough act of yours. It's not going to scare me off."

She remained quiet.

"I'm still going to chase you until I convince you to marry me."

Changing the subject, A.C. asked. "So what do you do?"

"I'm a chemist."

Settling back into her chair. "Wow. I'm impressed."

Paul laughed.

"I am," she insisted. "Your job must really be interesting."

"I think so. I create fragrances."

"Now I'm really impressed. Perfumes are my one weakness. I know most women are loyal to only one scent. But not me, I have to have several different kinds."

"Let's see. You have one for each mood, or something like that, right?"

Grinning, A.C. questioned, "Now how did you know that?"

"You're not as difficult to figure out as you'd like to believe."

It was almost as if Paul could see deep into the depths of her soul. That's why he made her so nervous, A.C. realized. But he also intrigued her.

Throughout the rest of the evening, Paul continued to surprise her with how well he seemed to know her. A.C. found they shared a lot in common. She also found that she was very attracted to him as well. He would be an interesting diversion during her stay in New Orleans. After that, she would never see him again.

The cold shower did little to cool Andre's ardor. He'd acknowledged a while back that Raven had the ability to get beneath his skin. If only he could just write it off as lust . . . but he couldn't. Andre couldn't deny that they had no future together either.

They were going to have to find a way to coexist as Julian's parents. Maybe one day, Raven would be fortunate to find love—maybe she would even marry. The thought disturbed Andre greatly. However, he had to be fair. If he wasn't going to marry her, then she deserved to find happiness with someone else.

As for him, Andre wasn't sure he would ever marry. All other women paled in comparison to Raven. She was in his blood, ruining him for anyone else.

Picking up his sketchpad, Andre carried it with him over to the desk in his bedroom. He sat down and began to draw, creating on paper, the object of his thoughts.

When he finished, Andre stared down at the image of Raven.

His discussion with her earlier had certainly painted her in a different light. Andre realized that she was as much a victim in all this as he was. However, it also reaffirmed for him that it was imperative that he raise Julian, despite his feelings for her.

At the moment, however, Julian had no idea that Andre was his father. As for him, he had fallen in love with the little boy. Spending time reading and playing with Julian were some of the best times for Andre in a long time.

Pulling some papers out of the desk drawer, he read over the legal documents once more. The thought of raising Julian thrilled him. When he thought of Raven and what this would do to her, Andre felt somewhat guilty, but he hoped to make her understand that this was best for Julian. The child would be safe from harm.

He put the documents back in the drawer, then got up and went to Raven's room. He needed to talk to her some more.

She was surprised to see him standing there. "Is everything okay?"

André couldn't imagine what she must be thinking when she opened the door. He was sure Raven didn't expect to see him standing there. "Do you mind if I come in?"

She stepped back to let him enter. "No, of course not."

"There's something I want to discuss with you." He followed her over to the bed and sat down beside her. "I meant to bring this up when I was here earlier, but I forgot." He paused a moment before continuing. "I think we should tell Julian that I'm his father."

"When?"

"Let's give it a couple of days. I want to spend some time alone with him first."

Raven agreed. "I think that's best."

"How do you think he's going to take it?"

"He's a little boy, Andre. Julian just wants to be loved." Patting his arm, she added, "It's going to be fine. You'll see."

Andre hoped she was right. "I'd like to take him out tomorrow—maybe find a toy store."

Nodding, Raven said, "Sure, if that's what you want."

"We won't be gone long."

"That's fine." Raven's expression was unreadable.

"You're sure you don't mind?"

"He's your son, Andre. You should get to know him."

He noticed her state of undress for the first time since coming into her room. Her short hair was wet and her skin damp. Andre caught a whiff of the scented shower gel she liked to use.

Raven had not changed much at all. She always wore the same body spray, used the same bath and shower gel and lotion. *Night Blooming Lilies*. It was her favorite.

"I'm sorry. I didn't realize you were getting ready for bed."

"I just got out of the shower."

Andre jumped to his feet. "I'll leave you then. Good night, Raven."

"'Night, Andre. Tomorrow A.C. will be picking me up. We're going to the gym."

"I don't know whether I should say good luck or have fun."

"How about both?" She walked him to the door. "I'll see you in the morning."

When Andre stepped out into the hallway, he found Julian standing there. He bent to pick him up.

"What are you doing up, little man?"

"Want some milk, please."

Raven smiled. "Just a little bit, Andre. I don't like to give him much to drink after eight."

He nodded. "You heard your mother. Just a little."

Julian smiled. He wrapped his arms around Andre's neck and laid his head on Andre's shoulder.

Andre's heart turned over in response.

Thirteen

Raven and A.C. spent the morning at the gym working out. Afterwards, A.C. showed Raven several ways to defend herself. She was extremely attentive and followed A.C.'s instruction to the letter.

"You're a quick learner," A.C. stated with a smile. "I like that."

They went through a few more techniques.

"Very good," A.C. complimented. She showed Raven another routine. "Now you try it."

They called it quits after two hours passed.

"This is enough for today. You're going to be sore tomorrow."

"I really appreciate you helping me like this. I feel so much better knowing that I'm going to be able to protect myself." Raven stretched slowly. "I won't let Lucien have power over me."

"The last time I talked to Andre, he mentioned you've had some trouble sleeping ."

"Sometimes," Raven admitted.

"I can find a therapist if you'd like someone to talk to, Raven. You're suffering from posttraumatic stress syndrome."

She shook her head. "No, I'll be fine. This is therapy for me—learning to protect myself and my son."

A.C. embraced her. "Just remember that you're not alone. You have me and Andre."

"I'm not going to depend on someone else. I'm determined not to be a victim."

"I understand totally." A.C. handed Raven a towel.

"Thanks." She patted her face and the back of her neck. "Andre told me that you went out with Paul."

Shrugging nonchalantly, A.C. replied, "We had dinner together. A girl's gotta eat."

Raven laughed. "I'm sure Paul doesn't see it that way."

"It was only dinner."

"Well, did it hurt that bad?" teased Raven. "My goodness."

A.C. gave in to her laughter. "No. Paul and I had a nice time. He wants to see me again. In fact, on the day that he showed up at the café, he told me we were going to get married a year from that date. Can you believe that?"

Raven's mouth dropped open in surprise. "He really said that?"

"Yeah. I don't know why he's trying to yank my chain like that."

"I think he might be serious, A.C."

A.C. looked at Raven as if she had lost her mind. "He doesn't even know me."

"Haven't you heard of love at first sight?"

"I've heard of it," A.C. admitted. "Don't believe in it, though."

Laughing, Raven shook her head. "I hope Paul is up to the challenge. He's certainly got his hands full."

They headed to the car. A.C. drove the short distance back to the house.

"Would you like to come in?"

A.C. shook her head. "I'm going shopping with my sister. I need some new clothes."

Raven gave a short laugh. "Don't tell me you're tired of those jeans and T-shirts you're always wearing. Mmm. . . . I wonder if meeting Paul has anything to do with this."

She and A.C. shared another laugh.

"No, he doesn't. I was planning to do some shopping before I left New York."

"Uh-huh." Raven waved good-bye and strolled into the house. She went looking for Julian. She searched every room on the first floor, but her son was nowhere to be found. Raven took the stairs two at a time to the second floor. The first room she checked was the nursery. It was empty.

She ran to her room. It was empty as well.

Panic raged through her. "Julian!" she called out. "Honey, where are you?" Raven checked every room but the two at the other end of the hall. She started toward the stairs, stopped, then turned around. One room was Andre's grandmother's room but the other one, she had no idea what was behind that door.

Raven ran up the length of the hallway without thinking and burst into the first room she approached.

The door opened easily, allowing her entrance in what looked like a mini art gallery of paintings that Raven had never seen anywhere. There was no time to stop and enjoy the artwork because she had a purpose—she was looking for her son.

Continuing on with her search, Raven started for the next door and was about to knock, but Andre's angry voice made her pause.

"You gave me your word you would never come up here. Once again, you've lied to me."

"Julian's missing!" she screamed hysterically. Panic surged through her. "Lucien's found us and he's taken Julian. . . ."

Andre crossed the room, shortening the distance between them. "Calm down, Raven." Andre shook her gently. "Julian's fine, sweetheart. He's outside in the back with my mother. That's why I came looking for you."

Raven burst into tears. "I th—thought . . . I thought he'd been kidnapped again."

Embracing her, he rubbed her back. "Julian saw that I was outside and he wanted to join me, so Mom brought him down. She thought it would be all right."

"It's fine. I . . ." She ran a shaky hand down her arm. "I'm sorry for overreacting."

Taking her by the arm, Andre led her to the door. "Come on. They're waiting for us outside. I think the three of us should have a picnic. I'll have Anna prepare a basket for us."

Raven could only nod. She was still very shaken. Rubbing her arms, she took several deep calming breaths.

When she went downstairs, she found Andre in the kitchen with Anna.

A huge picnic basket sat on the counter. While Anna moved around the space preparing sandwiches and potato salad, Andre picked up a jar of pickles.

"Should we take these?"

Smiling, Raven nodded. He remembered how much she loved pickles. Julian loved them too.

Laughing, he put them in the basket.

She heard Julian outside singing and relaxed. He was fine. Spurred by her son's song, Raven helped Andre and Anna with the rest of the food. "This is a lot of food."

"I don't know about you, but I'm hungry."

Ten minutes later, they joined Serene and Julian outdoors. Raven laid a blanket beneath one of the trees and placed the basket on top of it.

Julian ran over to inspect it. Pointing to the basket, he asked, "What that?"

"We're going to have a picnic. Do you remember the ones we used to have with Tee?"

He nodded. "I miss Tee."

Pulling him into her arms, Raven whispered, "I do too, sweetie."

"You all ready to eat?" Andre asked.

"I know I am," Raven stated. "How about you, Julian. You ready to eat?"

He nodded. "Sanwish please?"

Amused, Andre opened the basket. "We've got plenty of sandwiches. We even have your favorite—peanut butter."

Julian clapped his hands with glee.

Raven prepared a plate of food for her son. Next, she offered to fix one for Andre.

He declined her offer. "You go on and take care of you. I'll fix mine."

"You sure? I don't mine really."

"I know you're hungry, so go ahead, Raven. I don't want you passing out on me."

She knew he was teasing her and laughed.

After they had eaten, Julian ran off to play with his ball. Watching him, Andre said, "I think it's time we told him about me."

Raven agreed wholeheartedly. "Julian, come here. Mommy wants to talk to you." Gathering her son in her arms, she arranged him on her lap. "Do you remember asking me about your daddy?"

The little boy nodded. "Tee said I got a daddy somewhere. I don't know him."

"Who's Tee?" Andre asked in a low voice.

"Pansy. He couldn't say Auntie, so he just called her 'Tee.'"

"Tee's in heaven," Julian announced. "She went to stay

with the angels." He pointed toward the house. "I think she lives up there. I see an angel sometimes."

Raven glanced over at Andre. "He must be talking about your grandmother."

Andre nodded.

"Honey, I want you to meet your daddy. Would you like that?"

He nodded. "I want a daddy."

She took his tiny hand in hers. "Julian, this is your daddy. Andre is your father."

Julian turned his gaze to Andre. He didn't say a word, but just stood staring.

"It's okay, honey. Your father loves you. Remember how he came to get you when you were staying with . . . with Grandpapa?"

Julian nodded.

Andre spoke up. "Son, I am so sorry I hadn't come before now."

"Tee told me you would come," Julian whispered. "She told me you wuved me."

"Tee was a very smart woman. She's right." Andre stole a peek at Raven. "I do love you, son. I do." He held out his arms.

Without hesitation, Julian fell into his embrace. "I wuv you too, Daddy."

Raven smiled through her tears.

Over Julian's head, Andre's eyes met hers. There was a nice shine to his eyes that Raven had never seen before. Father and son together. It had been a dream of hers for so long.

Silently, she gave thanks to God.

Julian had fallen asleep almost the instant he'd had his bath. Andre had not read any more than the first two pages of *Thomas the Tank Train* before he started yawning.

He watched his son sleeping a moment longer before joining his mother and Raven downstairs.

"I have to leave for New York tomorrow morning," Andre announced.

"Do you really have to leave?" Raven asked. "You and Julian are just beginning to get to know each other as father and son."

"We don't want Lucien to figure out that we're together."

"How will you explain your absence?" Serene asked. "Surely the man knows you're gone."

"A.C.'s made it look as if I've been in London all this time. Carol will even back me up. In fact, the flight I'll be taking to New York originated in London."

Raven was still doubtful. "Do you think this will work? What about luggage? Your passport?"

"A.C.'s taken care of that as well. I even have a seat in first class."

"That young lady is good at what she does." Serene sipped her coffee. "Please be careful, son."

"I hope it works. Lucien's not stupid." Raven shook her head sadly. "I'll be so glad when this is finally over once and for all."

"Do you believe that Lucien Dupont will ever give up?" Serene asked. "I don't think so. Something drastic will have to happen."

"I'm hoping that it won't get that far."

"I think I have to agree with your mother. I'm going to talk to A.C. about this and see what she has to say. Maybe there's something else she can do." She stood up. "I'm going to give her a call." Raven excused herself and left to go upstairs.

"So Julian finally knows the truth?" Serene asked her

son when they were alone. "So Julian knows that you are his father and I am his grandmama."

"He knows," Andre confirmed. "He seems to have accepted it well."

"He is a darling little boy and he brings so much life to this house."

Andre stole a glance over his shoulder before asking, "Mom, what would you think of me and Julian living here permanently?"

Serene's face lit up. "Do you really mean it? You would leave New York? What about your work?"

He nodded. "I can paint anywhere. But I think this is a much better place for Julian to grow up. Besides, I want him to have a sense of family."

Putting aside the needlepoint she was working on, Serene eyed her son, "I noticed you haven't said anything about Raven. She is the boy's mother. Where does she fit into this picture?"

"She doesn't." Lowering his voice, Andre added, "I don't question her mothering skills, but Raven is still very much tied to Lucien Dupont. Mom, he kidnapped Julian to coerce her into stealing a painting."

"What painting?"

"The *Danse Macabre*."

Serene's mouth dropped open in surprise. She lowered her voice. "You haven't mentioned any of this to Mother, have you?"

Shaking his head, Andre answered, "No. And I don't intend to. She's been through enough."

"This is very important, son. Mother can never know."

"She won't."

"Does Raven know—"

Andre stole another peek over his shoulder. "No. I never told her anything."

"How do you plan to talk her into leaving Julian with you?"

"I saw an attorney before I left New York. I'm going to sue for custody."

Serene met her son's gaze. "I'm going to ask you something. Are you really concerned for your son's safety or are you being vindictive?"

"Mom, I'm only concerned for Julian's safety."

Serene rose to her feet. Moving to stand beside Andre, she said, "I believe that you have his best interest at heart. That's why you have to make sure this is the right thing to do. You can't just take a child from its mother like that."

"I've given this a lot of thought. Raven will have very generous visitation rights. I want her to remain an important part of his life."

"What happens if she chooses to remain here in New Orleans?"

"I don't have a problem with that. It would make the transition easier for Julian."

"So you would still sue for custody?"

Nodding, Andre replied, "I just think it's best that Julian remain with me."

"I have a strong feeling that Raven would disagree." Serene shook her head. "This is going to upset her."

"You're probably right, but hopefully she and I will be able to sit down and talk this out after she calms down. We both want what's best for our son."

"One word of advice, Son. I think you should really think some more on this. If you don't handle this correctly, Raven could run off with Julian and you'd never see him again."

"I won't let that happen, Mom."

"How are you going to stop her? Raven has complete legal

custody of her child. She's all he's ever known. Think this out, Andre. If you don't, you could lose them forever."

"I'm not trying to hurt Raven. I just want to make sure Julian's safe from Lucien's influence. His hold is still too great on Raven."

"Why don't you just give her a chance?"

Placing a reassuring hand on her arm, Andre promised, "I'm not going to make a move until I feel it's absolutely necessary, Mom."

"I'm praying it won't come to this. I hope you and Raven will be able to talk things through."

"I hope so, too."

"Is there any chance you two will be able to put aside your differences and get back together?"

Andre considered her question. "It's much too late for that, Mom. You know that we can't undo the damage of the past, no matter how much we may want to. I don't know that I can ever trust Raven with my heart again."

Raven got up early Thursday morning so that she could say good-bye to Andre. She found him coming out of his grandmother's room.

"How is she? I hope I didn't upset her the other day."

"She's fine."

Andre never seemed to want to discuss his grandmother with her. She changed the subject. "I'm going to miss you. So will Julian."

"I'll miss the two of you, too. I'll be gone for about a week or two."

"Be safe, Andre."

"I'll do my best." He gave her a rueful smile. "I'm going to say good-bye to my mom. Paul will be here shortly."

"I'll wake Julian up."

She was about to walk off, but he stopped her. "No, let him sleep. I've already been in to see him."

"Was he up?"

"Just briefly. He probably won't remember it though."

"I could go to the airport with you," Raven offered. "Paul could drop me off back at the house."

"That won't be necessary."

Andre left half an hour later. A.C. called to make sure that he got off okay.

"Raven, I've been thinking about our last conversation. I don't know why you didn't want to mention any of this stuff before."

"I didn't think you would want to help us."

"I'd already suspected as much. Raven, I know about your parents."

She swallowed hard. "What Lucien told me is true then? He said they were art thieves."

There was a slight pause before A.C. answered, "Yes." Another pause. "I'm sorry, Raven."

"How can we stop Lucien?"

"We can set him up."

"How?"

"You'll have to go back to New York. Make Lucien believe that you're ready to finish the job."

"Andre won't agree to this. He won't like it at all."

"That's the only way, Raven. Lucien's covered his tracks well. There's nothing we can do without proof. The only way we can get that proof is to catch him in the act."

Raven nodded in resignation. "When Andre gets back, I'll talk to him about it."

"If you want to be rid of Lucien—this is the only way."

Raven knew A.C. was right. She also knew that Andre would never agree to such a plan. He didn't want Michael caught in the middle.

Fourteen

"I'm leaving the day after tomorrow," A.C. announced. She and Paul had just finished their evening walk. Since that first date, they'd spent all of their free time together.

"So soon?"

"I need to get back to work." She tossed a handful of peanuts into her mouth.

"Have you ever considered moving to New Orleans?"

She shook her head. "Too many bugs. I don't like swamps and I especially hate snakes."

Paul burst into laughter with A.C. joining him.

The laughter evaporated into silence. They were standing in front of his house.

Wrapping his arms around her, Paul spoke up. "I hate to see you leave, Amethyst. I'm going to miss you."

Inclining her head, she asked, "Really? Sure you're not going to forget about me as soon as my plane takes off."

"Amethyst, there's something I have to tell you."

"What is it?"

"I've fallen in love with you. It was love at first sight, actually."

A.C. was speechless in her surprise. "You've only known me for a few short weeks." Backing out of his embrace, she started to tremble. "P—Paul, this is crazy. Don't do this."

"Look me in my eyes and tell me that you can't see the love I feel for you."

A.C. reluctantly met his gaze, then quickly looked away. She had never expected this declaration. What in the world could Paul be thinking?

"You know what I'm saying is true, don't you?"

She didn't respond.

When Paul prompted her again, she replied, "I have to go." A.C. walked over to her rental car and quickly unlocked the door.

"Why are you leaving?"

"I need to pack . . . Paul, I really have to go."

He grabbed her by the arm. "Don't, Amethyst. Don't run away from me."

"I'm not running. I didn't realize how late it had gotten."

Paul released her with a sigh. "Fine. Just remember this. I love you, Amethyst. It's not going to just go away. Whenever you're ready, you know where to find me."

"Good-bye, Paul." Her emotions were in a jumble and A.C. suddenly felt like crying. She quickly unlocked her car and drove off as fast as she could.

Paul was moving entirely too fast for her. She barely knew the man and now he was proclaiming his love for her.

He was crazy, she concluded. He'd lost all sense of reason. A.C. was glad to be going home to L.A.

Andre hadn't been home an hour when he received a visit from Lucien. Instead of inviting him inside, he blocked the entrance with his body and demanded, "What are you doing here?"

"Hello, Andre. May I come in?" He stuck his cane in the doorway to prevent Andre from slamming the door in his face.

"No. I just got back from a trip and—"

"You were in London," Lucien cut in. "So I heard."

"How did you hear that? I told no one I was going." He moved to stand closer to Lucien. "Are you spying on me now?"

"The reason for my visit is Raven. I'm looking for her and I thought you might know where she is. Surely, she's been in contact with you."

"Thanks to you, I have nothing to do with Raven."

Lucien studied Andre's face. "You almost sound as if you hate her. You are aware that she loves you more than her own life."

"I haven't heard from Raven and I hope I don't. Now that you have your answer, I want you to get out of here."

"If you should see or hear from Raven—"

"I'll tell her the same thing I'm telling you," Andre interrupted. "Go to hell!" He kicked Lucien's cane out of the doorway and closed it shut, hoping to God that Lucien believed him.

He stood with his back pressed to the door, listening. All he heard was a few mumbled words Lucien hissed to his bodyguard.

Andre eased over to the window and ventured a peek outside. There was no sign of Lucien or Cal. He released a sigh of relief.

Andre had only been gone for four days, but Raven missed him terribly. He might as well have been gone four years. A.C. had gone back to Los Angeles, so she really felt alone.

She'd thought that Andre would've at least called

them by now, but there had been no word thus far. She was getting worried about him. Raven debated over whether or not to give A.C. a call.

She became distracted when Serene entered the family room carrying an armload of freshly washed laundry.

"Have you heard anything from Andre?" Raven inquired.

"He's probably not going to call," Serene stated. "He may think that Lucien has his phone bugged. You know my son. He'll do whatever it takes to keep you and Julian safe."

"But we have no idea if he's safe. I'm worried about him."

"He'll find a way to get word to us."

Julian ran into the room. "Daddy? Want Daddy."

Serene picked him up. "Daddy will be back soon. Why don't you come with Grandmama into the garden? You can help me pick flowers. You like the flowers, don't you?"

The little boy grinned as he nodded.

Raven broke into a smile. "So you're going to help in the garden. Julian, you're such a big boy now."

"I like the flowers."

"Why don't you join us," Serene suggested. "It's a beautiful day."

"I think I'll stay in here and fold these towels for you."

"You don't have to do that, dear. Anna will be back shortly."

"I don't mind. Besides, Anna will have to start dinner soon."

"Well, come join us when you're done."

"I will," she promised.

Julian took Serene by the hand and was pulling her toward the door.

"I guess you're ready to go outside."

Biting back her laughter, Raven picked up a towel and began to fold it. Julian loved it here. He enjoyed the outdoors and running beneath the massive oaks. She imagined he was very much like Andre was at his age.

When she finished folding the towels, Raven got up and joined Serene and Julian outdoors. They were in the garden. Her son was laughing and chasing a butterfly.

Raven felt the hair on the back of her neck stand up. She glanced up. *Andre's grandmother. She's watching me*, she thought silently.

"Your mother, does she ever come downstairs?"

Serene glanced up. "Sometimes. Not as much as she should."

"I would love to meet her."

"Maybe you will. My mother has been through a lot, Raven. She's very fragile."

"I understand."

Placing a rose in her basket, Serene said, "She adores Julian."

"She's met him?" Raven asked in surprise.

"I believe so. I think Andre's taken him up to visit her."

Raven couldn't help but wonder why Andre never bothered to take her to meet his grandmother. She tried not to take it personally, but it continued to nag at her. Maybe he didn't think she was good enough.

Fifteen

"Why are you looking as if you've lost your best friend? You should be happy after leaving me to do all the work while you bask in the New Orleans sunshine."

Snapping out of her musings, A.C. muttered, "Huh?"

"A.C., what's going on with you?" Onyx demanded. "You've been walking around in a fog all day long."

Massaging her temple with her fingers, A.C. responded, "I'm just tired."

"I'm not buying that. Come on, what's up?"

"I met someone," A.C. announced. She leaned back in her leather chair.

"Like a man?"

A.C. didn't know whether or not to be offended by her sister's question. "Yeah, like a man. What do you think?"

"I thought you'd sworn off men. Lord knows I have."

Leaning forward with both hands on her desk, A.C. inquired, "Why is that, Onyx?"

"Oh no you don't. This is all about you. Now tell me all about this man." She made herself comfortable on the sofa in A.C.'s office.

"His name is Paul Robichaux. Before I left, he told me that he'd fallen in love with me."

Onyx's eyes grew large in her surprise. "Wow. So, what did you say?" She leaned forward.

"I left." A.C. dropped her eyes and pretended to go through her appointment book.

"Without saying a word to him?"

She wouldn't look at her sister. "I said good-bye."

Onyx shook her head and muttered a curse.

Glancing up, A.C. questioned, "What? What was I supposed to say to something like that?"

"How do you feel about him?"

A.C. shrugged. "We haven't known each other that long."

"You said that to say what?"

Standing up, A.C. made her way over to where her sister was sitting. She sat down beside her. "Onyx, I haven't known Paul a good two months yet."

"You've said that already. What you haven't said is whether or not you have any feelings for the man."

"He lives in New Orleans."

Onyx rolled her eyes in irritation. "A.C., do you love him?"

Silently she considered Onyx's question.

"Well?"

"I don't know."

"Honey, be honest. Not just for me, but for yourself."

"Onyx, it really doesn't matter. We live in different states. I'm not good with long distance relationships. There is no way this can work out. It just can't."

"How do you know?"

"It won't work, Onyx." A.C.'s tone brooked no argument.

"If you care for this man, don't walk away without trying to make it work."

She gave a short laugh. "You're one to talk. You won't even give a man your phone number." A.C. got up and stretched. She turned to face her sister. "Onyx, you need to practice what you preach."

"This is not about me, A.C."

"Paul and I have no future together. That's the end of this discussion. Now unless you intend to tell me what's

really going on with you—you'd better leave my office."
She returned to her desk and sat down.

Onyx got up and headed to the door. Just before she
left, she looked over her shoulder at A.C. and said, "I
made a mess of my life, A.C. I just don't want to see the
same thing happen to you. That's all I'm saying."

"Why don't you trust me?"

"This isn't about trust. It's about me, A.C. This is
something I just can't share with you right now. I need
you to respect my wishes on this, okay?"

A.C. nodded.

"Oh yeah . . . I'm glad you're back."

"Me too." A.C. returned her attention to her work, but
she couldn't concentrate. "Why did you have to ruin what
we had, Paul? Everything was just fine the way it was."

Her eyes landed on the telephone. A.C. resisted the
urge to call him. *What good would it do?* It certainly
wouldn't change things between them.

Andre returned to New Orleans ten days later. It was
Sunday around four P.M. when he strode into the house.
Hearing footsteps at the top of the stairs, he looked up.

"You're back!" Raven shouted as she flew down the
stairs and into his arms. "I'm so glad you're back. I was
so worried about you."

Andre eased out of her warm embrace. "I'm okay. I
would've called, but I had to be careful." He dropped his
garment bag on top of the suitcase.

"I know."

"Lucien came to see me, Raven. Shortly after I arrived
home. He must have had someone watching my place as
A.C. assumed."

"What happened?"

Andre told her. "I don't know if he believed me or not."

Wrapping her arms around her middle, Raven asked, "Why did you say that?"

"Nothing really. I just meant Lucien didn't let on one way or the other."

"Do you think he followed you to the airport?"

"Probably. I wouldn't doubt it."

"Then he knows where we are." Raven turned toward the stairs. "We've got to get out of here."

Andre grabbed her by the arm. "Calm down, Raven. If Lucien actually had me followed, then he believes I'm in London." He released her.

"How do you figure? They most likely boarded the plane with you."

"If they did, then they followed me to London and they were watching when Carol met my plane."

"Excuse me?"

"I was in London for a couple of days."

"With Carol?" Waves of jealousy washed through her. Were they still lovers? She wondered.

"Yes. We have to make this believable."

"Aren't you using her?"

"No."

Raven had her answer. Andre was still involved with her. She struggled to hide her disappointment. "Can she be trusted?"

His gaze met hers. "I can trust Carol with my life."

His response hurt Raven to the core. She looked away. "I just meant . . ."

"It's okay, Andre," she said a little too quickly. "I know exactly what you meant." She took a step backwards. "I'm glad to see that you're back. I . . . Julian missed you a lot." Right now, Raven just wanted to get away from Andre. She wanted to be alone.

"I missed him too."

"He's upstairs with your mother. They're playing with the train set you bought him."

"I think I'll go up and say hello."

A suffocating sensation tightened her throat to the point that Raven could only nod.

He stopped halfway up the stairs. "What are you getting ready to do?"

"Nothing in particular. Why?"

"After I check in with everyone, I want to sit down with you and talk."

"Sure. I'll be in the family room. Just come get me whenever you're ready." Raven was heartsick. She had a feeling that she already knew what Andre wanted to talk about. He was in love with Carol and would probably be joining her in London.

Or worse yet, maybe he was going to announce that he and Carol were getting married. The mere thought made her want to cry. Raven closed her eyes, her heart aching with pain from the rejection that was sure to come.

Andre had to admit that he'd missed Raven as well. In fact, he was having a hard time fighting his feelings for her. He still cared deeply for her even though he hadn't gotten past the hurt and distrust. It was time that he was honest with her—after all, he demanded honesty.

He watched her a moment before climbing the stairs to the second floor. Andre didn't miss the air of sadness surrounding her. It was almost as if she were grieving. He scratched the back of his ear in confusion.

He walked straight to the nursery and found Serene sitting on the floor laughing as she watched Julian play with his train.

His mother picked up a book and said, "Look Julian. It's Thomas."

"Thoma," he repeated. "Thoma Train."

Andre smiled. His son was the greatest gift Raven could have given him. He was determined not to miss any more of Julian's life.

Serene spotted him and gestured for him to come inside. "When did you get back?"

"Not too long ago." Andre strode to the middle of the room and picked Julian up. "Hello, Son. How are you?"

"Daddy . . ."

"I missed you. I missed you a lot."

Julian wrapped his arms tightly around Andre's neck. Andre smiled at his mother as he reveled in the feel of his son. He loved this little boy more than his own life.

Andre spent the next hour playing with Julian on the floor.

His next stop was to see his grandmother. She greeted him with a warm hug.

"I was worried about you."

"As you can see, I'm fine. There was nothing to worry about."

"What kind of trouble is this?" Antonia inquired. "Is there something I can do to help?"

"No, Grandmother. It's nothing you should concern yourself about. I will take care of everything. I promise." He owed her that much.

Antonia gave him a puzzled look.

"Raven would like to meet you, Grandmother."

She shook her head. "No, I can't." Antonia became agitated.

He wrapped his arm around her. "It's okay. You don't have to do anything you don't want to do."

Andre sought Raven out after leaving his grandmother's room. He found her outside on the porch. "I've been looking for you everywhere."

"I needed some fresh air." Looking over her shoulder, she asked, "Why do you want to talk to me?"

Her question caught him off guard.

"I thought maybe we could go somewhere and have dinner first."

"You just got back. Don't you want to spend some time with your family?"

He scanned her face. "Raven, is something wrong?" She looked terribly unhappy.

"No. Nothing's wrong."

"Then I have to assume that you don't want to be around me," he stated.

"That's not it at all. I just thought you would want to—"

"I want to spend time with you, Raven," Andre emphasized.

Her eyes widened in surprise.

"We really need to talk." He moved closer to her. "You've been after me to talk and now I'm ready."

"Okay. We'll talk. But you don't have to take me to dinner. I'd rather do it here. Right now."

"I know you're tired of this house. Let's go out. What would you like to do?" Her face was bleak with sorrow.

"I'd like to listen to some jazz."

Andre nodded in approval. "I know just the place."

"When should I be ready?"

"I'll make reservations for eight."

"What about our talk? Can't we just do it now?"

"Go on and get dressed. We'll talk later."

He watched her walk slowly past him. Raven looked like a woman facing her doom. Andre was puzzled by her strange reaction. He'd thought she would be pleased.

Raven didn't know quite what to make of Andre and the sudden change in his behavior. He had completely taken her by surprise. This was definitely not a good sign.

She was so nervous she could barely put on her make-up. Torment was eating at her from the inside.

Raven tried on three different pairs of shoes before she decided on which ones to wear. Why she was paying all this attention to her wardrobe, she had no idea. It wasn't as if Andre would notice or even care.

At seven-fifteen, she met Andre downstairs. Raven wasn't looking forward to this evening, but there was no avoiding it. He insisted on speaking with her tonight. Nervously, she ran her fingers through her short hair.

Scanning her from head to toe, he said, "You look exquisite."

"Thank you, Andre," she admired the black suit he wore. His dreads had been pulled into a ponytail. "You look very nice, too." Her mouth felt like old paper, dry and dusty.

Andre held out his arm to her. Putting her arm through his, Raven chewed on her bottom lip. Her eyes watered, causing her to blink rapidly.

He opened the car door for her. She got in, grateful for the few seconds alone. She composed herself.

Inside the car, Andre said, "Raven, seeing you again hasn't been easy for me."

Her eyes darkened with pain. "Do you want me to leave? If so, you didn't have to go through all this trouble—"

"Stop jumping to conclusions," Andre interjected quickly. "I'm trying to tell you how I feel. How I've been feeling."

She settled back into her seat. "I'm listening."

Andre kept his eyes on the road while he drove. "I never thought I'd see you again, Raven. When I did, I realized that I'd never resolved things between us. I think we need to do that now."

Little by little, warmth crept back into her body. "That's what I've been trying to tell you all this time. I feel the exact same way."

"I know. I just wasn't ready before," he admitted.

"I see."

"Do you?"

"Andre, I understand that you want to be a father to Julian. That's fine. I don't intend to stand in your way." Clearing her throat, she continued, "I also know that you want nothing to do with me."

"Raven, listen to me, sweetheart. I care about you."

"But?" She was on the verge of tears once again.

"But nothing. I want us to start over. Maybe we can find a way to become friends."

"You think we should be friends?" Raven almost choked on her words.

"Yes, don't you?"

He didn't want her out of his life. Relief swept through her. "I'd like that, Andre. I really would."

Andre reached over and took her hand. "So, do you think we can enjoy the rest of the evening, friend?"

Grinning, Raven nodded.

Andre and Raven spent the evening listening to the soothing sounds of Nicholas Payton. It had been a long time since they'd spent time like this.

Raven was on cloud nine. They weren't a couple, but maybe in the future . . . she glanced over at him.

"What is it, Raven?"

"I know it's none of my business, but are you and Carol lovers?"

"We used to be. We're just friends now."

Just like us, Raven added silently. At the moment she was too afraid to hope for more.

Sixteen

The tension between Raven and Andre was finally gone. He seemed more at ease around her now and she couldn't be more pleased. They were talking more—even laughing. A part of her still hoped for more, but for the most part, she was content with the way things were now. Last night, he had taken her to Harrah's Casino at the foot of Canal Street. Raven won a thousand dollars and lorded it over Andre for the rest of the evening.

They'd really had a good time last night. It brought back memories of the way they used to be with each other. She yearned to regain Andre's trust. It would take a while, Raven realized, but she was willing to be patient. She was not going to blow it a second time with him.

Andre and Julian were also becoming closer more and more each day, and there was nothing more Raven wanted other than to spend her life with Andre and their son.

Raven shifted in her bed trying to get comfortable. She couldn't sleep because Andre dominated her thoughts. Excitement engulfed her, although she struggled in vain to keep it under control.

She lay back in bed with her eyes closed. Raven finally gave up the idea of sleeping and climbed out of bed. She padded barefoot over to the window and peered out into the moonlit night. The moon was full, casting a soft glow over the city. She broke into a smile when one of the stars seemed to wink at her.

After a while, Raven grabbed her robe and slipped it on. She left her room and walked a few feet down the hall. She could hear the shower running in Andre's room. Good, he was still up.

Smiling, Raven slipped into Andre's room. He was in the shower. She made herself comfortable and waited for him to exit the bathroom. Memories of their last moments of happiness filled her. They used to be so close once.

When the shower stopped, Raven sat up. She shifted in the chair, pulling her robe closer. Andre would be out soon.

He was clearly surprised to find her in his room. "Raven, what are you doing in here?" He wrapped his towel tighter around him. "You couldn't sleep?"

She shook her head "no." "There's something I need to discuss with you."

Pulling his towel tighter, he said, "I'm sorry, I wasn't expecting company."

Raven grinned and replied, "You look fine to me."

Grabbing a pair of jeans, Andre headed back to the bathroom. "I'll be right back."

She jumped up and picked up the briefs he'd dropped in his haste. "You forgot these," she teased.

Muttering under his breath, Andre snatched them from her and strode briskly into the bathroom for privacy.

Raven burst into giggles.

He returned a few minutes later wearing the jeans. They eyed each other for a moment before Andre questioned, "What is it?"

"Huh?"

"You said you wanted to talk to me?"

"Remember all the late night talks we used to have?"

"I remember," he practically whispered.

Raven stood up and moved to stand just inches away from him. "I miss those days, Andre."

"I do too," he said softly.

Pacing back and forth, Raven tried to gather her thoughts. "I talked to A.C. about Lucien. I told her everything."

"What did she have to say?"

"A.C. thinks that the only way to stop Lucien is to set him up."

"Set him up how?" Andre's tone was coolly disapproving.

"By making him believe that I'll do as he wants. Steal the painting for him."

Andre was shaking his head. "No, I don't agree."

"We can tell Michael what's going on. He won't get hurt."

"I don't want him involved at all, Raven. There are too many people involved already."

"I'm sure Michael would appreciate knowing that Lucien is not at all the man he's always assumed he was," she argued. "I know I would want to know."

"Then why didn't you tell him before?"

"Because I didn't think he would believe me."

"And you think he'd believe you now?"

"I just wish we had some kind of proof," Raven murmured to herself. "There has to be some way to convince Michael that Lucien is not his friend."

A strange expression washed over Andre's face. He leaned against the chest of drawers, his arms folded. "We'll think of something, Raven. We'll find another way to get Lucien."

"I hope so. Because if we don't, I'm going to have to seriously consider disappearing with the help of A.C. and Preacher."

He pulled her toward him. He wrapped his arms around her. "It won't come to that."

Andre met her gaze. They stared at one another, each one caught in memories of the past.

Feeling bold, Raven placed the palm of her hand on his bare chest. "Seeing you like this brings back so many memories."

"Raven . . ."

"I know you want me, Andre. Why won't you admit it?"

His voice was hoarse. "Yes, I want you. To act on it would be wrong though."

"Why do you say that? I feel the same way. I want you to make love to me, Andre."

"Raven, I want you to understand something. First of all I want to take this one day at a time. It's possible we'll be able to become friends, but as for anything more . . . I have to be honest with you—it's not going to happen. With love, there has to be trust, no matter how much I may care about you."

She removed her hand and retreated a step. "I understand."

"I hope you do, Raven. We both have to maintain absolute control over our feelings. I don't want to hurt you, either."

Closing her robe, she said, "Andre, you know everything now. There are no secrets between us."

"I'm sorry, Raven. I just make it a habit of not repeating the same mistake twice."

"I want you to know something. I love you, Andre. You are the only man I've ever loved. That's not going to change. We have a son and he deserves two parents."

He didn't respond.

"Did you hear what I just said?"

"I heard you."

Raven couldn't stop her heart from aching. "But you have nothing to say?"

"What am I supposed to say?"

"That it means something to you. That you believe me. Just say something. I don't care what it is."

"I will always care about you, Raven."

"But you won't consider . . ." Raven couldn't even finish the sentence. She shook her head sadly. "I don't believe this." Her eyes filled with tears. "You are going to punish me for the rest of my life."

"It's late, Raven. Why don't you go to bed?"

Blinking back her tears, Raven agreed. She left Andre's room as quickly as she could.

Back in her room, she fell on her bed sobbing softly. Raven couldn't deny that she'd left herself wide open for Andre's rejection. She felt like a fool.

Warm waves of humiliation flowed through her, bringing on another bout of tears. The painful memories of the past rushed to the forefront and they caused her to cry harder. Raven cursed herself for believing that she and Andre could ever have a second chance. It was stupid on her part.

Sleep did not come easily for her. Raven was still awake when the sun burst through the darkness. She heard someone outside her door. Although she had a strong suspicion that it was Andre, she didn't make a move. She was too embarrassed to see him now.

Raven finally closed her eyes and surrendered to sleep out of pure exhaustion.

Andre stood outside of Raven's door. He'd come to her room shortly after she left his and heard her crying. It made him feel like a cad. He hadn't wanted to upset her, but he didn't want to give her false hope either. After a moment, he decided against disturbing her. Andre made his way back to his own room and climbed into bed.

Hours later, he remained wide awake. Andre got out of bed and strolled onto the balcony. He couldn't get Raven out of his mind. He couldn't risk letting her get too close because she could break his heart all over again.

Andre took off his pajamas and put on a pair of jeans and a T-shirt. He needed to get some fresh air. On his way downstairs, he paused at Raven's door, but decided once again to leave her alone. She was probably sleeping anyway.

The door to the nursery opened and he watched his grandmother come out. Andre didn't say a word, just nodded at her and smiled.

Antonia blew him a kiss and rushed to her room.

Anna was already up and moving around. She was in the kitchen getting breakfast started. She looked up when he entered the kitchen.

"You are up so early. Why don't you go back to bed?"

"I thought I'd get some fresh air. After that, I think I'm going to do some painting in my room."

"Are you hungry?"

"Not really."

"I'll make your favorite for you when you return."

He winked at her. "You're spoiling me, Anna."

They bantered back and forth for a while. Andre finally took his leave. He drove to a nearby park and shut off his mother's car. He settled back in the seat and closed his eyes.

Groaning, Andre put his hands to his face. He'd almost given in to his lustful urges and made love to Raven. It would have been a mistake. Maybe if he said it enough, he would believe it.

For the moment, they were in close quarters, so there was no way to keep his distance from her. Andre's heart was pounding fast. This was not going to work. He wanted Raven much too badly.

He sat there for a couple of hours, pondering his predicament. The last thing he wanted was to alienate Raven or cause her any pain. They were becoming closer until last night. Andre muttered a curse. He should have handled things differently. Now it was too late. The damage was done.

She'd been home almost three weeks and A.C. couldn't stop thinking about Paul. He was on her mind day and night. She picked up the phone several times to call him, but each time she chickened out and changed her mind. Besides, Paul hadn't bothered to call her either.

Maybe he was still angry with her. A.C. couldn't fault him—especially after the way she'd rushed off after his heartfelt declaration. Now she wished she'd handled the matter differently. They would never have a future together, but she shouldn't have dismissed him like that. She had no right to do so. Especially because she felt the same way. This made her just as crazy as Paul, she realized. *How could they be in love?*

Paul challenged her in a way very few men ever had. She enjoyed his company as well as their playful bantering back and forth. He was a good man, A.C. decided shortly after they'd met. And she'd fallen for him harder than she could've imagined.

But the fact remained that she lived here and he lived in New Orleans. Paul seemed content to stay there while she would not consider leaving Los Angeles.

Their relationship didn't have a chance. A.C. released a long, sad sigh.

Seventeen

After her disastrous episode with Andre three days before, Raven decided to keep her distance. Andre had made it abundantly clear that they had no future together and all they would ever share was Julian. That knowledge pained her greatly, but she intended to abide by his wishes.

She went downstairs, hoping that she would be able to avoid him. Lately he'd spent most mornings with his grandmother. After that, Andre would lock himself in his room working on some project.

"Good morning, Anna."

"Good morning to you. I trust you slept well."

"Somewhat," Raven admitted. "I didn't fall asleep until after daybreak."

"You poor dear. Why don't you go back upstairs and try to rest. I'll take care of Julian for you. I really don't mind."

"You're so good with him, Anna. Thanks for the offer, but I'm okay. I'll probably nap sometime during the day."

"Here's your cranberry juice."

Raven accepted the drink. "Thank you." She sat down at the breakfast table. "Have you seen Andre this morning?"

"He's upstairs in his grandmother's room."

"Oh." Raven had already assumed as much. She immediately jumped to the conclusion that Andre simply didn't want to be around her either right now. The revelation hurt her deeply and she struggled to hide her true feelings. "I guess I'll see him later then." She reached for a piece of toast.

"He should be down shortly. Andre planned to have breakfast with Julian."

Serene joined Raven at the table. "You're just not going to have toast for breakfast, are you? Anna made her delectable banana nut pancakes. You have to try them—they're divine."

"I'll try a couple. I'm not real hungry."

Pouring a cup of coffee, Serene eyed Raven. "Is there something wrong, dear?"

"No, everything's fine," Raven lied.

Serene was not at all convinced. "Are you sure? You look a little sad."

"I'm fine, really. I was just restless most of the night."

Serene let the matter drop. "I checked on Julian before I came down and he was sitting on the bed playing with his teddy bear. He's such a precious child."

"He's the love of my life. I don't know what I would do without him." Raven caught the strange look that passed over Serene's features and wondered what was behind the look. Before she could ask, Andre entered the kitchen with Julian in his arms.

"This young man's already bathed and dressed. He's ready for pancakes."

"Pancakes. . . ." Julian echoed. "Want pancakes." He grinned when he caught sight of Raven. "Mommy."

She rose up and came around the table to give her son a kiss. "Good morning, sweetie."

"Good morning, Raven."

Turning her attention to Andre, she said, "'Morning, Andre." She refused to look directly at him.

They sat together at the table in the breakfast nook. Serene and Andre carried most of the conversation while Raven sat quietly nibbling on her toast.

After breakfast, Raven and Serene took a quiet stroll around the estate.

"I love it here," Raven murmured. "It's so beautiful in New Orleans."

"The city is lovely. When I left Boston, I had some doubts as to whether I would stay, but I wasn't here a week before I decided this is where I wanted to live."

"Did you come back because of your mother?"

Serene nodded. "If it wasn't for Anna, she would be all alone here."

Raven longed to meet the elusive Antonia Savoy. She'd seen pictures of Antonia when she was younger and she was a very beautiful woman. Serene resembled her mother very much. She imagined Antonio was still striking, so why was she hiding?

Shortly after one in the afternoon, Raven found she could barely keep her eyes open. After putting Julian down for his nap, she laid down to take one, too.

She slept for two hours. She jumped up and went into the bathroom to wash her face and freshen up.

Serene knocked on her door before peeking in. "I'm going to pick up some things for Mother. Would you mind if I took Julian with me?"

Smiling, Raven answered, "It's fine. I know he'd love it."

"I'll keep him safe."

"I know you will."

Raven left her room ten minutes later and ran into Anna in the hallway. "Have you seen Andre?"

"He's in his room, I believe," the housekeeper announced.

"Thanks, Anna." She went to his room and knocked on the door. She knocked a second time before slowly opening the door and peeking inside. "Andre." she called out. Raven stepped all the way inside the room.

The recollection of what had happened the last time she was in there overtook her, bringing back unpleasant memories. Raven suddenly wanted to get out of the room as fast as she could.

Just as she was leaving, Raven's eyes landed on some papers lying on top of his dresser. They looked like legal documents of some sort. Unable to fight her curiosity, she picked them up and started to read.

"No . . ." Her heart was breaking. Andre was planning to take Julian from her. Tearing the papers into tiny pieces, she threw them to the floor and ran out, her tears nearly blinding her.

"Raven, what's wrong?" Anna questioned.

She couldn't even utter the words. Waving her hand in despair, she brushed past the housekeeper.

Downstairs, Raven went in search of Andre. He wasn't in the house, so she ventured outside. She found him sketching beneath one of the many hundred-year-old oak trees. She wiped her face with her hands and called out to him. "I want to talk to you," she snapped. Fury almost choked her.

His face a mask of confusion, Andre inquired, "What's up with you?"

"Julian and I are leaving, and don't you dare try to stop us."

Dropping the pad, he demanded. "To go where?"

Raven gave him a hostile glare. "I don't think it's any of your business."

"Julian is my son, too," Andre replied sharply. "You will not take him from me."

"Take him away from—" Raven stopped short. "You have some nerve. How could you do this to me, Andre?" She threw the words at him like stones.

"Do what?"

"You hate me so much that you would take my son from me?"

"I'm not trying to take Julian from you. I'm trying to keep him safe." Andre rose to his feet. "Raven, listen to me. I'm only trying to protect him. He's in danger as long as Lucien is roaming around."

Her thoughts were racing dangerously. She couldn't lose Julian. She wouldn't survive without her son. "I can leave the country. Go somewhere where Lucien can't find us."

"He found you in Georgia."

"We've been through that already. I won't let you take my son, Andre. He's all I h—have." Raven started to cry once again. "Please don't do this to me."

Her tears didn't affect him. "Doesn't he deserve to be safe?"

"I can keep him safe, Andre."

"You can see him anytime you want, Raven. However, we would have to be careful to keep his whereabouts secret."

"I'm not leaving him. I won't just walk out of my son's life."

"That's not what I'm asking you to do. Raven, I want you to be there for Julian. I know he needs you."

"I don't think you believe that. If you did, you never would've gone to an attorney behind my back." Waving her hands in dismissal, Raven uttered, "I don't want to talk about this anymore. I'm not going to let you have my son and that's final. " Turning on her heel, Raven stormed off.

Andre was right behind her. "Don't walk away from me."

She kept walking. "I can't deal with you right now."

He grabbed her by both arms. "If you leave, you risk endangering Julian. Surely you don't want that."

Raven's tone had become chilly. "You know I don't, but I'm not going to just sit here and let you take my baby from me."

Andre released her. "We'll talk about this when you calm down, Raven."

Raven was beyond listening to anything he had to say. "There is no need to talk about anything. I will fight you to the end. I won't let you have Julian. Do you hear me?"

"Raven . . ."

"I mean it, Andre. You will not take my son from me. You've only been in his life a short while. I've been there from the moment he was conceived."

"I didn't know about him," he countered.

"Because you wouldn't give me a chance to tell you."

"You could've sent a letter or something."

"You wouldn't have read it. Besides, it's neither here nor there. Julian and I have been together all of his life. Now you want to step in and push me away. It's not right." Wiping away a tear, Raven muttered, "Get out of my way. The last place I want to be right now is around you." She took several deep breaths before saying, "I never thought I'd say this, but I hate you, Andre. I hate you with my entire soul."

Serene handed Andre a cup of tea. "Raven was very upset when I got back. She looked like she'd been crying. Did you say something to her about wanting custody?"

"I didn't get a chance to. She found the papers." Andre had never seen her so angry before. He didn't doubt she meant it when she'd said she hated him.

"Oh dear." She sat down beside him. "I'm sure she was devastated."

"Mom, the look on her face . . . it was the look of betrayal and something more. There was this look of pain. The kind that runs so deep within—it can kill you." Shaking his head, he said, "I don't want to see that look on her face ever again."

"Was it the same look that was on your face when you found out the truth about her?"

"I guess."

"So where do you two stand?"

"I don't know," Andre admitted. "Right now I've got to find a way to keep her from bolting."

"You really think she'll leave?"

Andre could tell that his mother was worried. "No, not with Lucien on the loose, but then, I really don't know for sure." He took a sip of tea, pretending to be at ease. "I thought I was doing the right thing."

"And now?"

"Now I'm not so sure. Mom, she hates me."

"She didn't mean it, son. Raven said it out of anger."

"No, she meant it all right," Andre muttered uneasily. "I saw it in her face."

"You should go to her, Andre. Tell her that you've changed your mind." Serene glanced over at him. "You have changed your mind, haven't you?"

"I want to keep my son safe."

"What about his mother? Do you not want to keep her safe as well? Why can't she stay here too?"

"I didn't want to give Raven false hope."

"Son, I'm not trying to tell you what to do, but I think you shouldn't take Julian from his mother. Forcing her out of her son's life is not the way to deal with your feelings for Raven."

"You think that's what I've been doing?"

"Yes, I do. You've never been one to face your past."

"How can you say that to me?"

"It's the truth, Andre," Serene said gently. "Raven is

part of your past and you can't handle it. Look how long it took you to come back to New Orleans."

"It's not the same thing."

"I know that, Andre."

"Why don't we just change the subject?" he suggested. "This is getting us nowhere."

"I have one more thing to say. Before *you* lose your son, go and speak to Raven. Try to find a compromise. She is welcome to stay here as well." Serene's eyes were wet with tears. "Fix this before we lose Julian for good."

Raven couldn't concentrate on her novel, so she put it down. Tears ran down her face, but she didn't bother to wipe them away. She didn't have the strength. Never in a million years had she expected Andre to be so cruel. He'd planned all along to take Julian from her.

If she lost Julian, it was because of her own selfish reasons. She had to face the truth. Raven had come to Andre because she'd hoped once he found out about his son—he would come back to her. First and foremost, she'd needed his help, but it didn't stop there.

Just like her, Andre had had a plan of his own. The only reason he'd helped her was so that he could take Julian away from her.

Raven leaned back against the comfort of the plush pillows. She felt so alone right now, so misplaced in the world . . .

Andre walked by her room, took a step back and paused. "Can I come in?"

"I don't want any company," she replied without looking at him.

He stepped inside her room. "Raven . . ."

Anger rippled along her spine. "Please leave, Andre."

"How long are you going to act like this? It's getting us nowhere."

She swung her legs off the bed. "If you don't leave, then I will. We have nothing to talk about."

Andre shook his head vehemently. "I don't agree."

"I don't care," Raven snapped in anger as she stood up and headed to the door.

Andre blocked her exit. "*I'll* leave for now. But when you calm down, we are going to talk about this. Oh, and if you try to run, I'll have A.C. track you down. You will not take my son away from me. I'm hoping we can reach a compromise, Raven, but if we can't . . ." He turned and left.

Raven trembled. Andre was no better than Lucien, she thought sadly.

Paul was surprised to find A.C. parked in his driveway when he came home. He got out of his car, "When did you get back?"

"I had to see you," A.C. announced. Opening the door, she stepped out of the car. She followed him up to the house, but did not venture any further until he said, "Come in. You don't have to stand outside."

"Wasn't sure I was welcomed here anymore."

Standing in the doorway, Paul asked, "Why would you think that?"

"Because of the way I left things between us." She tried to depict an ease she didn't necessarily feel.

Paul gestured for her to have a seat.

A.C. refused. Noting the heartrending tenderness of Paul's gaze, she was overcome with longing. It had been a while since a man looked at her that way. "There's something I have to do first."

"What's that?" he asked.

She wrapped her arms around him. Paul bent his head and covered her mouth with his own. A.C. matched him kiss for kiss as his hands explored the hollows of her back.

"Does this mean that you love me, too?" he whispered. His breath was warm and moist against her face and her heart raced.

Pulling his face back to hers, A.C. murmured, "Shut up." Reclaiming his lips, she gave herself freely to the passion of the kiss. Paul's tongue sent shivers of desire racing through her.

They parted a few minutes later.

"How long are you staying this time?" asked Paul.

A.C.'s mouth was still burning with fire from his kiss. "Just for the weekend."

Giving her a mischievous grin, he pulled A.C. back to him. "Well, we don't have a moment to waste, do we?"

"No, we don't."

"What would you like to do?"

She took a step back and removed her shirt. "It's been a long time since I've been with anyone." A.C. unhooked her bra and tossed it to Paul. "Think you can bring it all back to me?"

Eighteen

Saturday morning, Andre stopped by Raven's room to see if she wanted to do some shopping.

"Leave me alone, Andre."

He gave an exasperated sigh. "How long are you going to keep this up?"

Raven glared at him in response. She was still very angry with him and couldn't stomach the sight of him.

"I think Julian is beginning to sense the tension between us. I don't think either one of us want that. We need to work this out for Julian."

"Don't dare use my son against me. Will you stop at nothing?" she snapped.

Andre released a long sigh. "I can see you're not ready to talk to me."

"You know, you're no better than Lucien. He was low enough to use my son and now you're doing it."

"Excuse me?"

"You're doing the same thing to me. Just like Lucien."

"How can you compare me to that man?"

"I'm tired of my son being held over my head. I love Julian and have been a good mother to him. His disappearance was due to something Lucien did—not me. There's nothing I could have done to avoid what happened."

"I know that, Raven. You're totally missing the point here."

"Then what is the point? I'm never going to agree with you, Andre. *Never.*"

A.C. and Paul spent the morning in bed. Snuggled up beside him, she stated, "Paul, there's something I want to say to you, too."

"What is it, honey?"

She sat up, pulling the covers to her chin. A.C. suddenly felt shy. "I never thought I'd ever say these words again. Never thought I'd mean them even if I did. Paul, I'm falling in love with you, too."

He kissed her. "That wasn't too bad, was it?"

A.C. shook her head.

"We belong together, Amethyst. I knew it the moment I saw you. I've been looking for you all of my life."

"There's something else, Paul. My job takes me all over the country. I live in Los Angeles and you live here. How are we going to make this work?"

"A cosmetics company has offered me a position in their Los Angeles office."

"When did this happen?"

"Right before I met you."

"Are you going to take it?"

"I wasn't sure about it initially, but now that I've met you . . . I'm ready to move."

"I don't want you to take the job because of me, Paul."

"I'm not."

"So, you're really going to move to L.A.?"

Paul nodded.

A.C. threw her arms around him. "I'm so happy." Perhaps they were meant to be together. Paul was going to move to Los Angeles. At least now they had a chance.

* * *

Four days passed and Raven was still not speaking to Andre. He decided to call a truce. He found her in the kitchen where Anna was teaching her how to make beignets.

She glanced his way when he entered, but didn't say a word. As he neared, Raven turned her back to him.

Anna glanced from one to the other.

"What do I do now?" Raven asked her.

Andre interrupted them. "Would you mind leaving us alone for a moment, Anna? Raven and I really need to talk."

"She's teaching me how to make beignets."

"It can wait, Raven," he stated firmly. "We need to talk."

"I'll go check on Julian," Anna announced. "He should be just about ready for his lunch."

Smiling, Andre said, "Thank you, Anna."

After the housekeeper disappeared from sight, Andre asked, "Feel like taking a walk?"

"No." Raven washed her hands in the kitchen sink and dried them on a paper towel.

He gave a loud sigh. "Raven, I'd like to talk to you. This has gone on long enough."

"We don't have anything to discuss, Andre. You've made your intentions very clear."

"We have a son together so we have to come to some type of agreement."

She didn't respond.

Andre took her damp hands into his own. "Raven, I'm sorry for hurting you. I really mean it."

She looked up at him then. "But it doesn't change anything, right? You're still going to take me to court, aren't you? You're still going to try and take my child?"

"Take that walk with me, please."

Sighing in resignation, Raven reluctantly followed Andre outside. "You know you talk about being honest, but you're no better than I am."

"What are you talking about? I never lied to you."

"You had an ulterior motive for helping me find Julian. You'd already planned to take him from me. The truth of the matter is that I still wouldn't know anything about it if I hadn't seen the papers. I certainly don't consider that being upfront. By the way, when were you planning to tell me that you were going to sue for custody? When?"

"I was waiting for the right time, Raven."

"Is there ever a right time for something like that?" she questioned.

Andre had to admit there wasn't. "I was trying to look out for Julian."

"By taking him from his mother. Andre, we've been through this. There's no point in rehashing it all."

"You've had your turn. Now it's mine. You're going to listen to me. I went about this the wrong way. I admit that. When I went to see my attorney, I felt it was the right thing to do. I should have said something sooner."

"It wouldn't have changed what I feel. You hurt me terribly when you kicked me out of your life, but now you've set out to destroy me by taking my son. Andre, how do I make you understand that there is no me without Julian. I love him more than I love my own life."

"I understand that, Raven," Andre said softly. "I really do."

"But you don't care about that."

"Raven, listen to me. I have considered everything you said to me the other day. I was wrong in how I handled this situation, but I was not wrong in trying to protect my son. I see the way Julian looks at you—honey, you're his world. I would not do anything to hurt him."

"So, what are you saying?"

"I'm not going to fight you for custody."

"You mean it?"

He nodded. "I can't stand seeing you look so sad. Raven, you are a wonderful mother. I see that."

"Julian is my best work."

"You've done a good job with him."

"Thank you for saying that, Andre."

"I mean it. I'm sorry I put you through this." He took both her hands in his. "For what it's worth, I really was trying to keep my son safe."

Pulling away from Andre, she said, "I guess I just didn't understand why it couldn't be a team effort. We are his parents. We could protect him together."

"I was worried about Lucien manipulating you. He's always been able to do so."

"Maybe when I was younger, Andre. The day I met you, I started to see my world in a different light. You helped me grow up. I'm not that same naïve little girl anymore. I'm just sorry you can't see it." Raven took a deep breath and exhaled slowly.

"I made mistakes. I will continue to make mistakes, Andre."

"So have I," he admitted. "I have regrets as well."

"Then how can you judge me so harshly? There have been moments when you tell me that you don't blame me for Lucien's actions—then you turn around and penalize me for being his goddaughter."

"No, I don't."

"Yes, you do, Andre."

After a moment, he said, "I'm sorry."

"Where does this leave us now?"

"I would like to start over, Raven. I am going to ask something of you, selfishly. I would like the chance to earn your trust again. I know that you want the same of me."

"Do you think we can start over and do it right this time? I have to admit that I'm not so sure. We keep messing up."

Andre heard the resigned tone of her voice. If he didn't act quickly he would lose her for good. "I don't want to give up, Raven."

She looked up at him. "I'm not sure I'm understanding you."

"I want to keep you and Julian safe." He stopped talking and shook his head. "It's not just that, sweetheart. I want the two of you in my life. I want you to be a part of my life."

Raven gave a bitter laugh. "You're something else, Andre. I won't give you my child, so now you're willing to—" She stopped short. Scanning his face, her expression changed. "No, that's not you at all. You wouldn't do something like that."

"No, I wouldn't. I mean it, Raven. I want to start over with you." Andre reached for her.

She fell into his embrace. "Do you think we can make it work this time?" she murmured against his chest.

Andre kissed her in response. He smothered her lips with demanding mastery. Raven quivered at the sweet tenderness of his kiss. When his mouth grazed her earlobe, she thought she might faint. Her thoughts spun out of control.

Raven could hear his heartbeat throbbing as Andre's hand moved gently down the length of her back.

"We're in the kitchen," she whispered between kisses. "I don't think we want Anna walking in on us like this."

Andre let out a soft groan. "I guess you're right." He released her.

"Why don't we go check on our son?" Raven suggested.

"Sounds good to me."

Stopping just outside Andre's bedroom upstairs, Raven pointed toward the room at the other end of the hallway. "Remember the day I was looking for Julian? When I went into that room, I noticed some paintings hanging in there. They were exquisite—at least from what I can remember. I was so frantic that day I didn't really get a good look at them. I was just wondering why you've kept them hidden away?"

Andre's eyebrows raised a fraction. "You think I painted them?"

She looked over her shoulder at him. "Didn't you?"

He shook his head. "My grandmother painted them."

Raven gave Andre a sidelong glance of utter disbelief. "They should be displayed throughout the house. They're wonderful."

"I agree wholeheartedly, but Grandmother wants them in her room."

Raven suspected there was much more to this story, but Andre wasn't saying anymore. He always seemed to act strange whenever she mentioned his grandmother. She was dying to know why.

Andre felt like a new man. He hadn't felt this good in days. Andre was glad he and Raven were back on speaking terms again. But it was more than that. They were back together and now he felt complete.

Serene tapped him on the shoulder. He turned around.

"It looks like you and Raven have patched things up. I'm so happy for you."

"You really like her, don't you?"

She smiled. "Yes, I do. I think she's a nice girl. But mostly because she makes you happy. I haven't seen you look this way in a long time."

Andre threw back his head and laughed.

"It's true. You wore your sadness like a badge. It broke my heart to see you that way," Serene said.

"Well, it's all in the past now. If things work out, she and I will make a home for Julian. Together."

"Are you still considering New Orleans?"

"I am, but I'll have to talk to Raven about it when the time comes."

"I understand. I would hate to miss out on seeing my grandson."

"You won't, Mom. You never have to worry about that."

Raven breezed into the room. "Am I interrupting?"

Patting the seat beside him, Andre said, "No, come sit down beside me. Mom and I were just talking."

"It's so good to see you two like this."

"I'm glad you approve," Raven murmured.

"Oh, I do. You two belong together."

Looking over at Andre, she said, "I think so, too."

Later that day, Andre and Raven visited the New Orleans Museum of Art which housed one of the largest decorative glass collections in the United States, in addition to collections of pre-Columbian and Native American art, Asian art and a wealth of European works.

Andre remembered how much Raven enjoyed viewing art collections and that she was a history buff.

"I'm going to take you to the New Orleans African American Museum if we have time."

"Great."

Raven was like a kid. She breezed from room to room, filled with awestruck wonder. Andre loved seeing her that way. He slid an arm around her.

Leaning into him, she murmured, "Thank you for bringing me here." Glancing down at the watch on her arm, Raven asked, "Do we still have time to go to the African American Museum?"

"I think so. Let's get out of here." Andre took her by the hand and led her out of the museum and to the car.

Nineteen

Paul peeked into a closet. "Thanks for all of your help, A.C."

"I didn't mind. Actually, it was the realtor who did all of the work. She faxed over the listings and I came to check them out."

Leaving the master bedroom, he stated, "I think I like the last house we saw best. It's spacious enough and I'm getting more room for the money."

A.C. glanced down at the thin stack of papers in her hand and then replied, "We have a couple of more to see unless you'd rather not."

"We can look at them, but so far, I really like the last one."

She smiled. "Come on, let's go see the next one."

"Which one did you like best, Amethyst?"

"I like the last one, too."

Heading out to the car, A.C. announced, "We've been invited to my friend's house for Labor Day." Inclining her head, she asked, "Interested in going?"

Paul gave a slight nod. "Sure, if you want to."

"There are a lot of them, but they're real nice people."

Paul burst into laughter. "A lot of them, huh?"

A.C. nodded. "Mrs. Ransom has ten children. Five girls and five boys. I think most of them are married and have children. Then there are the cousins and other relatives."

"I'm looking forward to meeting your friends."

Paul decided to make an offer on his original choice. They met with the real estate agent and went to dinner afterwards to celebrate.

Two days later, A.C. drove Paul out to Riverside for the Ransom's annual Labor Day barbeque.

They were met at the door by Ivy Ransom. "Mama was just talking about you. Come on in."

A.C. introduced her to Paul.

They headed to the patio where she introduced Paul to the rest of the Ransom family. The matriarch, Amanda Ransom, welcomed him warmly with a hug.

Kaitlin and Matt invited them to sit down with them.

"It's good to see you again, A.C. You've been on my mind."

"I'm fine, Kaitlin. I've been busy with a couple of cases. I actually had to call Preacher in on one of them."

"I spoke to him last night," Matt announced. "Sabrina's been sick a lot with this pregnancy, so they won't be here."

"I'm sorry to hear that." Giving Paul a playful nudge, she said, "Paul is going to be moving here soon."

"Really?" Matt asked.

"Yes," Paul stated. "I've taken a job with Cunningham Lake Cosmetics."

Kaitlin's eyebrows rose in surprise. "Are you serious?"

He gave A.C. a puzzled look. "Why? Is something wrong?"

"Kaitlin's sister Elle is married to Brennan Cunningham, III," A.C. explained.

Paul was astonished. "Talk about a small world. I had no idea."

"I almost told you, but I thought I'd let you meet Brennan first."

"Is he here?"

"He and Elle should be here shortly," responded Kaitlin.

"How are the twins?" A.C. inquired. "They're almost two, right?" She caught sight of Matt watching her. She wanted desperately to wipe that knowing grin off his face. The only thing that saved him was the fact that she could tell he was truly happy for her.

"Brennan and Elle are here," Kaitlin announced. "Come on, Paul. I'll introduce you to my brother-in-law. He no longer works in the family business."

Standing up, Paul acknowledged, "I'd heard that."

They left A.C. and Matt alone at the table.

"You can stop grinning like a Cheshire cat now."

"You're in love," Matt stated. "I'm really happy for you."

"What is it? Am I wearing a sign or something?" A.C. looked over her shoulder.

Matt burst into laughter.

"It's not funny." She poured herself something cool to drink. A.C. loved the tangy taste of Mrs. Ransom's homemade lemonade.

"Girl, I haven't seen you look this happy in a very long time."

Paul returned to the table saying, "Amethyst, you've got see the twins. They are charming little guys—"

"Amethyst," Kaitlin and Matt said in unison.

She sent a glare their way.

Matt held up his hand. "Hold up! Your name is Amethyst. In all the years that I've known you, I never knew that."

"You never asked," she shot back.

"Yes, I did. And if I remember correctly, you said your

name was Alison." He shook his head in surprise. "Amethyst."

"Just drop it, Matt."

"It's a beautiful name, A.C.," offered Kaitlin. "I like it."

"So do I," Paul interjected. "It suits her."

A.C. downed the last of her lemonade. When she saw that Matt was trying to hide his smile, she tossed a napkin at him.

Two nights after Labor Day, Raven woke up in a sweat. She'd had another nightmare about Lucien. In each one, he'd found her and Julian. Andre would always come to their rescue right before she woke up. This time though—he came to save them, only he took Julian with him.

She had no idea what time it was. In the darkness, she could just make out the silhouette of the dresser. The clock on the nightstand read 4:25 A.M.

Fear made her move slowly. Raven folded the covers back and climbed out of bed and strolled over to the window. Peering out, she could find nothing out of the ordinary. Relieved, Raven made her way back to bed.

She didn't get into it though. Julian ran across her mind and Raven decided to check on her son. Donning her robe from the foot of the bed, Raven slipped it on. She carefully made her way to the hall and down to the nursery.

She gasped when she walked into the nursery. There, sitting in the white rocking chair was a woman dressed in black. She reminded Raven of the Madonna with the way her scarf was draped over her head. She immediately assumed that this woman had to be Andre's grandmother. "Hello," she whispered. "I'm Raven—"

"I know who you are," the old woman interjected. "I

come here every night to watch over the baby. He's such a charming little boy. Andre was just like him at this age."

"Thank you for watching over him."

The woman stole a look at Raven, but quickly turned away. "I'm sorry if I scared you."

Moving closer, Raven responded in a loud whisper, "I just didn't expect to see anyone in here. Mrs. Savoy, I've been wanting to meet you."

The room was enveloped in silence.

Raven made her way over to the bed. She bent over and placed a kiss on Julian's cheek. She glanced over her shoulder. "I'm going to go back to my room, Mrs. Savoy. I know he's in good hands." She added, "I'm sure that chair can't be too comfortable. Why don't you get in bed with him?"

"I'm fine. I'll stay in here for another hour or so, then I'll return to my own room."

"Thank you again, Mrs. Savoy."

"He's family, child. We protect our own at all costs."

The realization came to her that Andre shared the same mindset with his grandmother. He would protect Julian at all costs—including suing for custody. She had to admit she would feel the same way if the roles were reversed.

That revelation gave her some understanding of where Andre was coming from, but the fact remained that Raven had no inclination to relinquish her son to him. Instead, she planned to do all that was necessary to insure that Lucien could never come near him again.

Andre glanced up when Raven entered the studio the next morning. "How did you find me?"

"Your mother told me you were here. What are you doing?"

"Working on this." He gestured for her to come closer.

Raven stared at the canvas. "It's a picture of Julian chasing a butterfly. Andre, it's lovely." It was a perfect rendition of their son.

"It's the look of innocence."

Raven nodded in agreement. "You've captured him beautifully. You did this entirely from memory?"

"No, not really. During one of the times we were outside, I took some Polaroids of Julian." Andre showed them to her.

"I can't wait to see it when you're finished."

"So you really like it then?" he questioned.

Nodding, Raven replied, "I do. It's going to be beautiful, Andre." She strode over to a nearby stool and climbed onto it. Perched regally on the chair, she announced, "I met your grandmother last night."

Andre stopped what he was doing. "Where did you see her?"

"She was in Julian's room."

Nodding, Andre said, "She visits him every night."

Raven didn't hide her surprise. "You knew?"

"Yes. She enjoys watching him sleep."

"I don't think she likes me, Andre. She would hardly talk to me and she wouldn't even look in my direction."

"Raven—"

"It's okay," she cut in. "I understand. It's because I'm not a part of this family."

"My grandmother will warm up to you. Just give her some time, okay?"

"Andre, I know where I stand. I've accepted it."

"She will come around, Raven. I promise you."

"If and when she does, I'd really like to see her paintings. Do you think she'll let me?"

"Maybe one day."

Her shoulders slumped down in defeat. "I feel like I

have the plague or something. I'm constantly under a microscope."

Andre walked over to her. "You shouldn't feel that way, sweetheart." He embraced her.

"That's easy for you to say."

Bending his head, Andre kissed her. "I'm sorry if we've made you feel that way. We meant well. All of us."

"All I want is a normal life, Andre. And love. I want someone to love me unconditionally."

Andre started to massage her shoulders. His gentle touch sent currents of desire through her. Raven's senses reeled as if short-circuited.

Before she knew what was happening, he'd slid her shirt off her shoulders and down her arms. When she'd discarded all of her clothes, he locked the door, and then removed his own clothing. Raven's impatience grew to explosive proportions, causing her to push Andre down to the floor before climbing on top of him.

Raven sat up intentionally and went into Julian's room to wait. She wanted to speak with Andre's grandmother. It was important to her to have Antonia Savoy's approval.

The old lady took one look at her and turned to leave.

"Mrs. Savoy, wait! I just wanted to talk to you."

"No . . ."

"Please . . ."

Antonia hesitated long enough for Raven to reach her. In the dim lighting, she made out the scars on the woman's face. So this was why she hid herself from the world. Antonia was ashamed of her scars.

Raven didn't miss the pain etched in Antonia's face; such pain and humiliation. She was suddenly filled with guilt over having discovered the old woman's secret. The last thing Raven wanted to do was hurt her more. Reaching out, Raven wrapped her arms around Antonia. "You are still as beautiful as you looked in that picture downstairs, Mrs. Savoy," she whispered. "I just wanted to tell you that. I'll leave you now." Blinking back tears, Raven left the room.

Instead of going back to her own room, she went to Andre's. She couldn't really define the reason why, but she just didn't want to be alone right then. Her emotions were all over the place after seeing Antonia Savoy's face. What the poor woman must have endured, no one could ever imagine. Raven wiped her tears with her hands before knocking.

Andre was surprised to find her standing at his door. "Is something wrong?" He stepped aside to let her enter.

"No. I just needed . . . I needed to see you."

Turning her around so that she faced him, Andre asked, "What's going on with you, Raven? You look a little pale."

"I know why your grandmother hides."

His expression instantly became guarded. "What are you talking about?"

Raven eyes filled with unshed tears. "I saw her scars. What happened to her?"

"She was burned in a fire," Andre answered as if that was all to it. "A bad fire."

Tears rolled down her face. "Oh no."

"She was severely traumatized by what happened. That's why we have to be so careful with her."

"I understand."

"When did you see my grandmother?"

"Not too long ago. Before I came to your room."

"I see."

"I was in Julian's room when she arrived. I left immediately because I know how much she loves to spend time with him."

"She loves that little boy so much. She's a different person whenever she's around him."

"I can tell."

Raven stifled a yawn.

"Want me to walk you back to your room?"

She frowned. "Can't I just stay here? I don't want to be alone tonight."

"Raven, I don't think that would be a good idea."

"I'll sleep on top of the covers. I promise to keep my hands to myself."

"It's . . ." Andre began.

"Please let me stay," Raven pleaded. "I'm not trying to seduce you, I promise."

Gesturing toward the bed, he said, "Go on. You should get some sleep. You've been looking pretty exhausted lately. Mom mentioned it to me a couple of times. So has Anna."

Raven did as she was told. After settling beneath the covers, she propped up the pillows and lay there watching Andre.

He undressed before climbing into bed. Andre stared up at the ceiling.

Raven stretched and yawned. "Thanks for letting me stay."

"No problem." Turning his back to her, Andre yawned.

"I'm surprised you were still up," she murmured sleepily.

"I was working on the painting of Julian. It's almost finished."

Raven yawned again, causing Andre to follow suit. They both started laughing.

"I'm sorry. I'm so tired, but I'm also restless. I just can't seem to relax."

A thought occurred to Raven. "Maybe I'd better go

back to my own room. This is your grandmother's house and I don't want to disrespect her." She sat up and swung her legs out of bed. "I know we made love in the studio . . . I just don't want to be disrespectful to your mother or your grandmother. They mean a lot to me and I care what they think."

"You're sure?" Andre asked.

She nodded. "I'll be okay in my own bed." Raven came around to his side of the bed. Bending down, she kissed him. "See you in the morning."

Andre glanced over at the clock. "It's already morning."

"Then I'll see you later today." Raven headed to the door. She turned and gave a quick wave before leaving.

Twenty

Paul temporarily moved in with A.C. The house he'd purchased needed some work before he could move in.

He was awed by the friendliness of the Ransoms and the way they made themselves available to help him with painting the house and redoing some of the carpeting. The house was ready two weeks later.

He took a bench off the truck and carried it into the house. Paul placed it in the foyer with A.C.'s approval.

"I've already made up your bed in the guestroom. I didn't bother with your room."

Smiling, Paul replied, "You could have done that one, too. In fact, I'd like your help in decorating."

A.C. pointed to herself. "Me?"

"Why not?"

"Onyx had to decorate my place. I'm not the one to ask when it comes to decorating. You would be better off asking my sister."

Matt entered the house carrying two chairs. "Where would you like these?"

"In my office." Paul pointed out the direction. "It's the last room down the hall."

A.C. planted a kiss on his lips. "I'm going to miss you, Paul. It's been fun having you at the condo."

"I appreciate you opening your home to me."

She smiled. "You're so sweet and so old fashioned . . . I don't know what I'm going to do with you."

"Try loving me. That's all I ask. Think you can handle that?"

"I do love you, Paul. You know that."

A.C. led him over toward the balcony. She opened the sliding glass doors and stepped outside. He followed her.

"I hope you're going to like it here in Los Angeles."

"I do too. It's a big change from New Orleans, I have to admit."

She nodded in agreement.

Paul wrapped his arms around her. "Amethyst, I can be happy with you anywhere in the world. Don't ever forget that."

They stood on the balcony staring out at the city of Los Angeles for another few minutes before going back inside.

A.C. went upstairs to make up the bed in the master bedroom while Paul went out to the moving van.

A few days later as Raven walked out of her bathroom, she was startled to find Antonia Savoy sitting in her room.

"Did I scare you, child?" The old woman asked.

"A little," She admitted. "I didn't expect anyone to be in here." In broad daylight, she could see that Antonia's scars were much worse than she first thought. "But I'm thrilled to see you again," she added quickly.

Antonia placed a hand to her face. "They're hideous, I know."

"Oh no," Raven quickly assured her. "Your scars are most likely nothing compared to the ones branded on your soul. I know they don't even touch mine."

Antonia eyed her. "Do you love my grandson?"

Raven met her gaze. "I love Andre with all of my heart. I don't think that I could ever love another man the way I love him."

"If that is true, you will have to fight for him, you know?"

Raven shook her head. "He doesn't want me. I believe that the only reason—no, I *know* that the only reason I'm here is because of Julian."

"He still loves you, Raven. Despite anything he may tell you."

Raven's spirits lifted. "Do you really think so? He hasn't mentioned love to me."

"He does love you. He just has to know that he can trust you. Trust is very important in this family."

She reached over to place her hand over Antonia's. "Thank you for telling me this. It means so much to me."

"I have a very strong feeling that you are a good woman and you have a good heart."

"Mrs. Savoy, why won't you come down and have dinner with us? Your family misses you."

"I . . . I don't know, child."

Squeezing Antonia's hand, Raven said, "There's no need to hide. Your family loves you. I can hear it in their voices every time they speak of you. Scars mean nothing to them because they can see past them. You are so fortunate, Mrs. Savoy to have such a loving family. I would give anything to have been so lucky."

That night, Antonia Savoy surprised everyone by joining the family for dinner.

Serene escorted her mother to the dining room table. "I'm so glad you decided to leave that room of yours. I hope this is the first of many."

Antonia gave a little smile. "You sound as if you've missed me," she teased.

"I have," Serene admitted. "We've had some of our best conversations during dinner."

Julian pointed to Antonia. "That's my angel, Mommy. She watches over me."

Smiling, Raven murmured, "I know."

Antonia delighted everyone with tales of her early days in New Orleans. Raven found her to be thoroughly entertaining.

After dinner, Andre took Raven by the arm and led her over to the huge window in the dining room. "What did you say to my grandmother?" he asked in a hushed whisper.

"I don't know what you mean."

"How did you get her to come downstairs?"

"I told her how much you all love her and how lucky she was to have such a loving family. Besides, you said she would come down when she was ready." Shrugging, Raven added, "I guess she was ready."

Andre disagreed. "I think it was more than that, but I'm going to let it go for now."

Lowering her voice to a whisper, she said, "Andre, you can trust me on this. I had nothing to do with it. Honest. Your grandmother made up her own mind."

"Thank you, Raven."

"Why are you thanking me?"

"Because you were able to reach Grandmother in a way nobody else could."

"I still don't think it had anything to do with me."

"Would you like to go out later?"

Raven glanced up. "Sure. I don't mind."

"Julian's going upstairs with Grandmother. She's letting him paint."

She broke into a smile. "Really?"

Andre nodded. "Anna's going to give him his bath and will put him to bed for us."

"She's such a sweetheart. Does the poor woman ever rest?"

He laughed. "Anna says that if she stopped for too long, she would probably die."

Raven shook her head in amusement. "I'm going up to my room to shower and change. I can be ready in half an hour."

"Don't forget to put on your dancing shoes, sweetheart. We're going to dance the night away."

Breaking into a smile, Raven murmured, "I'm looking forward to it."

Twenty-one

The weeks flew by rapidly now that Raven was getting out more. Halloween had crept upon them and Serene wanted to take Julian trick or treating. Although Raven had never made much of this particular day, she allowed him to go.

She agreed upon the condition that Serene would not allow Julian to eat any of the candy. Raven preferred that he only eat what they'd purchased. She didn't allow her son to have a lot of sweets anyway. For snacks she usually gave him veggie sticks and raisins, sometimes fruit.

Raven and Andre rented a couple of movies and settled down together in the family room. She wasn't much of a horror buff, but she knew how much Andre enjoyed them, so they compromised and rented one love story and one horror film.

Love and Basketball always made her cry. Wiping her eyes with a tissue, Raven uttered, "I just love this movie. I could watch it over and over again."

"It was good," Andre acknowledged. "But now we're getting ready to watch a real movie."

Raven bit her bottom lip. She prayed that she wouldn't have nightmares after the film.

She missed most of the movie because she had her hands over her eyes. Andre teased her unmercifully.

"I can't believe you're such a wimp," he joked.

Raven tossed a small handful of popcorn into her mouth. "That movie was horrible, Andre."

Laughing, he pulled her into his arms. "Forget about the movie for now. There's something I need to tell you."

"What is it?"

Andre's voice was filled with emotion. "I still love you, Raven. As much now as I did four years ago."

Her eyes filled with unshed tears. "Why are you telling me this now?"

"Because I believe that I've been somewhat unfair to you. I may have even been too harsh in my judgment of you."

Raven wiped at her tears.

"But more importantly, it's the way I really feel about you. I figure if I want honesty, I need to be honest in return."

"I'm so sorry, Andre. For everything."

"I shouldn't have thrown you out like that."

"It's all in the past. I never blamed you for the way you reacted. You felt betrayed and I don't blame you."

"I should have listened to you. I should have given you a chance to explain."

"We can change the past, Andre. We can bury it and start over. I'd like that." Raven slipped her arms around him. "I love you so much."

Bending his head, Andre kissed her softly on the lips. "Raven, I don't want Lucien in our lives. The things he's done to you and then kidnapping Julian like that . . . if I ever see him . . ." He let the threat hang in the air.

"You don't have to worry about Lucien. He's out of my life for good."

"I mean it, Raven."

"I won't let you down, Andre. I will never ever give you reason to doubt me again. I promise."

*** *** ***

Two days later, Andre answered the ringing phone from the studio extension.

"Andre, it's me."

"A.C., how are you? Are you keeping my cousin straight?"

"Paul and I are fine, Andre." She paused a moment before asking, "Are you alone?"

"Yeah, I'm in the studio. Why?"

"Your town house has been trashed. I received a call early this morning from a contact. Are you positive there was nothing there to connect you to New Orleans?"

"Nothing. I've always been careful not to bring attention to my family, anyway. We don't need the past coming back to haunt us."

A.C. nodded in understanding. "How's your grandmother doing?"

"She's fine. She met Raven. It seems the two are becoming fast friends."

"So, how are things between you and Raven?"

He grinned. "Great. We're going to try again."

"I'm so glad to hear that. I think you two belong together."

"I think so, too. I've never loved another woman the way I love Raven. I can't put it into words, but the woman does something to me." Andre broke into a short laugh. "She's definitely in my blood. The last three years were hard for me. I alternated between loving her and hating her."

"More like you hated the fact that you loved her so much and couldn't stop."

"Right. That's it exactly."

"A.C., do you think Lucien is behind what happened?"

"Yeah, I do, Andre. This is going to have to stop. You

two can't keep hiding in New Orleans. Something has to be done to put Lucien behind bars."

"There's nothing we can do, A.C. The last thing we need right now is to have Raven get involved in this plot. I have a bad feeling about it."

"Why?"

"I feel like Lucien's trying to set her up. Until we know the rules, we shouldn't try to play his game."

"You feel this strongly about it?"

"I do, A.C. I don't want Raven involved until we know everything."

She gave a heavy sigh. "Okay. I don't agree with you on this, Andre, but I'll do as you wish."

"Thank you. And A.C., please don't say anything to Raven about the town house being ransacked. It would only scare her. She's still having trouble sleeping and if she hears this, she'll never let Julian out of her sight."

When he got of the phone, Andre went downstairs to talk to his mother. He found her in the family room watching television with his grandmother. "Where's Raven?"

"She upstairs with Julian," Antonia announced. "She reads to him about this time every day. She seems to be a good mother."

"She is. I admit I had some doubts initially, but I was wrong. About a lot of things, it turns out."

Serene turned to her son. "Andre, do you think that's the right thing to do? Keeping this from her?"

"I think so. For a little while, anyway. Raven's paranoid enough."

"I won't mention it, but I think you should tell her soon, Andre. For all you know, Raven could be entertaining thoughts of returning to New York."

He looked shocked. It wasn't something he'd considered. What if she didn't want to stay here in New

Orleans? "Has she said anything to you about going back to New York?"

Shaking her head, Serene answered, "No. I'm just saying that you two have to remain on the same page at all times in order to stay safe. So it's important that you communicate the danger to her."

"I will. Just not right this minute. I'll do it when the time is right."

Looking her son squarely in the face, she inquired, "When is the right time to tell someone that his or her life is in danger, Andre?"

After taking a walk with Antonia Savoy through the huge rose garden at the side of the house, Raven brought up the subject that had been on her mind for a while now.

"Andre told me the pictures hanging in that room next to yours are your work."

Antonia gave a slight nod. "They are."

"I think they're exquisite, Mrs. Savoy. You have a rare talent."

"Thank you for saying that, dear. You are very kind."

"I mean it. Your work is stunning. I can see the similarities in your work and Andre's. He definitely took his talent after you. Would you mind . . ." Raven was suddenly hesitant. "I mean, I'd like to see your paintings again. That is, if you don't mind."

"I would like that a lot, Raven. Come."

Upstairs, Raven noted the way the paintings sparkled with clear outlines in careful modulations of white, blue, yellow and lavender. "This is beautiful, Mrs. Savoy. Breathtaking, actually."

"Thank you, dear."

Raven strolled around the room. "They are all much

too beautiful to be hidden. These paintings should be shared with the world."

Antonia gave a tiny chuckle. "You make this old woman feel good."

"I'm not just saying it. I really mean it." She peered closer. "You know, your style is very similar to Pierre Delacroix's work."

Antonia didn't acknowledge her comment. Instead she asked, "Would you like to see some of your son's work? He loves painting." Antonia led the way over to an easel near the window. "This is his latest work of art."

Smiling proudly, Raven stared at the canvas. "Julian's becoming quite the artist, I see."

"He loves to paint."

"I guess he takes after his parents."

Antonia didn't hide her surprise. "You paint also, Raven?"

She nodded. "Yes, ma'am. I'm not any good, but I find it very therapeutic." Raven turned back around to admire another one of Antonia's pictures.

"You are a very gifted artist, Mrs. Savoy."

Antonia smiled, but there was still a shade of sadness behind her eyes. Raven wondered at the reason.

Andre found her in the library. "What did you do today?"

"I spent the day with your grandmother. She's such a sweetheart, Andre."

"I think so."

"She showed me her paintings today. I don't understand why she insists on hiding them. It's almost as if she doesn't have any confidence in herself."

"Grandmother's been through a lot. I think in time she may change her mind."

Twenty-two

Christmas was eleven days away. Raven and Andre went in search of the perfect tree for Julian.

"I'm loving Christmas New Orleans style," she stated. She and Andre had attended several concerts at the St. Louis Cathedral and throughout the French Quarter carolers serenaded them as they strolled from the art galleries to the bistros.

"How would you feel living here?"

"You would leave New York, Andre?"

"As I told you before, I can paint anywhere. Julian loves the house. This city is a good place to raise a child."

"You're seriously considering this, aren't you?"

He nodded. "There's been a lot of ugliness in that house. Julian has changed all that."

"The fire?"

"Yes," Andre muttered.

"You're still not ready to talk about it?"

Glancing her way, he said, "Not really. I hope you can understand." Taking her hand, he continued, "You never said whether or not you want to stay here."

Looking into his eyes, Raven replied, "My place is with you, Andre. You and our son are my family."

He kissed her. "I love you, Raven."

"I love you, too." She paid no attention to the friendly

glances she and Andre received. Raven only had eyes for him.

They found their tree and purchased it. As soon as they arrived home, Julian squealed with joy.

Serene, Antonia and Anna joined them in the living room to help decorate the tree. Raven couldn't have asked for a more perfect night. Everyone looked so happy, even Antonia.

The next day, Andre helped her and Julian into a garland-draped streetcar to take a tour of the historic Garden District mansions decked in holiday splendor. Even Julian seemed to enjoy the tour.

"We're going to take Julian to see Papa Noel," Andre announced.

"Is that your version of Santa Claus?" she asked.

"Yeah. According to legend, he arrives each year in a pirogue—that's a Cajun canoe, guided by the light of huge bonfires on the Mississippi River."

"Julian, you're going to like that, sweetie. We're going to see Papa Noel."

Her son burst into joyous laughter and it was like music to her ears. Raven picked Julian up, hugging him close to her. "I love you so much, my baby boy."

Paul greeted A.C. with a kiss. "I thought you were going to be here an hour ago. Was traffic that bad?"

Dropping her backpack in a chair, she shook her head. "No, it wasn't traffic. I didn't leave the office when I'd originally planned. I had a last minute meeting with a client."

"Well, I'm glad you're finally here." Wrapping his arm around her, Paul's lips caressed her check. "Amethyst, I missed you like crazy."

She turned in his arms. "Honey, I missed you, too."

He peered at her. "What's wrong?"

"Paul . . . honey, I'm going to have to go out of town on business for a few days."

"When do you have to leave?"

"Tomorrow."

"Where do you have to go?"

A.C. pressed her lips to his. "Let's not spoil what's left of this evening by talking about my job."

Paul stepped away from her. "Why do you always do this to me, Amethyst? What is the big secret?"

"I just don't like discussing my job with anyone." A.C. walked away from him. "I don't want to argue with you, Paul. Let's just enjoy tonight."

"I think we need to discuss this. Why are you so secretive about your work? You're a private detective, right?"

"Yes," she answered curtly.

"I just want to know where you're going."

"I have to go to Chicago. Are you satisfied now?" She glared at him in anger. "You know, Paul, maybe this isn't going to work out between us. I'm not going to report to you about my comings and goings."

He looked offended. "Excuse me. I guess I thought we were a couple. I can see I was wrong."

Her arms folded across her chest, A.C. shook her head in frustration. "Don't start that crap with me, Paul. We are both adults. I don't ask you to give me a rundown of your schedule when you travel."

"You don't have to," he countered. "I tell you anyway. I even make sure you have a copy of my itinerary."

"Paul, I'm not used to answering to anyone." Walking over to get her backpack, A.C. stated, "This is not going to work. Let's just forget about it."

He stood in her path. "Why do you always run away?" Shoulders slumped, he said in defeat, "I love you, Amethyst. But I'm not going to be your lap dog. I'm a man. I thought I was your man." Paul stepped off to one side. "I'm all for independence, and I'm not chauvinistic. What I want is a partner. A companion. Until you're willing to meet me halfway . . . forget where I live."

A.C. was speechless in her shock.

Raven went in search of Andre. She wanted to show him Julian's latest work of art. Hearing voices in the library, she headed in that direction. Andre was in there talking to Serene.

"Have you heard anything more from A.C.?" Serene asked her son.

"Nothing. Not since she told me Lucien had someone trash my apartment. The whole place has been ransacked."

"He had to be looking for something."

"Most likely he was looking for a clue as to where Raven and Julian might be hiding. A.C. isn't sure whether or not Lucien believes that we're together."

"Is this man as dangerous as you say?"

"A.C. said that Raven's friend's death was not an accident. It was murder."

"Oh, dear. All of you are in real danger."

"He has no idea where to even begin looking for us, Mom. He won't be able to find us here in New Orleans. Not right away."

"He's not just going to give up. Not a man this powerful. He has the money and the resources to find you all." Serene shook her head sadly. "You may have to leave the country and change your names."

"We're not going to run for the rest of our lives, Mom. I'm going to find a way to put Lucien away for good."

Listening from the hallway, Raven couldn't stop the trembling within her body. It was true. Pansy had been murdered. Lucien was responsible for the death of her very best friend in the entire world.

Onyx showed up on A.C.'s doorstep three days after she got back. She followed her sister upstairs to the master bedroom.

"Feel like talking?" Onyx asked as she sat on the edge of the bed. "You've been so quiet since you returned from Chicago. I haven't even seen Paul around." She gave a short laugh. "For a while, I thought you two were joined at the hip."

"We broke up." A.C. settled back against her pillows.

"What happened?"

"Paul wants to know where I'm going, where I'm staying, and when I'm coming back."

"What's wrong with that?"

A.C. sighed loudly. "I'm not married to the man. He doesn't need to know my business."

"Honey, you do know that you're no longer CIA. Paul loves you, honey. It's okay to tell him about your trips. It's not like they're top secret."

She considered her sister's words. "I overreacted, I know. I don't know what came over me, Onyx. I just lost it."

"You're a team player until it comes to love."

"You really believe that?"

"Yeah, I do. A.C., you're scared to death. You lost Gennai tragically and you're scared that something could happen again. You love Paul, but you're pushing him away."

"Now I've lost him. He told me to forget where he l— lives." A.C.'s voice broke miserably. "I . . . It's over. I ran him off."

Onyx handed her a tissue. "Dry your eyes, sis. All is not lost. You and Paul love each other. You'll work it out."

"I hope you're right."

Andre left jewelry store after store. He was looking for the perfect Christmas present for Raven. He was shopping for an engagement ring. It was time they became a family, permanently.

A ring caught his eye. It was propped regally on a stand covered in black velvet, and gleamed brightly. The stone, a heart-shaped diamond, set in eighteen-carat gold, overshadowed the other diamonds in that collection. Andre decided he would buy that one for Raven.

She would love it, he knew. This time, nothing would stand between them.

Twenty-three

"I just love Anna's gumbo," Serene announced as she scooped up a spoonful of sausage, shrimp and rice.

Antonia agreed. "She's a wonderful cook. Just a dear."

Raven wasn't paying attention to them. Her mind was still on what she'd overheard earlier. She played with her food as she stared off into space. Lucien wasn't going to give up. He would search and search until he found them—only this time, he could go after Andre.

"You haven't touched your food, child," Antonia stated.

Raven didn't respond.

Serene touched her hand gently. "Dear, are you okay?"

"Huh?" Raven eyes met hers. "I'm sorry, did you say something?"

"You have eaten a thing. Are you feeling okay?"

"I'm fine. I guess I'm not as hungry as I first thought."

"You've got to at least taste Anna's gumbo. It's delicious." Antonia stuck a spoonful into her mouth.

Raven took a bite. She loved seafood and savored the taste of shrimp and crab, along with chunks of sausage and chicken. "This is good." She took another bite. Then another. She was acutely aware that both women were watching her every move.

Antonia smiled in response. "That's right, child. Eat. You could stand to gain a few pounds as it is."

Raven was still troubled, but she continued to eat. The gumbo was wonderful and she managed to enjoy it.

When she was done, Raven retreated to her room. She wasn't good company and wanted to avoid any questions that might come up. Andre still had not said anything to her and she knew it was only because he didn't want to upset her. He knew she would be scared.

There had to be a way to get Lucien out of her life once and for all. Short of killing him, that is. Raven didn't want to live her life in fear and she didn't want any harm to come to Andre, so she had to come up with a plan of some sort. She was so close to having the family she'd always dreamed of and there was no way she could just sit back and allow Lucien to destroy her dreams.

Two hours passed before Raven came up with a solution. She wouldn't be rid of Lucien until she did exactly as he'd asked. She would have to steal the *Danse Macabre.*

Andre decided to take Julian and his mother Christmas shopping. They invited Raven along, but she declined. This provided the perfect opportunity for her to leave. As soon as they had drove off, Raven ran up to her room and placed a call to the airlines. She reserved a seat on the next plane leaving for New York. Afterwards, she began to pack. Raven wanted to be gone long before Andre and Julian returned.

Going back to New York was a big risk, but one she couldn't afford not to take. Raven had to end things and she had to do it quickly. She would steal the painting and then come home to Andre and their son. Lucien would be out of their lives once and for all.

She finished her packing and sat down to write a note to Andre. He was going to be furious with her and she feared losing him. However, Raven couldn't live with herself if something were to happen to him. Pansy was dead because of her. She prayed for Andre to understand her reasons for going back and that he would forgive her. Raven also hoped he would understand her reasons for not involving him.

She changed quickly and was ready to leave. Grabbing her suitcase, she headed to the door. Antonia stood in her path. It was apparent that she'd been about to knock.

The woman glanced down at the luggage in her hand and asked, "Where are you going, child?"

"I need to go back to New York, Mrs. Savoy. If I don't, Andre and I will never be able to move on with our lives."

"Do you think this is a good idea?"

"No," Raven admitted honestly. "But I don't have any other choice. I have got to do what Lucien wants or he'll never leave us alone. The next time it won't only be Julian. Lucien may go after Andre and I can't let that happen. I have to keep them both safe."

"Do you really think this man will keep his word to you? The man is a criminal."

"I used to think so. Now I'm not sure. Still, I don't see any other way out of this."

"If you steal this painting, Raven, it will only be the first of many that you will have to steal. He will hold your family over your head. It's what you value most. You will never be free of this man. And what good are you to Andre and your son behind bars? You could be placing yourself in even more danger if you're caught."

Confused, Raven asked, "What do you mean?"

"The police or the FBI could offer you a deal. Lucien Dupont is powerful enough to have you killed before you could talk. I suppose there is the Witness Protection Program . . ."

"I just want to live my life with Andre and Julian. Mrs. Savoy, I don't know what to do."

"What does Andre have to say about all this?"

"He doesn't know. I left him a note."

Antonia took her by the hand. "Come with me, child. Let's have a talk."

Raven was rooted to the spot. "Mrs. Savoy, I have to go."

"This won't take long. There is something I think you really need to know before you leave. Perhaps it will save all of you."

"I don't understand."

"You mentioned something the other day in my room. You compared my work to that of Pierre Delacroix. Do you remember?" When Raven nodded, Antonia cleared her throat and announced, "He was my brother."

Raven's mouth dropped open in surprise. "Pierre Delacroix, the painter?"

Antonia nodded. "My full name is Antonia Delacroix Savoy."

"I had no idea. Andre never said a word."

"He wouldn't. We have been very careful to sever all ties to the Delacroix name."

"But why?"

"Because of all the pain that comes with it." Antonia took Raven by the hand once more. "Pierre was a wonderful painter in the beginning, but after two years, that all changed. Critics made him the laughing stock of the art community."

"There was a low point in his career," Raven recalled. "What happened during that time? His work changed drastically. The paintings were dark—almost sinister."

"Pierre Delacroix became nothing more than a mean drunk and a bad gambler. The alcohol changed him and his work. He was miserable and had attempted suicide twice. He was my big brother and I hated all the pain I would hear in his voice. My husband had gone. Serene, her husband, and Andre were living here at the time, so I went to Paris to take care of him. Six months after I arrived, Pierre got cleaned up and started to paint again. But his depression showed in his work. I decided he needed a change of scenery so I convinced him to come back to New Orleans with me."

"Is that when he produced the *Parisian* series?"

"So everyone thought."

"I'm afraid I don't understand."

"Pierre's work just wasn't the same. It was still very droll. It looked as if he'd lost his zest for art." Antonia paused a heartbeat before continuing. "My brother didn't paint the *Parisian* series. I did."

"What?"

"Pierre was heavily in debt and very depressed. His own work had stopped selling and no one would even acknowledge him anymore. He needed money badly. I used to work on my own paintings in this studio while he worked on his. One day, I decided to throw caution to the wind and let him see one of my paintings—not knowing the trouble I'd unleash. He convinced me to let him take one of my paintings as his own. In return, he would help me with my own career. I don't know why I believed him, but I did." Antonia's eyes filled with tears. "He told me my own work was amateurish and worthless, but with his name affixed to it, the painting would be considered a masterpiece. As he talked, I could once again see the light in his eyes. You must understand that I loved my brother deeply and I wanted him back."

"Why did you believe him? Your work is beautiful. And perfect for that period. Pierre knew that."

Antonia gave a slight shrug. "I didn't know any better. He was my brother—the great Pierre Delacroix. There was no reason for me not to believe him. I trusted my brother. I thought he had my best interests at heart. When our parents died, Pierre took care of me and gave me a great education."

"I understand how you must have felt. Lucien has always made me feel that I was nothing without him. Like you, I not only trusted him, but I believed that I needed him. He was the only person in the world who loved me, so I thought. It wasn't until I met Andre that I learned otherwise."

Her eyes filling with tears, Antonia murmured, "These scars. These are because of my brother."

"What do you mean?"

"I want to show you something."

Raven followed Antonia toward one of the paintings. She watched as the woman lifted the framed artwork off the wall. To her surprise, there was another painting beneath it. Raven gasped in surprise.

"Outside of Pierre, Serene and Andre, you are the only other person to ever view this painting. This is the real *Danse Macabre*."

Shaking her head in confusion, Raven uttered, "I really don't understand."

"I hid this painting from Pierre. You see, I'd made two. I knew Pierre would want it. As you can see, the two paintings are not identical."

"I can tell. The colors in this one is much more vibrant, and the other one seems dark and depressing. It reminds me of Pierre's previous works. But more obvious is that in this painting there are five dancers instead of four."

"I believed this one to be my best work and I didn't want to see my brother's name on it. Quite by accident, he saw it one day and immediately claimed it as his own. I gave him the copy, but I should have known that I wouldn't be able to fool him." A lone tear rolled down her cheek. Antonia placed a hand to her breast and squeezed her eyes shut as if to block out an unwanted memory.

"What happened?"

"He demanded the original, of course. When I wouldn't give it to him, he became enraged. We were up here arguing. He was throwing things and cursing—I'd never seen him so angry. The noise must have awakened Andre, because he came running in here. He was only five at the time. Pierre yelled for him to leave and the poor child was so frightened that he fell, knocking a candle off the table. The fire started up the curtain and quickly blocked the doorway. Poor little Andre, his pajamas caught a spark . . ."

"Oh my goodness. How horrible."

"I couldn't bear the thought of my beloved grandson being burned, so I rushed to save him at the risk of losing my own life. I barely escaped with the child, but my brother was not as fortunate. I haven't slept well since— I still hear his screams as the fire ripped at him. But I think its Andre who has suffered more. He blames himself and Pierre."

Raven embraced her. "I'm so sorry, Mrs. Savoy." Now she knew the reason behind Andre's nightmares.

Antonia cut into her thoughts. "Your godfather—he is after the *Danse Macabre?*"

"Yes. It's ironic, now that I think about it. All this time he's been after a fake."

"It's time for the truth to come out. That's the only thing that will save this family."

"You mean everything? Your brother will be labeled a fraud."

"We will only tell what we have to, Raven. However, if it all comes out, then so be it. Pierre was a fraud."

"Are you sure about this, Mrs. Savoy?"

Antonia nodded. "This is what I think we should do. . . ."

Andre was going to propose that night. As soon as he and Julian returned home, he arranged for his son to have an early dinner.

"Mom, do you mind having dinner with Julian? Invite Grandmother, too. Raven and I will have a late dinner. Just the two of us."

Smiling, Serene nodded. "Tonight is special, I see."

"Very special. I'm going to ask Raven to marry me."

"I'm so happy for you both. She's a lovely girl, Andre."

Kissing his mother on the cheek, he murmured, "I'm going upstairs to ask her now."

"Congratulations, dear."

He took the stairs two at a time. Reaching the second floor, he knocked on Raven's door. "Honey, are you here?" He eased open the door and peeked inside. The room was empty.

He walked over to the bathroom and it was empty, too. Andre left and went to his own room. He immediately spotted the note lying on his pillow.

Tearing open the envelope, Andre quickly read the contents. Dropping the letter on the floor, he ran back to her room, and threw open the closet. Some of her clothes were gone. He muttered a curse.

Serene came bursting into his room. "Mother's gone! I've checked all through the house and she's not here."

"Raven's gone, too."

"Do you think that Lucien—"

"She left a note, so I don't think she's been kidnapped. It sounds as if she went willingly."

"Where did she go?"

"Back to Lucien."

"He could have forced her to return with him. Perhaps Mother tried to stop them."

Anna joined them. "Raven and Mrs. Savoy left together in a cab. I think they were headed to the airport. One more thing, Mrs. Savoy took one of her paintings."

Andre ran the short distance to the room where his grandmother's paintings hung. He checked each one carefully. When he returned, he was furious.

"The *Danse Macabre* is gone," he announced when he returned. Somehow Raven had found out where the real one was hidden. This had been the real plan all along. Andre felt betrayed once again. Anger welled up in him.

He reached A.C. on her cell phone. "Where are you?"

"In New York. Why?"

"I'm on my way there."

"What's going on?"

"I'll explain as soon as I get there. Can you meet my plane?"

"Sure."

"In the meantime, I need you to find Lucien Dupont."

"Not a problem."

He hung up. "Raven, if anything happens to my grandmother, I'll never forgive you," Andre muttered to himself.

Twenty-four

Michael Garner was the first person Raven called when they arrived. She made arrangements to meet him for drinks.

"Do you really think he'll help us?" Antonia asked.

"I think so, but then again, I don't know. He and Lucien are very close."

"We have got to make him believe us. This plan won't work without Michael."

Standing up, Raven embraced Antonia. "I'm going to talk to him before I bring him to the suite. Give us half an hour."

"Good luck, dear."

Michael was already in the bar when she arrived. He rose to his feet and greeted her with a kiss. "Hello, Raven." They sat down facing each other across the table.

She spoke first. "Thank you for meeting with me on such short notice, Michael."

"I have to tell you that I was surprised to get your call this afternoon. I was under the impression that you'd left New York."

"I did. I'm afraid it was rather sudden."

"I see. Are you back to stay?"

"No, I'm not. Michael, I have to apologize to you. If I misled you in any way, I'm sorry."

"You still love Andre."

"Very much."

Michael's eyes never left her face. "Are you two back together?"

Raven smiled and nodded.

They gave the waitress their drink orders.

"I'm happy for you two then," Michael stated. "He's a good man. I have to confess, however, that I'd had hopes to replace him in your life."

"I'm sorry."

"Don't be. You are with the man you love and the father of your child. I had a chance with the great love of my life. She's gone now. I will move on, but I won't ever love another woman the way I loved Anne."

When their drinks arrived, Raven said, "Michael, I have to know something. Can I trust you? I mean really trust you."

He gave her a strange look before replying. "Of course you can trust me, Raven."

"Even if it means going against Lucien?"

"Yes."

"Michael, I'm in trouble. Real trouble."

"I kind of suspected that, Raven. Is there anything I can do to help you?"

"Lucien is not the man that you think he is."

"I'm not sure what you mean."

"Lucien is a murderer and a thief."

"Are you sure? Lucien Dupont?"

"He's covered his tracks well, Michael. I know that it sounds far-fetched, but it's all true."

"Lucien has killed someone?"

"I don't think he did the deed, but I believe that he ordered her death."

"You make him sound like a character from *The God-father.*" Michael burst into laughter. "Your godfather . . ."

"He had my best friend killed. Lucien kidnapped my son in order to force me into stealing the *Danse Macabre.*"

Michael's mouth dropped open in shock.

"He wanted me to seduce you so that you would be distracted. The reason I disappeared is because Andre and I rescued our son."

"Lucien Dupont?"

Raven nodded. "He and Beatrice have been stealing paintings for years," she announced.

"How do you know this?"

"My parents were paid to do the stealing. Beatrice would make a copy of the paintings and have the forgery put in their place. Rarely did the owner ever realize the switch had ever taken place. In fact, there's only one in-cident I remember. A Picasso had been stolen off of a private yacht in France. Lucien was questioned, but nothing ever came of it."

"This is incredible."

"After Beatrice died, Lucien wanted me to take her place. My painting was never quite good enough, so he taught me how to steal them instead. This was the way I was supposed to earn my keep, so to speak."

Michael shook his head. "You're saying that Lucien is behind some of the major art thefts from around the world?"

"Everything I've told you is the truth. I know for a fact that Lucien has a Rembrandt worth millions in his col-lection, as well a Vermeer, a Van Gogh and two Degas. The *Bouc Mucicien* by Chagall has been missing for years, but I know where it is."

"Lucien has it?"

Raven nodded.

"What happens to the originals?"

Shrugging, Raven answered, "I'm not really sure. Lucien's kept a few for his own personal collection. I think the others were smuggled all over the country through some underground network." Raven leaned forward. "Michael, there's someone I think you should meet. She's upstairs."

"Who is she?"

"She's Pierre Delacroix's sister. You really should hear what she has to say."

After a moment, he agreed and rose to his feet.

Michael followed Raven toward the elevators. She knew he didn't believe her—he probably even thought she was a little bit crazy. But soon the truth would be out.

Raven made the introductions. "Michael, this is Antonia Delacroix Savoy. Pierre's sister."

They shook hands.

"Mrs. Savoy, it's an honor."

When they were all seated, Antonia said, "I understand you own the copy of the *Danse Macabre.*"

"*The copy?*" Michael glanced from one woman to the other. "What's going on?"

"The painting you own is not the original, Michael," Raven announced softly. "Mrs. Savoy has the original."

His disbelief was evident in his face.

"Mr. Garner, I'm about to tell you something that you may find very hard to believe, but I assure you it's the truth." Antonia took Raven's hand into her own as she began her story.

When she was done, she rose to her feet slowly. "I brought the original *Danse Macabre* with me. If you have the one you own analyzed, you'll find that it's painted over another painting."

"I have a certificate of authentication."

"Authentication is a process," Raven explained. "It's a tricky business with no guarantees. The panel members often don't have the experience and I'm sure they're overwhelmed by the number of applications they receive."

"I did it to hurt my brother," Antonia explained. "*Danse Macabre* was my best work ever and I just couldn't let him have it." She stood up and unrolled the painting that lay on the sofa beside her.

Raven eyed the painting. The original was brilliant in color and by contrast, the one hanging in Michael's house had colors that were muddy. Antonia was clever in creating the copy. In the original, her rendering of people was exacting, their facial features clearly delineated in modulated tones of raw sienna and ochre. The copy had been heavily painted and was a mess of darkened shadows.

Michael stared at the painting. "It's beautiful."

"Mr. Garner, you are free to take the original. It's yours, but we need the other one."

He tore his attention away from the painting. "Why?"

"It's the one Lucien wants," Raven explained. "I find it fitting to give the fake to a thief. Mrs. Savoy painted them both so I won't call it a forgery, but that's what he intended to leave you with. It's his calling card."

Michael was shaking his head.

"Mr. Garner, please feel free to have your copy analyzed. You'll see that all I've told you is true. Raven and I simply want to make things right . . . for everyone. Your copy is worthless, but the original . . ."

He appeared to be thinking it over.

"We really need your help, Michael. Lucien deserves to go to prison, but we can't do it without you. And you paid millions for a fake. You deserve the original painting. After all, you paid for it."

"What is it you want me to do?"

"I need to get into your house to steal the *Danse Macabre*. Andre told me that your brother-in-law works for the Art and Theft Bureau of New York. Is this true?"

"Yes."

"Good. There has to be a way we can trap Lucien. I want him in prison where he belongs. I'll even testify in court."

"Do you have a plan in mind?" Michael asked.

"I do. I just don't know if it'll work. I need you to tell me that." Raven laid out her plan.

When she was done, Michael uttered, "There may be a way. . . ."

Andre was furious with Raven. When would he ever learn? She was not the kind of woman a man could trust. She was still a liar.

Where was his grandmother? When he checked her room, he found that the original *Danse Macabre* was gone. Had Lucien somehow found out the truth? Perhaps this was their plan all along.

His imagination was running rampant. Andre clenched his hands into fists as he headed out to the car. He was taking a flight to New York in an hour. He had a strong feeling he would find Raven there.

During the drive to the airport, Andre tried to clear his head. None of this really fit. Why would Raven involve his grandmother? What happened to the real painting? Unless . . . unless she thought it was a fake. Maybe she was going to replace Michael's painting with this one. Andre shook his head in his confusion.

Half an hour later, he was seated on the plane.

Andre's mind was still troubled. How in the world would he find Raven and his grandmother? He wished now that he'd told A.C. what was going on. She would know what to do in a situation like this.

Andre was consumed with his thoughts throughout the short flight to New York. Raven took his grandmother to New York along with the original painting because somehow she'd convinced Antonia to give Lucien the real painting. No, his grandmother wouldn't have done that. Unless it was to keep her family out of harm's way.

As soon as he landed, Andre placed a call to his mother, and then he checked his messages stored in his home phone. There was a call from Michael Garner.

Raven had gone to meet with him and Michael feared she was in over her head where Lucien was concerned. Frowning, Andre wondered what he meant by that. Michael then announced that Raven would be at his house that night.

Andre planned to be there as well. He called A.C. on her cell phone and repeated what Michael had said.

"You're not going alone," she stated. "Lucien and his people are dangerous. I'll meet you in New York."

Twenty-five

Seated in the hotel suite, Raven said, "It's time for me to call Lucien. I hope I can be convincing." Michael had been gone for fifteen minutes.

"You will, dear," Antonia assured her. "So much depends on this."

"This has got to work, Mrs. Savoy. It just has to because I can't keep living my life in fear." She tried to swallow her panic.

"Everything will work out fine."

Raven took a deep breath and dialed. When Lucien answered, she announced, "It's me."

There was a slight pause on the other end. "I must say this is a surprise. Where have you been, Raven dear?"

She struggled to remain pleasant. "I needed some time away. I had a lot to think about."

"You have always been willful. So tell me. How is Julian?"

"He's fine, Lucien. And he's safe. Knowing that, I can now concentrate on the job you want me to do."

"The job?"

"Yes. I plan to keep my end of our little agreement."

"I see."

They were silent.

Raven broke the silence. "You haven't changed your mind, have you?"

"I'm just stunned. I assumed you'd gone back into hiding."

"No. I just wanted to put some distance between you and my son. Julian is my life and I wanted to be sure he was safe from harm."

"I assume Andre aided you."

"You can assume whatever you like, Lucien. This has nothing to do with Andre. I simply want to get this over with so that I can move on with my life. You will keep your word, won't you? You will stay away from me and Julian?"

"If that is your wish."

"I want your word, Lucien."

"How do I know if I can trust you, Raven?"

"I made this call, didn't I? I could have stayed in hiding."

"Yes, I suppose you could have."

"Lucien, I'm going to do it tonight. I had dinner with Michael and he's going away on business. In fact, he's most likely on his way to the airport." Raven knew Lucien would call to verify all she'd told him.

"I must go, Raven. I'll call you back in a few minutes."

True to his word, Lucien called her back. "You're ready?"

"I am. I've studied the floor plan and the security systems. I'm as ready as I'll ever be."

"When do you plan to hand over the painting?"

"Tonight. Right after I get it."

"Why don't you hold onto it for a few days?"

"I don't want to, Lucien. I intend to hand it over and be done with the entire matter."

Raven worked quickly. She was in and out of Michael's house in a matter of minutes. She released a huge sigh of relief that everything had gone according to plan, thus far. "It's almost over," she whispered over and over to herself.

Just as she unlocked the door of her rental car, she felt someone grab her arm. A scream trembled to her lips.

Her assailant covered her mouth with a gloved hand.

"Be quiet, Raven. It's me."

She whipped around. "Andre! What are you doing here?" Placing a hand to her chest to still her rapidly beating heart, she muttered, "You nearly scared me to death."

He stared pointedly at her. "I should be asking you that same question."

Raven was overcome with panic. "You've got to leave. Lucien could have someone watching me."

"I'm not going anywhere without you. Where is my grandmother, Raven? I know she came to New York with you."

"She's back at the hotel. Please Andre, I'm asking you to trust me on this."

"Raven . . ."

"Please, Andre. I know what I'm doing. This is the only way Julian will be safe. Now I need you to leave."

"I'm not going anywhere. Michael said you were in over your head."

His announcement stunned her. "He called you?"

Andre nodded. "He didn't tell me what you'd planned though."

"I don't have much time. I need you to leave, Andre. If you love me, then I'm asking you to trust me, too. I'm going to make everything right. Just trust me for once in your life. After tonight, Lucien will never bother us again."

"What's this?"

"It's the *Danse Macabre*. The real one."

"What?"

"Your grandmother gave it to Michael."

This time he was the one surprised. "She did?"

"Andre, please leave. I'll explain everything to you later." She quickly told him the name of the hotel where his grandmother was staying.

"I'll keep my distance, Raven, but I'm not going to leave you alone. Lucien's capable of murder."

"I know. I overheard you telling your mother that he killed Pansy. That is why I came back to New York. It has to end tonight."

"You're right. It does have to end tonight." Andre climbed into the backseat of the car.

"What are you doing?"

"I'm not letting you go alone. Now get in and drive. No one will know I'm back here."

Raven did as she was told. She had to admit that she already felt better with Andre in the car with her.

"You are one of the most hard-headed women I've ever met," Andre fussed. He was crouched on the floor.

"I wanted to keep you and Julian safe."

They drove the rest of the short distance in silence.

Right before Raven parked, she said, "We're here, Andre. Now please don't be a hot head. Michael and his brother have everything under control."

"I still don't like this. I don't trust Lucien. I'm glad A.C. is here."

She gasped. "A.C.'s here?"

"Yeah."

"I've got to go. Lucien just arrived. Wish me luck."

"Honey, I want you to be careful. Julian and I can't lose you."

"After tonight, Lucien will be sitting behind bars." Raven stepped out of the car and headed down the nearly vacant parking lot. Lucien and Cal stood near the limo that had delivered him.

Raven glanced around covertly. *"Where in the world were the cops?* she wondered.

Finally, she and Lucien were standing face-to-face.

"I have to admit that you've surprised me, my dear. I never really believed you would do it," Lucien announced with a grin. "Steal for me."

"I owe you, but that debt is now paid in full." Raven held up the canvas. "Once I hand this over to you—you are out of my life for good."

"Are you sure that's what you really want? Where would you be without me?"

"I want nothing else to do with you, Lucien. I kept me end of the bargain and I expect you to do the same. You gave me your word."

"Raven, I can make you a very rich woman. You can educate Julian in the best schools . . . surely you want to give him a good life. I gave you a life of wealth—"

"And one filled with pain. How could you claim to love me, Lucien? Why would you want me to live a life on the run?"

"You didn't get caught, did you?"

"Not tonight."

"I am a very careful man, Raven. It's how I've managed to get away with stealing masterpieces all this time. I will take care of you. I always have and I always will."

She shook her head. "No, Lucien. After tonight you're out of my life for good. I appreciate your taking me in when my parents died, but that's it. It ends tonight." Raven walked over to him and held out the canvas. "Here is your painting."

Lucien took it and smiled. "Raven dear, this is only the beginning." He grabbed her by the arm. His voice was deadly. "Haven't you figured it out yet? I own you. If you want Andre Simone to see another day, you'd better do everything I tell you."

Snatching her arm away, Raven asked, "What? You're going to kill him like you did Pansy? She never did anything to hurt anybody."

He shrugged nonchalantly. "She was in the way."

Raven slapped him. "I hate you, Lucien."

Andre had seen enough. He wasn't about to stand still and let Lucien harm Raven. Just as he was about to make his presence known, Andre felt the nudge of a gun in his back.

"Don't make a sound," the voice whispered.

The place was soon flooded with light. There were men with guns everywhere. Andre turned and the man identified himself as a policeman.

Shocked, Lucien turned to Raven. *"You did this?"*

"You deserve whatever you get," Raven announced. Pulling up her shirt, she revealed that she'd been wearing a wire.

"You ungrateful tramp!"

"Your words can no longer affect me, Lucien."

He pulled out a gun and grabbed Raven. "I'll kill her," he yelled. "I will kill this betraying bi—."

Raven made eye contact with Andre who stepped out of hiding. He was not going to let Lucien take her from him. He would die first before he let Julian be robbed of a mother. "Let her go, Lucien. It's over. You no longer have a hold on her."

"I should have known you were somewhere near by." He pressed the gun closer to Raven's temple. "I will have the pleasure of killing her right here in front of you."

Pleading, Andre held out his hands. "It doesn't have to be this way. If you kill her, then your life is over, Lucien. There are police everywhere."

A.C. pulled Andre back. "Don't get any closer. Let the police handle this."

"No, I have to do someth—" He caught sight of movement. Cal was going for his gun. "He's got a gun!" Andre yelled.

A.C. gave a slight nod of her head and suddenly, Raven elbowed Lucien before dropping to the floor.

Andre was shoved to the ground as well. He heard shots ring out and panicked. Had Raven been shot? "Raven!" he screamed. He tried to get up, but A.C. wouldn't let him until the shooting stopped.

Raven lay on the ground in a fetal position with her eyes closed and her hands placed to her ears. When she finally opened her eyes, she found Lucien lying near her, covered with blood.

"Lucien!" She crawled over to him.

He was still breathing and his eyes were open, staring at her. He looked as if he was trying to say something. Raven moved closer.

"Get away from him!" Andre shouted.

Police surrounded them. Raven grimaced at the sight of blood seeping from Lucien's body. He was still trying to tell her something. Raven leaned in closer.

When one of the policemen tried to pull her back, she snatched her arm away and shouted, "No! He can't hurt me now." Crying, she placed her ear to his mouth.

Andre soon realized that Lucien was struggling to breath. Gradually, his chest stopped moving. Raven let out another grief-stricken cry.

Lucien was dead.

Twenty-six

Back at the hotel, Raven took a long bath while Andre was in the other bedroom checking on his grandmother.

Raven sat on the edge of the bed in one of the fluffy robes the hotel provided its guests. Rubbing her arms, Raven tried to warm her body. She felt so cold—not just on the outside, but on the inside as well.

She heard a key in the lock and knew it was Andre. Raven gave him a mournful smile when he sat down beside her.

Slipping an arm around Raven, he questioned, "What are you thinking about?"

"Lucien. I hate the way this all ended. It was not supposed to go down this way. I never wanted to see him killed."

"It isn't your fault, Raven."

"I know. Lucien wanted to die. That's what he whispered in my ear. He said he wouldn't have survived prison."

Andre was not as sympathetic. "I don't feel sorry for him. Lucien got what he deserved."

"I don't know what I'm feeling right now," Raven confessed. "I just wanted him to go to prison or back to France. I thought maybe it would scare him enough that he would stay out of our lives for good."

"He's gone, Raven. *For good.* Lucien will never bother us again."

"I know. He wasn't always nice to me, but I still loved him. At least up until the past few months, anyway. After he took Julian, I started to hate him."

Taking his hand, Raven inquired, "Andre, why didn't you ever tell me about the fire?"

He gave her a surprised look. "What are you talking about?"

"The fire that your uncle died in."

"Grandmother told you?"

She nodded. "Honey, it wasn't your fault. You were just a frightened little boy."

Andre suddenly seemed caught up in memories of the past. "I never should've gone into that room. I just didn't like the way he was talking to her. He had no right."

"You never liked him, did you?"

"I hated Pierre Delacroix," Andre stated. "We were all very happy until Grandmother brought him into our home. He was a mean drunk and he made her cry all the time."

"She loved him, Andre. He was her brother and she loved him."

Andre's eyes were filled with pain when he looked at her. "He would have killed her, Raven. I saw it in his eyes. I didn't accidentally knock over that candle. I did it on purpose because I wanted to scare him. I didn't know the fire would get out of hand like that." A tear rolled down his cheek. "I wanted to save her, but instead I nearly killed her."

"You're wrong, Andre."

Raven and Andre both turned around. Antonia stood in the doorway. She moved toward them. "Child, you didn't cause the fire. It was an accident."

"But I . . ."

Antonia shook her head. "Andre, you were a little boy. *A scared little boy.* The only thing you did was trip and fall. Pierre had destroyed the studio; there was paint, rags and canvas scattered everywhere." She wiped away his tear. "It was bound to happen. Pierre was a crazy man that night. Perhaps if I'd just given him the painting all of this could have been avoided."

"I didn't do this to you?"

She shook her head. "No, you didn't." Antonia put a scarred hand to Andre's face. "Stop carrying this burden. It's all over now. Finally, the past is laid to rest. Leave it there and never pick it up again. You have Raven and Julian now. Look toward your future."

After giving them both hugs, Antonia retired to the adjoining bedroom. But before she left, she winked at Andre and said, "I'm looking for some much needed good news tomorrow morning."

"I just love your grandmother. She is such a sweetheart," Raven said after Antonia had gone.

Andre agreed. "She's finally agreed to let me pay for her reconstructive surgery. She's tired of living in the past, too."

"That's wonderful news." Raven suddenly looked sad.

"Honey, what's wrong?"

"I was just thinking that I don't have any family except Julian."

Clearing his throat, Andre said, "There's something I want to say to you, Raven. I was going to do this the day you left."

"What is it?"

"I was wrong about you. I'm sorry for that. You reached out to me all those years ago and I threw you out of my life. You were carrying my baby and I treated you like trash."

"You had no way of knowing."

"I should have trusted you."

"It's the past, honey. Andre, I understand. Really, I do."

"I love you. I want you to know that, Raven."

She stroked his cheek. "I know that, Andre."

"You and Julian mean the world to me. I want to spend the rest of my life with the two of you. Raven, I'm asking you to marry me."

"You want to marry me?"

"Yes, I do." Andre pulled out a ring box. He opened it to reveal the stunning ring he'd bought a few days before. "This was supposed to be one of your Christmas presents, but I think that this is the perfect time. I hope you like it."

"Like it? Honey, I love it. It's beautiful."

Andre placed it on her finger. "I promise to be a good husband and father."

"I love you," Raven murmured softly. "I promise to be a good wife and mother, Andre. Forever and always."

It had been a long night for A.C., but outside of Lucien's death, she was pleased with the way things had turned out. She'd taken her shower and was getting ready for bed.

A.C. pulled down her bedcovers. When a pillow accidentally hit the phone, she felt a sharp knifelike pain slice through her. "Paul, I miss you so much."

So why don't you call him? Her heart inquired.

"The hell with pride," she muttered. A.C. climbed into bed and placed the phone on top of the comforter. She dialed quickly before she lost her nerve.

When Paul answered the phone, she said, "I'm taking an early flight out in the morning."

"Are you coming here?"

Questions like that irritated her. "Yes," she snapped. "Why else would I call you, Paul?"

"You can lose the attitude," he shot back. "If anybody has a right to be angry, it should be me."

"I didn't call to argue with you. If you don't want to see me, then just say so. I'll catch a flight home instead."

"Do what you want to do, A.C. It's what you always do."

Paul slammed the phone down in her ear. He'd called her A.C. That was a bad sign.

The next morning, Raven announced, "Before we leave, I need to do something."

"What's that?" Andre questioned.

"I need to give Lucien a proper burial."

Andre opened his mouth to object, but Antonia stopped him by saying, "He was her family. I understand how she feels. It was the same for me. Even after all that Pierre had done to me, I wanted him to have a proper service. I arranged it from my hospital bed, although I didn't attend."

"This is the final chapter in my life with Lucien. I have to put it to rest."

Andre nodded. "Whatever you want, sweetheart."

Antonia glanced down at the ring on Raven's finger. "Congratulations to you both. I'm happy to see that my grandson's made the right choice." She embraced her. "Welcome to the family, dear."

Smiling, Raven murmured, "Thank you, Mrs. Savoy. It means so much to me to hear you say that."

Twenty-seven

Serene and Julian met them at the door. "I'm so happy to see that you're all okay. Anna and I were so worried."

"We're fine." Andre gave his mother a brief overview of what happened while Raven played with their son.

"Oh my goodness. How dreadful for you all." Serene took her mother's hand. "I was so afraid for you. But I have to tell you how proud I am of you."

"It is time for the truth to come out. I've never wanted to tarnish my brother's name but . . ." Antonia's voice died.

"Pierre used you, Grandmother. He was a fake." Andre's tone was harsh. "Do not waste your tears on him. He doesn't deserve them."

"What happened to the painting?" Serene asked. "The real *Danse Macabre?*"

"The rightful owner has it."

Serene looked at her mother in confusion. "What are you talking about?"

"Michael Garner. He paid millions for the copy, so I gave him the original. He's calling them *Danse Macabre* I and II. "

"Michael wants to see more of her paintings," Raven announced.

"Really?"

Antonia nodded. "He loves all of the pieces I did. He didn't like Pierre's earlier works."

Serene was ecstatic. "That's wonderful."

"I think so," Raven stated. "You have such wonderful work and you've kept it hidden from the world. It's time to come out of hiding, Mrs. Savoy."

Andre agreed. "Like you told me, it's time to face our futures."

Antonia put a hand to her face. "It will take some time to . . ."

"Grandmother, why don't you let me find a plastic surgeon for you? We'll get the best in the world. I've heard of a man in Los Angeles."

Serene reached over and took her mother's hand. "Andre's right. We can get you the best."

"I'll do it," Antonia agreed. "Now no more talk about me. Andre and Raven have something to tell you."

"What is it?" Serene asked with a smile on her face.

"Raven and I are getting married," Andre announced.

"That's wonderful news." Serene got up to hug them both. "I knew it was coming. I just knew it."

Antonia called for Anna, who joined them seconds later. "Andre and Raven are engaged. Could you make us something nice to celebrate?"

"Congratulations. I will make something special for dinner."

Raven ran her fingers through Julian's curls. "Mommy and Daddy are getting married. We're going to be a real family, sweetie."

Julian giggled in response.

Raven broke into laughter. "I know, honey. I feel the exact same way."

A.C. arrived at Paul's condo early Christmas morning. When he opened the front door, she held up a beautifully wrapped present. "Merry Christmas."

"Same to you," he uttered politely. "What are you doing here?"

"I . . . I was hoping that we could talk—"

"Talk or argue," he threw in.

"Paul, I love you and I want you in my life. I've been miserable without you."

He moved so that she could enter the condo. "What are you saying?"

She turned around to face him. "I'm sorry. I've been on my own for so long, Paul. I'm not used to this."

"I wasn't trying to take anything away from you. I wanted to compliment you—be your companion, your lover and your friend. I want you to respect me like I respect you."

"I do, Paul." A.C. paused a moment before continuing. "I was scared."

He moved until he was just inches from her. "You don't have to be scared. I love you, Amethyst. I'm not going anywhere."

Her eyes filled with tears. "I was so afraid that I'd lost you."

Paul wrapped his arms around her. "We're going to be okay, sweetheart. We are."

A.C. wiped her tears. "Here, open your present."

"Only if you open yours."

"You bought me a present?"

Paul handed her a tiny box. A.C. knew what it was. Her eyes met his as she took the gift. She unwrapped it slowly, savoring her final moments of total freedom. Her suspicions were correct. Inside was an engagement ring.

"Will you marry me, Amethyst?" Paul practically whispered the proposal.

"You'll get your answer after you open my gift to you."

Grinning, Paul tore into the large box with relish. Inside was another box. He laughed. "Okay, you're a funny one."

Five boxes later, Paul was down to the last gift. A box the size of the one he'd given her.

"Open it," she urged.

He did as she requested. Smiling, Paul said, "I have my answer."

St. Simons Island, Georgia

It was a beautiful April day and Raven believed that it had been especially created just for her wedding. In less than an hour, she would realize her dream; she and Andre would be man and wife. They'd chosen St. Simon's Island because of the meaning it held for both of them.

A soft knock interrupted her thoughts. It was A.C. "You look beautiful."

Standing in a strapless ivory gown with a wispy cloud of tulle draped around her shoulders, Raven smiled. "Thank you. So do you, by the way."

A.C. was her bridesmaid and looked stunning in a deep purple gown. Her long hair was pulled back into a bun surrounded by sprigs of baby's breath, giving her a romantic glow. "Are you ready?" she asked.

"Yes. I've been waiting on this day for a very long time."

She accepted the elaborate bouquet of flowers A.C. held out to her. "In a few months, we'll be doing this again." Paul and A.C. had announced their engagement shortly after the New Year and would be getting married in July.

Raven followed A.C. out of the dressing room and into the alcove of the small chapel. She was about to walk down the isle to her destiny.

* * *

Andre's eyes grew wet when he glimpsed Raven coming down the aisle. He couldn't remember ever seeing her look so beautiful or so happy.

She loved him. He'd known that particular truth, but today—their wedding day . . . the realization suddenly hit him more deeply than ever before.

Raven had stolen his heart from the moment he had laid eyes on her. Andre had never known love until Raven. Very soon, they'd say the words that would bind them together for life.

Andre couldn't wait. He glanced over his shoulder and winked at Paul.

Raven now stood beside him. Together they faced the minister.

Half an hour later, the ceremony was over. Mr. and Mrs. Andre Simone turned around to face their guests. Michael Garner was the first to offer his congratulations. "I'm very happy for you both."

"No one is more happy than I am," Raven stated. "I've lived my entire life for this moment."

Andre kissed her. "So have I, sweetheart." When he could finally tear his attention away from his bride, he said to Michael, "I'm glad you could share this day with us. Thank you for coming."

While Andre and Michael talked, Raven bent down to pick up her son. "You were such a good boy today. I'm so proud of you."

"I wuv you, Mommy." Julian threw his arms around her neck, hugging her tight.

Andre wrapped his arm around them as the photographers snapped pictures, capturing the early moments of the rest of their life together.

Twenty-eight

Sunday, July Sixteen

A.C. removed her sunglasses when she glimpsed her father and sister getting off a chartered plane.

"Turquoise, it's so good to see you," she murmured as she embraced her sister.

"You, too."

A.C. hugged her father next. "Hello, Daddy."

"My little girl is getting married," he teased.

"Daddy . . ."

"I'm happy for you, A.C. I really am."

"I know, Daddy."

"When is Pearl getting in?" Turquoise wanted to know.

"She flew in last night. She and Onyx spent the morning shopping, but they plan on meeting us at my place."

Turquoise surveyed her from head to toe. "I don't believe it. You're absolutely glowing. I don't know if I've ever seen you look this happy." She shook her head in amazement. "This Paul must be quite a man."

Catching her sister's double meaning, A.C. shot her sister a look before they both burst into laughter.

Walter Richardson cleared his throat noisily. "Why don't you girls save that kind of talk until you're all together . . . and alone."

More laughter erupted.

"Wow. In three days you're going to be a married woman. Tell me, how does Paul feel about your work?"

"He's not exactly crazy about it, but he says he's getting used to it."

"What brought on that change of heart?"

"I've agreed to farm out the more dangerous work to our operatives."

"I see."

Lowering her voice as they walked, Turquoise questioned, "A.C., how's Onyx?"

"Why do you ask?"

"Her last case took a lot out of her." She stole a peek across her shoulder at their father. "I can't say anymore than that."

"You know more than what you're saying. I'm worried about our sister, Turquoise, so tell me what's going on with her."

"I think you should let Onyx tell you."

A.C. let the subject drop for now as she drove them to her condo. She knew her sister didn't want to discuss Onyx in their father's presence.

When she had her father settled in his room, she and Turquoise headed to hers. They weren't in their long before A.C. stated, "I know you didn't want Daddy to overhear you, but he's not in here. So tell me what's going on with Onyx." Closing her door all the way, she continued, "She fell in love with Kenison Moore, didn't she?"

After a moment, Turquoise confirmed A.C.'s suspicions. "I don't know if she was in love with him, but she did become involved with him. A little boy was born out of the union."

Swallowing her surprise, A.C. asked, "So where is he? This child?"

"Kenison found out about Onyx, just before she could

be pulled out. I think Kenison was going to have her killed, but something went wrong and Onyx escaped. She went gunning for Kenison, but when she found him, she couldn't shoot him because he held their son in his arms. He left the country with the baby and we haven't been able to find him."

"You couldn't keep your nose out of my business, could you?" Onyx demanded as she burst into the room, Pearl on her heels.

A.C. turned to face her sister. "It's only because I care about you."

"Because *we* care about you," Turquoise emphasized.

Onyx surprised them all by bursting into tears. Pearl wrapped her arms around her. "It's going to be okay."

Wiping her eyes with the palm of her hands, Onyx disagreed. "It'll never be okay. Not until I find my son."

"You should tell Daddy, Onyx," Turquoise advised. "He needs to know."

"Why? So he can call me a failure . . . a disgrace to law enforcement."

"Onyx, he wouldn't do that," Pearl countered. "Daddy's not like that at all and you know it. Or at least you should."

"Pearl's right. Daddy will understand," interjected A.C.

Onyx glanced over at A.C. "I'm sorry for yelling at you like that. I know how much you care about me." She put a hand to her face. "I'm so ashamed. I don't know how I could have fallen for him like that. I wanted so much to believe that he was innocent."

Turquoise wrapped an arm around her. "Don't be. Things like this happen all the time. It's even happened to me once, but as much as it hurt, I made the case."

Pearl glanced over at her sister. "Really?"

Nodding, Turquoise replied, "Sure it has."

"I just want my son. Kenison can rot in hell for all I care. I just want my baby back."

"We're going to find him, Onyx," their father stated from the doorway. "I have some people on it as we speak."

They all gasped in surprise.

Turning, Onyx questioned, "You know?"

Walter nodded. "I've known for a while. I just wish you'd felt as if you could come to me. Honey, I understand. That's why I wanted you pulled off the case a long time ago."

"We're going to find my nephew," Turquoise vowed.

"Yes, we are," A.C. murmured. To her father, she asked, "Have you come up with any leads?"

"Nothing definite, but I'm not giving up."

"Onyx, do you have a picture?"

"Yes, I do." She pulled a picture from her wallet and showed it to them.

"He's beautiful," A.C. murmured. She vowed she would hunt down Kension Moore and destroy him—if it was the last thing she ever did. The man would pay for the heartache he'd caused her sister. As she gazed from one sister to the other, A.C. could tell from their expressions that they were all thinking the same thing.

After Turquoise and her father freshened up, she took everyone to lunch. Seated in The Cheesecake Factory, they made small talk while waiting for their food to arrive.

"When are we going to meet this wonderful man of yours?" Turquoise asked.

"He should be on his way over here."

"You're going to be a beautiful bride. You'll look just like your mother did on our wedding day."

"Do you still think about her, Daddy?" A.C. questioned.

Nodding, Walter responded, "Not a day goes by that I don't think about her. All of you look just like her."

Paul arrived a few minutes before their entrees. He sat in the empty seat beside A.C., who quickly made the introductions.

He raised his hand, signaling the waiter. Paul gave his order without ever glancing at the menu.

"You must eat here a lot," Turquoise observed.

Grinning, Paul nodded. "Amethyst and I love this place."

"I told you," Onyx said. She gave a short laugh. "I never thought I'd see the day."

Frowning, A.C. inquired, "What are you talking about?"

"Nobody calls you Amethyst except for Pearl, so we just can't believe that Paul . . . I guess it must be love. I was certainly never brave enough to call you anything other than A.C."

"She loves being called Amethyst," Paul announced.

A.C. gave him a pinch on the arm. "Stop instigating."

He laughed.

Watching him, A.C. burst into a round of laughter. Life with Paul was certainly not going to be dull. Her family seemed to like him as well.

The previous week she'd gone out to visit Gennai's grave. A.C. had stayed in the cemetery for a couple of hours just talking about Paul. She wanted Gennai to know that all was well with her. That she was going to be fine.

God had given her a second chance at love and she was so grateful. She would never forget Gennai, but she knew without doubt that Paul was her future.

Raven reached over and took Andre by the hand. He turned his attention to her and smiled.

"How are you feeling, sweetheart?"

"I'm fine." Raven was ten weeks pregnant and prone to morning sickness throughout the day. For the moment, she felt fine. She leaned forward and said, "A.C. is a beautiful bride. Look at her."

Andre agreed. "She and Paul look very happy. I'm glad they found each other."

"Thanks to you," Raven added. "You gave them that little push and you know it."

Feigning innocence, Andre said, "I have no idea what you're talking about."

Raven laughed.

They sat watching as Paul and A.C. had their first dance. They were so happy that they almost seemed to float across the floor. It reminded Raven so much of Andre and her on their wedding day just three months before. The thought brought a tender smile to her face.

Her eyes scanned the room, stopping briefly on a nearby table. A.C. had introduced her and Andre to the Ransom family. Raven met the gaze of the woman called Kaitlin and she smiled. She was granted one in return.

She spied Preacher and waved. He waved back. She admired his wife's beauty and noted the strong resemblance between her and Regis Ransom. Raven made a mental note to ask if they were sisters.

"What are you thinking about?" Andre cut into her thoughts.

Raven glanced over at him. "Nothing really. I was just checking out the wedding guests."

"What about them?"

"Just that they are an attractive group. Our wedding wasn't as big as this one, but you know what? I can still feel the love and joy glowing throughout the room. Weddings have a way of bringing that out."

"I think family has a way of doing that. I'm sorry you

didn't grow up around yours, sweetheart. I can't imagine how that must have felt."

"I'm not going to dwell on it because I have you, Andre. You more than make up for my lack of family. I have never been so happy."

"I will always be here for you and our children."

Raven smiled. "I know that, Andre."

She heard Julian's laughter and turned around in her chair. He was playing with Antonia. Raven marveled over how well Andre's grandmother looked. The second surgery has removed most of the scars from her face and had given Antonia the confidence she needed. She no longer hid her face behind scarves, although she wore gloves to conceal the badly burned hand.

Antonia had recently had her first showing and the response to her work was astounding. She was busy at work on another project, she entitled, *The Wedding Series,* inspired by the many weddings she'd attended in recent months. Her life was beginning anew while Pierre Delacroix's deceit would be buried somewhere in history.

Andre rose to his feet. "Do you think you can hold up long enough for one dance?"

"I think so." She stood up.

Hand in hand, Raven and Andre walked toward the dance floor. They joined A.C. and Paul as they celebrated new beginnings. For Raven and Andre, it was the creation of a new life and for Mr. and Mrs. Paul Robichaux, it was the start of a life together.

Dear Readers:

There are no words to explain how I feel when a book comes to an end. The characters are so much apart of my life—it's almost heartbreaking to see them leave. As always, I hope you have enjoyed my latest story. Many of you requested another storyline involving A.C. Richardson. . . . I promise this is not the last you'll see of her and her sisters. Thank you for your unselfish support and remember that you are all in my heart. Don't forget to visit my website www.jacquelinthomas.com for updates on upcoming releases and book signings.

Blessings,

Jacquelin Thomas

BIOGRAPHY

Jacquelin Thomas is the author of nine romance novels and two novellas including, *Hidden Blessings, Love's Miracle, Undeniably Yours* and *With A Song In My Heart.* She has also written two inspirational fiction novels, *Singsation* and *The Prodigal Husband* and is a contributor to the newest edition of the Women of Color Devotional Bible. She lives in North Carolina with her family and is currently at work on her next project.

More Sizzling Romance from *Jacquelin Thomas*

MORE ROMANCE FROM
ANGELA WINTERS

__**A FOREVER PASSION**
    1-58314-077-8   **$5.99US/$7.99CAN**

__**ISLAND PROMISE**
    0-7860-0574-2   **$5.99US/$7.99CAN**

__**SUDDEN LOVE**
    1-58314-023-9   **$4.99US/$6.50CAN**

__**KNOW BY HEART**
    1-58314-215-0   **$5.99US/$7.99CAN**

__**THE BUSINESS OF LOVE**
    1-58314-150-2   **$5.99US/$7.99CAN**

__**ONLY YOU**
    0-7860-0352-9   **$4.99US/$6.50CAN**

Call toll free **1-888-345-BOOK** to order by phone or use this coupon to order by mail.

Name_____

Address _____

City_____ State _____ Zip _____

Please send me the books I have checked above.

I am enclosing $_____

Plus postage and handling* $_____

Sales tax (in NY, TN, and DC) $_____

Total amount enclosed $_____

*Add $2.50 for the first book and $.50 for each additional book.
Send check or money order (no cash or CODs) to: **Arabesque Romances, Dept. C.O., 850 Third Avenue, 16th Floor, New York, NY 10022**
Prices and numbers subject to change without notice.
All orders subject to availability.
Visit our website at **www.arabesquebooks.com**.